PRAISE FOR *CHILDREN OF GOD*

Exquisitely wrought stories that dwell deeply in place and character—this is a revelatory collection.

—T.C. Boyle, author of *Outside Looking In: a Novel*

David Lynn is a master at unpacking the nuances of encounters between characters of varying identities. These precise, finely-observed stories are filled with unexpected insights.
—Amitav Ghosh, author of *The Hungry Tide* and *Sea of Poppies*

This is a terrific collection. What is most impressive is the way Lynn renders deeply and sharply the lives of these people while keeping a calm hand over all. There are no tricks here, no literary high jinks or post-modern acrobatics. There are only heartbreaking stories of people about whom we grow to care, no matter their caste or calling, their family or fortune. These stories matter.

—Bret Lott, author of *Jewel* and *The Difference Between Women and Men*

In this immersive collection David Lynn shows himself expert in charting the subtle shifts of internal weather that condition the climate of our lives. In India or America, home or away, we are under the skin of his characters, close to their pulse. Alert and perceptive, Lynn is a fine craftsman, who leaves his reader both wiser and more unsettled.

—Hilary Mantel, author of *Wolf Hall* and *Bring Up the Bodies*

The stories in *Children of God* are graceful and astute, beautifully written and keenly intelligent. David Lynn has given readers a collection to celebrate.

—Ann Patchett, author of *Commonwealth* and *Bel Canto*

There's no rushing in the work of David Lynn. He takes his good time telling us his stories, which he seems to discover as he writes them. The result is magical. We find ourselves transformed into Coleridge's wedding guest, held in the thrall of tales, like the Ancient Mariner's, that deal with the human essentials—courage, cowardice, fear, self-inspection, love. In the title story, "Children of God," in "Year of Fire," "Naming the Stones," "Mistaken Identity" and the breathtaking "Divergence"—in all the stories, really—Lynn writes with a sympathy, an intelligence, and a touch so beautifully subtle, we are aware of a story's power only after we've finished, and we realize we've been someplace we've never been before, even if we've lived there all our lives. This is a wondrous collection.

—Roger Rosenblatt, author of
Making Toast and *Thomas Murphy: A Novel*

In *Children of God*, David Lynn reveals just how deeply he understands, as one story so perfectly puts it, "the fragility of this enterprise. Living." These are complex, richly-rewarding stories that reveal a mastery of detail, line after amazing line, leading you toward an understanding of what it means to be alive.

—Kevin Wilson, author of *Baby You're Going to Be Mine*
and *The Family Fang: A Novel*

Children of God

CHILDREN OF GOD

NEW & SELECTED STORIES BY
DAVID H. LYNN

BRADDOCK AVENUE BOOKS

UNCOMMON BOOKS · UNCOMMON READERS

Printed in the United States of America
10 9 8 7 6 5 4 3 2 1

FIRST EDITION, May 2019

ISBN 10: 1-7328956-2-1
ISBN 13: 978-1-7328956-2-1

With thanks to these journals and magazines for original publication of the stories:
Blackbird, Glimmer Train, Kansas Quarterly, Michigan Quarterly Review, New England Review, Salmagundi, Southampton Review, Triquarterly, Virginia Quarterly Review, Yale Review

Book design by Savannah Adams
Cover design by Rick Landesberg

Braddock Avenue Books
P.O. Box 502
Braddock, PA 15104

www.braddockavenuebooks.com

Braddock Avenue Books is distributed by Small Press Distribution.

For WFS, ALSL, and EMSL, now and always.

ACKNOWLEDGMENTS

With deep thanks to those helping this collection come into the world: my brilliant and tireless agent, Valerie Borchardt; Rick Landesberg for designing the memorable cover with inspiration from the border of Wendy Singer's Indian shawl, and Rebecca Kiger for the photograph that made it possible; and my friend and colleague Sergei Lobanov-Rostovsky who wrestled the stories into a kind of sensible order.

CONTENTS

CHILDREN OF GOD

NEW & SELECTED STORIES

PART ONE:

NAMING
THE
STONES

Divergence

Just as he was swinging his leg over the bike, Shivani brushed past and whacked him on the rump.

"Watch yourself," she cried.

Jeremy Matthis bobbed up and onto his saddle. He'd caught his wife in a few strokes, swooshing past her on the street, and already he was marveling at the lightness of the new frame, the smooth response of derailleur and gears. At the first corner they cruised, slowing for a glance each way. Again he pushed ahead, wobbling lightly—the balance was entirely different from his ancient touring bike.

This would take some getting used to. And not just the new bicycle. He was entirely prepared to sacrifice the summer to countless adjustments, now that his book had finally appeared in the spring and, not coincidentally, the trustees of Ransom College had just this past weekend confirmed his tenure in the Classics department. For months he'd been predicting that promotion would alter nothing, that he wouldn't feel in any way transformed once it had been granted. Yet already in the stretch of a few days he'd discovered how faulty that reasoning had been.

It seemed that over the course of many years a tightly woven mesh of stress and anxiety had gradually and ever more tightly caged his heart, his lungs. Mostly he'd been unaware of the binding, except for the occasional snapping awake at four in the morning, sucking for air. Over these last few days that invisible harness had finally begun to loosen, to fade, shadow becoming shadow becoming light. Each time his lungs filled with air seemed almost a revelation, perhaps the start of a new life.

A decade and more earlier, he'd steal an hour on hard-packed country roads in Virginia, digging with his old ten-speed to grind away the frustrations, dead ends, and humiliations that are the dues paid in grad school, and just such a bicycle as the one he was riding had been his dream. An expensive dream he'd scarcely ever acknowledged aloud. Two days ago, however, he'd arrived to meet Shivani for a celebratory dinner at their favorite restaurant, a trattoria on High Street. She'd spotted him through the large front window and was standing in her black dress and pearls by their special table with one hand on the blue-and-silver Italian bike, a bright bow on its seat.

Not until today had there been a real chance to get out on the road. They spun down to Main and sliced along an alley to the back entrance of a coffee shop where their small group of friends were already gathered. Marty, Gretchen, and Lee were there, standing with their own bikes.

As Jeremy swung onto the sidewalk, Owen Thurlow emerged from the shop with a cup of coffee. "Nice wheels," he said, saluting the new bike. "I must be paying you too much."

"Since when are you paying him at all?" Shivani demanded. "I thought he was teaching just for the love of it. Anyway, this baby comes out of my check from the Attorney General."

The Provost saluted her in turn.

Everyone other than Owen was satisfied with water bottles and eager to be away. So soon they were mounted again and cutting over to the Alum Creek path. The day was gray, an occasional faint drizzle keeping them cool but slicking the pavement. It took less than five miles of occasional weaving and dodging before they'd left the city behind, along with its joggers, baby strollers, and dog walkers. They were flying now across the rolling, open country of central Ohio, the river meandering near and away again from the old rail path.

"Hey, Fancy Pants, quit showing off," Owen grunted loudly.

Jeremy swiveled and tossed him a wave. The machine he was riding yielded such a pure joy that, without quite realizing it, he'd been out front and pressing his friends beyond their usual pace. He eased, coasting so that Gretchen could swing into the lead. As he drifted back to her side, Shivani was breathing hard but wouldn't grant him the satisfaction of admitting it. She was also smiling broadly.

"So?" she said.

"Yeah," he said. "Nice."

He was feeling strong and swift—he'd remember that afterward. The rhythm of the ride, the entire day, was perfect. There was satisfaction even in the way his sweat was wicking efficiently into the breeze, except for this one annoying patch high on his brow, just under the lip of his helmet. He flicked at it with a finger, and in that instant spied the groundhog ambling out of tall grasses along the river. This too he recalled later. How it raised its snout, spotting them in turn.

Maybe Jeremy was caught up in his own momentum, rhythm, surprise—he hesitated. Had he started to call out? The muscles in his throat tightened later when he recalled the instant.

For its part, the animal froze as well. Considered. Then with astonishing quickness hurtled its bulk of rolling muscle and fat across the path. Dodging Gretchen, it rammed heavily into Shivani's spokes.

*

His eyes were already open. This he realized. But only gradually would they tighten toward focus, and only partly. The pounding pulse in his head throbbed more painfully as his vision cleared. But someone was just then sticking a finger in his eye, pushing one lid up and the other, and he was figuring she was a doctor—who else would poke him with such casual deliberateness?—and so this was a hospital. And he was in a hospital. Okay.

When he woke again he remembered the hospital right off. His own lack of surprise, of curiosity, surprised him. The dimmed light in the room seemed to thrum at the same rate as the thud of pain in his head. A woman was hovering between him and the light, looking for something in his face, studying him. Was this the doctor again? He started to ask and then, the effort too exhausting, fell back and far away. The woman glanced to the side, and then someone else, Shivani, was hovering too, closer. He felt her kiss on his lips.

"Hey," she said softly and held a straw to his mouth.

Water was good. He sucked after more.

"What the fuck," he tried to whisper, water dribbling down his chin.

Next time, or maybe the time after, that's when he began to realize something was wrong or at least different. Though he couldn't put his finger on it. Couldn't put a name to it.

Shivani had been speaking for a while, he realized this too, but his attention was drifting. He tried hard to appear attentive.

"Do you remember?" she asked. She was asking him.

"Not sure," he mumbled. He was proud of that answer—it didn't give him away.

"You saw it just before, right? The groundhog."

The groundhog he did remember.

"Sure," he said.

"I didn't—that's the thing. I felt Gretchen swerve and the thump as it hit my front wheel and then I was pitching over. Darling, brave Jeremy—you tried to catch me. So we were both going down. Owen and Lee ran right into us and down into the mangle. What a mess." She sighed and he could tell she was struggling not to cry.

He didn't know what to say.

He remembered the groundhog.

"Your helmet split on the pavement just like it's supposed to, but you were knocked cold anyway. The rest of us were nothing but cuts and scrapes." Shivani was struggling with her own helplessness.

He closed his eyes. Her voice, its elite Delhi-wallah cadence, more British than the Queen, was scraping, grating— annoying. It had never bothered him before. He knew that. But all this emotion, the concern and guilt, was radiating from her too. Demanding a response in kind. Was he supposed to provide sympathy?

A quick surge of anger shivered him. His head was throbbing harder.

The flame of his little rage expired almost instantly, leaving him frail, a spent wick on the hospital bed. He could not move.

Jeremy groaned. Shivani stroked her cool hand across his forehead.

She had been at his bedside when he woke—he remembered this too—and he'd recognized her right off, her eyes tired, the stylish flair of her short hair, unusually mussed in the non-time of the hospital.

He'd known who she was.

He'd been glad to see her, truly, to sip the cool water through a straw, grateful not to be alone in this strange place.

But now as he considered, and he was panting lightly through his mouth, he realized that even in that first moment awake he'd also felt—what?—different. Distanced. Dislocated. Watching this lovely woman from very far away. His wife. Hugging a silk shawl against the arid chill. Someone he knew so very well. And yet it seemed as though a tether between them had snapped, like a tendon torn at bone hinge.

A question occurred to him and he opened his eyes once more. "How long?" he whispered.

She hesitated, searching his face. "You've been here two weeks."

That stopped him. It took a while to make sense.

"Two weeks? I was out for two weeks?"

Shivani nodded, and now she was looking sad and worried and guilty again and relieved all at once, tears in her eyes.

He turned his head. He figured the groundhog must have got away free and clear.

*

"You remember the groundhog?" This time it was Owen Thurlow, his pal the Provost.

He managed not to roll his eyes. "Sure," he sighed.

And all he didn't remember: the shell of his helmet splitting. Cell calls to 911. The medevac copter. It had become a crazy therapeutic catechism, his wife and friends reciting the sequence over and over. Chanting the story of all that had swirled about while he remained an unconscious witness. As if capturing it in ever finer detail might somehow penetrate to the heart of the matter. As if grasping precisely what had happened would bring him to himself. His old self.

It was beginning to drive him crazy.

Did they sense the truth?

He would listen graciously, or pretend to, hiding his boredom and occasional flaring annoyance as best he could. The flashes of emotion, unwilled, unprovoked, unreasonable, were also unnerving. All his life he'd prided himself on his cool. Unlike other teenagers years before, unlike many adults to this day, he'd never allowed his emotions to run riot. This was one reason he'd been convinced that the silent libraries and controlled classrooms of the academy were his destiny.

Of course, the recitations also helped Shivani and Owen and Gretchen feel better about the outcome. Obviously. That annoyed him too.

So this time it was Owen Thurlow resurrecting the damned groundhog.

A question struck him only now. "Why the hell did it take me so long to come out of it?" Jeremy demanded, as if he needed to get to the bottom of some truth buried from his gaze, his voice both hoarse and sharp.

Owen seemed startled. "Well, you just didn't wake up, not that first evening. The neurologists wanted to stabilize you. So they induced a coma to play it safe." He hesitated before going on, as if this next verged on something more intimate. "I mean, Jesus, Jeremy, your brain was all bruised and swollen—it needed time to heal. But even that turned out not to be enough," he said, as if trying to convince the patient after the fact. "Dr. Wainwright finally persuaded Shivani you needed surgery—she opened a patch of skull to relieve the pressure."

He lay still and considered. The image struck him as odd, as eerie: contemplating his own head laid open. It dizzied him. Tears welled up out of nowhere, trickling onto his cheek. He'd never been one to weep, certainly not in front of others. He swatted at them with one hand, an I.V. tube rattling awkwardly along. Thurlow seemed not to notice.

From his first waking, nurses had been swabbing a wound on his head and changing the bandage every few hours. He'd assumed a gash from the original accident.

And all along there'd been this headache behind his eyes, radiating deeper and deeper still, and it had never entirely disappeared. Now its presence seemed almost reassuring. Along with the thrum of his blood and the steady breaths in his chest, one after another.

He'd never felt so fully the fragility of this enterprise. Living. He blinked away at a fresh rush of tears.

A day or two later he was being examined by Dr. Wainwright, the same neurologist who'd brought him back into the world. She must have been 40 or 45, he guessed now, her tinted auburn hair cropped short. She was checking his eyes again, the stitches in his itching scalp. As she bent close over him in a lab coat and hospital fatigues he smelled a faint mix of sweat and detergent and peppermint.

"There's this thing," he said.

"Mmm, hmm," she said, shining a pocket flashlight into his other eye.

"It's hard to describe, to explain."

"Mmm, hmm."

"I just don't feel like myself."

She flicked the flashlight off. "Are you experiencing discomfort? Nausea?"

That distracted him for a moment. "Well, yes, actually—there's some nausea. And sort of a constant headache. But that's not what I mean."

"Okay." She seemed only partly listening.

"The thing is, I don't feel like my old self. It's like I'm not the same me any more, if that makes sense. Something's gone all haywire." He was speaking softly. Could she even hear him now? His lips were dry.

This was hard. He closed his eyes. But the struggle to mold words around it was already helping him grasp the slippery thing itself—the strange feelings of dislocation. As though he was staring out at the world from an angle slightly askew to what he'd ever known before. At least trying to explain the deeply unnerving sensation to Dr. Wainwright made it more real, more than just a vague unease.

If this had also taken on the tones of a private confession, as much as a plea for advice or explanation, it was because he felt, well, guilty—as if he were somehow responsible for what had happened. Though he couldn't imagine how. It occurred to him suddenly that if he were Catholic he'd be having this chat with a priest—that notion provoked a snort of laughter. Which shot a bolt of pain through his head.

He winced and lay silent, panting lightly, for a few seconds while she was making notes on his chart.

"For one thing," he murmured, taking up the thread again, "I've been having these crazy, veering emotions—wild swings, from rage to a kind of weepy sadness. It's pathetic." He sighed. "I've never been that kind of guy."

Still no direct response from the doctor. She was glancing at a bank of monitors.

"Yeah," he went on. And it's also how I'm seeing my friends. Even my wife. Like they're strangers. I mean, I do know them. I'm just not relating the same way. About them. Even about myself."

A flash of heat flushed through him as he lay there. His cheeks burned and his brow was slicked with sweat. It might have been another burst of emotion but felt more physical than that. He wanted a sip of water. He wanted this woman to stop examining him for a moment and demonstrate some concern or at least pay him some attention.

He wasn't sure she'd even been listening. But now she did step back, a hand on the stethoscope draped over her shoulders. She studied him seriously—an odd look, almost as if she hadn't until this moment taken him in as a whole person beyond patched head, bruised brain, dilated pupils.

Nodding, she shrugged. "Yes," she said. "I hear what you're saying. This is all very uncomfortable and confusing—I can well imagine. But given the trauma you suffered, these feelings of, let's call it disorientation, aren't uncommon. And each case is so different. How symptoms manifest—there's never any predicting." She patted him on the leg.

"My guess is you're experiencing a response to severe concussion. Believe me, Professor Matthis, it could be so much worse. As the injury fades, as your brain heals, many of these unhappy feelings will almost surely lessen and even disappear entirely."

"Okay," he said, wanting to believe her. "But it sure doesn't feel like it's heading in that direction."

She hesitated, fumbling a roll of mints from her side pocket and slipping one into her mouth. Glancing at him again, she considered. "I do have one piece of practical advice, if you don't mind my offering."

His eagerness was only too clear.

"Now understand, this part lies outside my expertise. One of the clinicians or the chaplain may say something different. But I've seen other situations resembling this, and my suggestion is, keep these feelings to yourself, at least for the time being. Think of yourself as having been wounded—recovery is always going to be slower than you like. And for better or worse, confusion is part of that process. It's understandable. Everyone understands."

Jeremy lay quietly, considering as best he could. His energy had already spent itself again, and weariness was beginning to crush him.

She looked at him directly. "What I'm saying is, if you rush to share your—what?—your sense of all these emotional changes with your wife and friends, isn't it likely they'll only feel hurt and rejected? Not to mention more guilty that they're all right and you're not.

"So," she became brisk and businesslike again, picking up his chart. "What's the point in upsetting everyone at this stage, when things may go back to the way they were?"

"Sure," he whispered, closing his eyes. "You're right."

"What I can say with some confidence is that you're healing very nicely—as rapidly as we could hope."

Even the shaded light in the room had begun to throb through to the back of his head.

At some point Dr. Wainwright must have drifted away to other duties.

Oddly—it seemed odd to him—whenever he woke alone in the night he never doubted his own sense of himself. His consciousness would tug free of the suck of heavy, vivid dreams that vanished without trace even as he broke through their surface. For a few moments he'd lie still in the dry air and dim light, thirsty, taking stock, trying to recapture for an instant an image, a feeling, that had already faded beyond his grasp. He was also relieved to be alone.

The last monitor and I.V. drip had been detached, leaving him untethered. He moved his legs up into the sheet, lifted his arms. Their heavy thinginess, the constant need to pee despite the catheter, these were reassuring. They implicated him in being who he was, lying there, and the me-ness of the self he was considering. It provided a kind of animal certainty of the here and now. He might doubt everything else, but not that.

On one such occasion he awoke deep in the night and his head felt clear, with an alertness, a sharpness he'd forgotten could exist. Exhilarated, he sat up and breathed deep. He was hungry. It was cold in the ward. And a new thought struck: wasn't *himself* some sort of amalgam of memories collected from boyhood on? Were the ones flicking about in his head still his? What a bizarre notion, he thought. Whose else might they be?

Almost without volition, a haphazard inventory flared, wild, charged with no little terror and fretting, leaping from one memory to another. What traces of himself might have disappeared entirely, lost forever? One recollection chased and tumbled into another by chance or association or no reason at all.

That ugly moment when Sandy Greenwalt, like him twelve years old and training in the same bar mitzvah class outside of Pontiac, had one day opened the desk drawer in his friend Jeremy's bedroom. Who knew why? Looking for a pencil? But there lay exposed before the two of them the complicated army knife Jeremy had swiped off Sandy's bedside table some weeks earlier, naked and accusing. All the little blades and screws and bright red shell with its silver cross. He could no longer recall the why of why he'd taken it, or even the scene of theft. But, oh, how vivid that scalding instant of discovery and shame had remained.

Without citing that precise example, Jeremy had often spoken over the years to his students about such peculiarly human capacities, often displayed or discussed in the very texts they were studying. The Greeks delved especially deep. That the memory of something shameful or embarrassing might eternally kindle a blaze of the original agony, piercing if brief. Stranger still to consider that the events themselves, distant in time and space, no longer existed anywhere except within the precincts of an individual skull.

Sandy Greenwalt, and this too Jeremy never mentioned to students, had died long ago. A terrible death in a ditch, the rain water only inches deep, him having crawled from a car wreck he hadn't caused. So no one alive could testify against Jeremy any longer. No external correlative to the theft or the terrible instant of exposure in his bedroom survived. Even that damned Swiss knife was surely lost forever, buried in some unknown landfill. He alone remained custodian of the sin and shame after all these years.

Except now there'd been a singular, revolutionary adjustment: cracking his skull on an asphalt bike path had apparently cauterized the memory. Oh, the original scene could still be summoned in detail—Sandy Greenwalt, long limbed and thick lipped, shaggy red hair, opening the drawer. The jerk of recognition and accusation in his eyes. Jeremy not saying anything, just closing the desk and walking away. But the burning guilt that had haunted him for twenty years and more had vanished, not even a shadow of it lingered, almost as if the memory did indeed belong no longer to him but to someone else entirely. No matter that it existed only in this head wobbling on these shoulders. It was an eerie sensation, as if he were peering in on someone else's private life.

His skin itched. He'd already sat up in the hospital bed and flung off the sheet. Now he slid heavily down and sat heavily in a padded chair by the window. His legs and feet were cold. He realized he was trembling and also that a flood of panic unlike anything he could remember was welling into his chest and throat.

Another memory came unbidden to test him, one with higher stakes: his first glimpse of Shivani Chatterjee nearly eight years earlier. Its details had been reliably seared into his synapses.

Hot and frustrated, he'd been killing time on a block of dumpy bookstores and rundown bars across from the university, instead of laboring in the library's un-air-conditioned stacks. The decisive chapter of his dissertation lay waiting, half-drafted in a spiral notebook, half-scattered about the airless carrel on note cards. An hour rifling through the same boxes of dusty books that had been on limp display for many months yielded nothing. Not that he expected any treasures. At last he was pushing open the shop's front door and stepping warily into the ferocious sun, when this tall, thin figure strode past him purposefully on the sidewalk, arms swinging, bangles tinkling, fresh and light and oblivious to any heat. She wore a sleeveless sundress like all the southern girls, but a silk scarf, magenta and blue-bird blue, rippled at her throat.

And he's following her. He finds himself *following* her, trailing along behind. It's already something more than curiosity. He's never done such a thing. It's not at all who Jeremy Matthis is or has ever been. Yet it's so matter of fact, as if he's been waiting for this all along and never had a choice. Turning into an alley, she tugs open the side door of the Methodist Church, and before the screen can slap shut he scoots forward and slips inside too, right on her heels. Where wouldn't he have followed?

She's arrived, it turns out, to attend a monthly meeting of the local Amnesty International chapter. Some ten or twelve other good and earnest souls have fluttered in as well. Okay, he's all for this—he's decided in an instant. He'll pen letters of protest to all the oppressive governments on the planet, just so he can share the same musty air with this woman.

A cascade of dark brown with a hint of henna, Shivani's hair reaches her waist—she's still unmarried of course—with a ribbon of the blue-bird blue gathering it at the back of her long neck. A trio of delicate gold bangles, the ones that had captured him on the sidewalk with their tinkling dance, they dance, sliding up and down at the wrist of one elegant arm.

Had she noticed him before the meeting began? Eight years on and he still didn't know for sure—she'd laugh, treasuring the mystery of her own thoughts in that Methodist church and the question of whether she'd even been aware of his presence. She never let on.

More important, whether he was recounting the tale at a dinner party or the memory was scratched alive by a certain scent of rose (or mildew), it had always conjured as well a trace of his original breathless desire. Of the sexual dazzle. The delight in his own bold chutzpah. Something, too, of the dismaying worry throughout that interminable Amnesty session—there'd been so much political outrage to set down on paper—that when the instant finally presented itself and he mustered some brilliant *hello*, she might simply dismiss him out of hand like some furtive stalker. However faint, these feelings flashed along the sinews of his being, part of the fabric of his identity.

Tonight the images of that far-away moment did flair vividly—sharper, cleaner than anything he'd seen or remembered in the long, fuzzy days since the accident. Tall and slim and elegant, Shivani came striding past him, turning at last into the church's screen door. He remembered his own shoes sinking into the asphalt on that torrid afternoon. He must have followed her down the stairs—that he couldn't recall—but he certainly did remember the musty basement and the smoky rose of Shivani's cologne. Only later did he learn that her sister faithfully supplied it twice a year from a certain stall in Connaught Place.

Jeremy sat panting in the padded chair. And as he spied now the further truth, a new truth, seeping through, he drew his legs up in the hospital gown to his chest and squeezed tight as if to shut it all away. For it came to him that, vibrant or not, this memory like the other had been leeched dry of emotion at its heart. Though he might recall every detail, he felt nothing. The magic that had drawn him to Shivani and bound them together from that distant start, the fatedness and wonder of it all, had belatedly flashed out, fading gray, ashen, leaving behind only the tatty, worn shell of habit and everyday life.

He might have moaned, but that seemed too dramatic. He felt too little. A strange distance or mutedness had been draped over his past, creating a chasm between a former Jeremy Matthis and the person he felt himself to be in the here and now. He had changed. That was the thing. His life had changed. Not a lot. But enough.

It now seemed to him that from the very first moment of waking days earlier, before he'd known where he was or what had happened to him, he'd been flung out stumbling on a journey over which he had no control or compass or guiding star. All he could manage was a kind of awkward staggering forward in the dark. Yet in this late night of the hospital ward, an unmapped land lay stretching before him.

He was slightly dizzy and his head ached. He realized he was shivering again. Pushing himself up from the chair, he climbed back into the bed. He was breathing hard, and he wrapped his arms about himself. Sleep offered no refuge. His mind remained sharp and clear, and it was racing.

Only two hours later, never having slept, Jeremy Matthis rose once more and showered for the first time, with difficulty, in the tiny bathroom. He dressed in clothes that Shivani had brought several days earlier to cheer them both with anticipation of his release, whenever that might be, back into the world. But it was a new world he now intended to enter, making a place for himself as best he could. He carried the largely empty suitcase with him.

He announced his intentions at the nurses' station, and after they had remonstrated and warned as he knew they must, they pointed him to the office where he would sign his release, absolving them, the hospital, its doctors and administrators of all responsibility. Responsibility for himself was precisely what he intended to assume. When the final form was presented for his signature, he wrote the name Jeremy Matthis with a sense of eagerness and a bit of fear, because he suspected it might be the last time. He hadn't yet decided what would take its place. Of what he would say to Shivani when she surely found him. He knew only that this was the journey, that this was the right path, wherever it might lead him.

Year of Fire

On a slow night, a warm night, Natalie would perch on her bar stool, propping first one foot and then the other on the next stool over. It was a different pair of stiletto heels each night of the week. She'd rotate through them, gold to lipstick red to candy pink. So she'd be leaning forward, foot cocked precariously as she touched up her nails (which already matched the shoes du jour). And since it was a warm night and she was between sets anyway and there were no customers to flirt into buying her the Fox Hole's version of champagne, she'd let her blouse hang open. You might could see through it all buttoned up, she'd say, but it sure weren't no friend to any breeze that way.

Duncan Boothe was tending bar and his wife had left him and he was doing his best simply to wipe down the bar and clean a glass or two and try not to stare or imagine what he could be doing with Natalie. On one of those nights early on—he'd only been at the Fox Hole for a month—Natalie shook her head and laughed.

"Shoot," she said. "You're a cute guy, Duncan, you sure are. Sweet too. I'd take that problem off your hands—the one in front of you—but then I'd have to be helping out the other guys who work here. Know what I mean?"

He nodded, frozen but his face hot, wondering how she'd made out the problem, what with the bar between them. And sweet he didn't feel.

"It's the funniest damn thing, the way you boys go ape over a girl's boobs." She was shaking her head again, thoughtfully. "Never made any sense to me, but I guess I can't complain. Not for that, I'd be working with my dad over at the Six Mile Ford plant. Most likely I'll wind up there anyhow, once they've dropped." Most all of Natalie's sentences lilted up at the end as if she were asking a question. "Fatty tissue—that's all they are, you know? Just sacks of fatty tissue. I learned that in junior high. In Roanoke, before we moved up here for the work."

Duncan was still nodding. But after a while, when he realized what she'd done, he was grateful to her. She'd set him free. *Fatty tissue*—it's all he needed. For the rest of that year he was able to spend four nights a week with Natalie and her friends without wrestling that particular problem, most of the time.

Later that same night she came back to him and his problems. "So why'd your wife go and leave you? What was her name?" She dragged deep at her cigarette. "Ginny, wasn't that it?"

"Jenny," he said.

"Yeah. Ginny. You all must have been fighting bad. You didn't smack her, did you?" Natalie looked him up and down. "No, you ain't the type. I *know* the type."

She knew the type. Twenty-four, two kids, her second husband already flung free. Duncan had gotten some of her story already. But how did she come to hear about Ginny/Jenny? Had he let something slip? Since when had he become the object of study? It made him plenty uneasy, the tables turned.

He didn't have the Fox Hole in mind when he launched his first clumsy researches by wandering down to Eight Mile Road and Woodward Avenue a few weeks earlier. But Jennifer had already decamped, his classes at Kingsmount Academy wouldn't resume before Labor Day, he wasn't writing poetry, or nothing but crap. So when a faint flutter of inspiration tickled him, bourbon-induced or not, he figured there was time to kill and nothing to lose. A book: that's what he could do. It would be an exposé of sorts. Not literature. Something more journalistic, about life in a bar like this and the girls who worked there, and the guys who drank there, and maybe something about what the life in the bar could say about life in a city that had just torn itself apart. Who knew, it might even make him some money. Teaching in a private school paid nothing, and his family, the Boothes, had ceased supplementing his income months before.

Eight Mile was where the city ended and the suburbs began. Those couple of blocks along Woodward Avenue, the main north-south artery, were a kind of no-man's-and-everyman's-land of liquor stores and strip joints, cheap motels and, on the other side of the avenue, a sprawling public cemetery. Up until that summer most of the traffic headed south from the still sparse suburbs to the professional buildings downtown and to auto plants across the city, to the Grand Circus Theater for a movie, to Greek Town and to Hamtramck for Polish pizza. But one July morning the traffic jolted to a halt in amazement and terror and then fled, once and forever, in the other direction. Caught up in the sharp tidal surge, other white families who still lived in the city followed swiftly behind, away from the riots that over several days had burned out great swathes of the old black neighborhoods.

In the wee small hours of that first morning, the cops had raided a blind pig, one of those unlicensed neighborhood joints for drinking and playing cards. It wasn't a big deal to begin with—those raids happened most every night. But this one went wrong—white cops bungling and then shooting to cover it up. The city exploded. Who would have guessed it had been seething with black anger and despair for months and years? Not the police apparently.

Not Duncan Boothe. A straight drag fifteen miles up Woodward, Kingsmount Academy might have been on another planet. What did any of this horror have to do with the handful of faculty and their families who remained on the sprawling estate through the summer? Along with the others, Duncan and Jenny followed reports of the riots on one of the school's big black-and-white television consoles, witnessing the chaos and destruction on the tube like the rest of the nation. It was distant, the burning city, remote. Yet it was also so disorienting—this was *their* city after all, not Newark or Watts. Like everyone else, downtown was where they shopped, stood in line for new movies, ate Chinese egg-fou-yong, watched the Tigers play ball.

It was as if the napalm flames half a world away in Vietnam, which they'd also been witnessing on television, had suddenly burst from the safe quarantine of the box before them. Duncan had been living in dread of Vietnam, afraid of a plunge into its swamps and tunnels and fire fights against his will. This is what kept him yoked to teaching at the school, where his family's local influence had managed, so far, to replace his college deferment. Which meant that Duncan had his own full measure of anger and despair.

The burning city seemed sinister and fascinating, impossibly distant and yet near at hand, and somehow it just didn't feel real.

Except that Michael Rosen, about to be a senior at Kingsmount, lived with his mother not so far from downtown. Early that same first morning of the disturbances, he'd journeyed by bus, only slightly ahead of the crest of violence and its faster spreading repercussions, up to the school library for what was to have been a single summer's day—he was giving Jenny Boothe a hand with new entries in the card catalogue. It was Jennifer, hearing the news first from an English teacher who rushed in to share and then on her radio in the small office off the main reading room, who called Michael from the catalogue to listen with her. Together, silent, heads bowed, they followed the early reports.

His neighborhood was a mix of elderly Jews and recently arrived Blacks, and it wasn't all that far from 12th Street and the fires that were creeping from charred block to block, with invisible snipers on the roofs, with milling, angry crowds shouting at the cops when they weren't looting, weren't dying. Michael's mother was trapped there, or more likely in the hospital where she was a delivery-room nurse. They couldn't get any word. Again and again he dialed the heavy black telephone on Jenny's desk, only to be met with the grating signal for tangled circuits or, more disconcerting, merely a hollow silence. Nor was there any way to slip past the National Guardsmen ringing the city like a tourniquet and find his mother for himself. Not that Jenny would let him try. A couple of times he threatened to set out on his own. But the buses had ceased running after several were seized, burned, their stricken hulks dragged into barricades. He had no car of course. Jenny would have wrestled him to the ground in any event. Michael had no doubt of that and neither did her husband.

So they took him in for the time being. It was true that their cottage at one end of Faculty Row was dark and cramped at the best of times. Duncan was certain that, had they asked the headmaster, Henry Hopkins, he would have made a place in the empty dorms for one of the school's star pupils. But Jennifer wouldn't have it. She and the boy had become friends over the past couple of years. In between classes he would drift into the library's office and they'd chat about this and that. After a while he even managed to satisfy his daily work duty—each Kingsmount student, no matter how privileged, had some such responsibility—by shelving books or reading the stacks. Jennifer wasn't about to abandon Michael Rosen to an empty dorm, not knowing whether his mother was safe, not knowing whether his house would survive. So in the late afternoon the three of them hiked to Faculty Row together. As they entered her home, even before starting dinner, she tucked some sheets into the couch and strung a blanket across a line in the small living room as a measure of privacy for the boy.

Duncan had stumbled in on them once, a year or so earlier. Jennifer and the boy were sitting face to face in her office, next to the leaded windows overlooking the quad. Deep in conversation, they flustered when Duncan appeared through the door, as if they'd forgotten where they were, as if he'd caught them at something. And yes, a pang of resentment—of raw jealousy—did flare in his throat and chest and thighs. Because they were intimate, this sixteen or seventeen-year-old boy and Jenny, twenty-four or twenty-five herself. Michael was pale, tall and rail thin, gawky, with a big head and a shock of dark hair and dark, deep-set eyes. Jennifer's reddish-blonde hair was gathered back in a haphazard pony-tale, stray wisps defying any rubber band. She had a broad face, lightly freckled, a pixyish nose, and grayish-blue eyes that, at that moment with Michael, seemed full of warmth and gaiety. And without seeing it he knew she had a little cleft, an ancient small scar on her upper lip. It was that tiny flaw that Duncan had never had an answer to. It had slain him in college, overcoming Jenny's steelworking father in Ohio and her impatience with his own lack of either an ability to do hard work or a clear ambition towards something else.

They, Jenny and the boy, were intimate but not sexual. Duncan knew that. Sex was never the issue. He understood it thoroughly and almost wished it weren't true—that they'd trespassed in that more predictable way so he could at least possess that to lord over them. Because jealous he was. When had Jenny and he last shared that kind of intimacy?

"Are your grades so good you can afford to skip study hall, Mr. Rosen?" he demanded, sounding every bit as mean as he felt.

Startled, blushing furiously, the boy gangled to his feet and fled, glad to get away.

"He *adores* you, Duncan. Why can't you see that?" Jennifer said.

The truth of this was not a surprise. Over the past couple of years Michael had signed up for any course of Duncan's that was available, from poetry to journalism to the Victorian novel. He'd done very well and his grades reflected it. But there was something more about the boy, a neediness, a hanging on every word, that Duncan found distasteful. He supposed the boy was looking for a father figure or at least an older brother. But that wasn't a role he sought. It demanded too much. Kingsmount didn't pay Duncan enough. Why not let Jennifer do that too, he thought bitterly.

"Adoration's not what I need," he snapped, mean again and sad and wanting to reach out to her and just not able to.

Afterwards, a day or two later while he was marking some papers at the kitchen table, Duncan realized what it was he'd also spied in that instant of bursting in on them quite unintentionally—what it was they shared. The insight struck with a marrow-numbing clarity. So obvious, how had he not seen, not understood this before? Jenny and Michael were bound to each other precisely because they both felt like outsiders at Kingsmount. They didn't belong, didn't fit in, no matter how hard they tried. (Unlike him, Duncan Boothe, scion of the founding family.) Bound by this burden, they'd adopted each other. Yet—and here was the irony—the boy wanted desperately to belong. Not Jenny. She'd never felt at home.

At Princeton she'd been foolish enough to believe Duncan's impersonation of a poet—one of the roles he'd inhabited over the years. He grew his hair long, let his Brooks Brothers collars fray. He played acoustic guitar quite well. She was tough, prosaic, political—and passionate. As the anti-war movement began to grow, she attended rallies, carried petitions. For his part, Duncan had no problem with any of her beliefs, not that he took them all that seriously either. He certainly didn't defend the war—and had no intention of joining the fighting if he could avoid it. Torching his draft card in a slight drizzle outside her residence hall was an impulse, an inspiration—it worked magic, brushing aside her reservations about who he really was.

That last year in the east they were happy and the world seemed open and beckoning, full of possibilities. It was only much later, looking back, that he might have realized that Princeton had not been the launch pad to greater things, glory as a poet or success in real estate or on Wall Street, as everyone anticipated for him, but rather the apex of his personal trajectory. After graduating a gradual slide began, unanticipated and unperceived at first, as back to Kingsmount he brought his bride. This was all he could think of, falling back on the influence of his family—his indomitable mother—to replace his deferment from the draft. Him returning, the not-quite-prodigal son, not yet anyway. He was one of the elect, one of the Boothes.

Jennifer loathed his family, especially his mother. She was a Boothe by marriage, but now that her in-laws had passed away she was more Boothe than mere blood might ordain. She ruled husband, family, Kingsmount, through checkbook and ruthlessness. What wasn't to loathe?

Less than a year after he intruded on them in the library it was a hot, muggy July and the industrial city only fifteen miles south was on fire. Michael Rosen was trapped on the right/wrong side of the barricades, and they took him in. The decision wasn't Duncan's and he didn't make the offer, but in truth most of the time the boy's presence in their lives over those few days wasn't a burden. Most of the time, of course, they weren't actually in the cottage together, tripping over one another. When they were, say at dinner, the situation seemed natural enough, almost a regular little nuclear family. Jenny would be bustling about assembling some kind of casserole of noodles and cheese. Michael would stand and watch helplessly, wanting to help her. But the kitchen was too small.

After a bourbon, however, or after a second one, Duncan would be watching the boy watch his wife or her showing him how to test the pasta or where to find something in a book, and suddenly having Michael in his house wouldn't seem so natural or okay. Little intimations would detonate behind his eyes. Them and their damned intimacy, their shared understanding. Him and his damned failures. He clenched his teeth to keep the rage hidden.

On the second evening, after a quick drink for Duncan, the three of them strolled from Faculty Row with a few of the other families up to the campus. Naturally, some of the other teachers had televisions of their own, but already they had developed this little ritual—it seemed they should be witnessing the city's destruction together in one of Kingsmount's common rooms. Weren't they a community, after all?

It was one of those evenings in midsummer when the light lingers, fading so slowly that it can't possibly disappear entirely before dawn. The estate was green and lush, the heavy-leaved chestnuts bending under the weight of their own glory. That day, however, the reality of the catastrophe had first begun to intrude even on Kingsmount as something more than an abstraction, a story. The stink arrived, invisible at first, followed by the coarse, gritty testimony of smoke and cloud overhead. So as the families strode through all the summer majesty of elms and oaks and cypress, past the Scandinavian sculptures and fountains, and through the modern gothic boys-school architecture to Marquis Commons, the acrid fumes hung faintly in the air. Some covered their mouths and noses or tied kerchiefs around their children's faces as if they were playing cowboy bandits. Some simply breathed, drawing the stink into their lungs as if this were their due, their fate.

For a long time that evening the small gathering of twelve or fifteen adults (their younger children playing outside on the lawns), sat in solemn horror, watching the great box of the television, no one saying much. The sound was turned down as well. Scenes flashed across the bottle-thick tube, water arcing through the air towards buildings aflame and crumbling, Molotov cocktails arcing through the air and landing in a blast of fiery splinters, ragged scrums of protestors or looters splintering away from police batons and tear gas. Occasionally they'd spy a sniper on a roof or a body flopped broken in a smoking lot.

"Hell of a way to accomplish a little urban renewal," Duncan muttered, half to himself. It was merely a throw-away joke. Smart-ass irony. Not very funny, not very subtle, bad taste of course, lousy timing. But how big a deal? He wasn't even trying to lighten the mood. He never really intended anyone to hear. But out it flashed like a dark fist clenching all his anger, his resentment, the dour despondency that for months had been tightening its grip around his throat. The black-and-white images of their city being wracked by protest, violence, and flame, like the kindred images of destruction half a globe away, might have been a projection of the despair gnawing his own soul.

Jennifer heard. (He didn't realize until a moment later.) She'd been perched next to him on an over-stuffed couch, but now she drew away as if sniffing something worse than the smoke settling its ash invisibly about them. Shock, disbelief, scarred her face, not so much for the brutish comment itself as at the sudden eruption of recognition that it had brought her: as if the fist had physically struck and she knew him for what he was.

He felt a yellow-green sick, a shudder. Or better: not a shudder but a hard thud to his chest that rang hollow, except for the lard of self-pity that seemed to sit heavily in that cavity. He knew in an instant that something was more than just wrong. Jennifer was staring at him as if she hadn't actually seen him for a long time. Most disturbing was the faint smile—out of sync with the look in her eyes—that flickered about her mouth with a hint of relief. This had been one of those rare and unexpected moments when a stiff key turns in the soul, a decisive click that changes everything.

*

It turned out that Michael Rosen's mother was perfectly safe. After another day or so, that's what they discovered. Grueling shifts at the hospital had swept her along fourteen, sixteen hours at a rush. Given the sudden flood of wounded and ailing, they'd shifted her from delivering babies to a ragged sort of triage in an emergency area that had spread across most of the hospital's main floor. Naturally, Mrs. Rosen was plenty worried about Michael too, hoping he'd reached Kingsmount safely before the surging tide of violence crashed over him but unable to know for sure. Finally, in a momentary lull, one of the other nurses was able to slip away to her home in Lincoln Park where she could place a phone call to the school's switchboard.

And that was that. Two days later Michael went home—his neighborhood had been spared, but the streets were littered with debris and largely vacant, the smells of wet ash and urine blowing in from a few blocks away. The summer withered. Jennifer and Duncan watched each other stumble through the dying paces of a routine that seemed empty, that made them miserable. Duncan watched as well with a numb passivity, seeing the choreography play out with an apparent inevitability, lamenting it, and feeling sorry for himself.

Again and again he recalled that single frozen moment after he'd betrayed himself in Marquis Commons by speaking aloud and how Jenny recoiled on the couch. Perhaps if he'd reached out to her just then? But he wasn't capable of reaching out. He knew that for many months now she'd been the one reaching out towards him, again and again, and now the futility had sucked her dry. They stumbled through their paces. No more blow-ups. No more fights or really much conversation of any kind. They were kind to each other in their shared misery, even thoughtful, sensing that it would soon be behind them.

And then in the deeper heat of August she was gone. A single bag. A bus ticket. She took hardly anything with her. There wasn't even the need for a forwarding address, at least initially, because she didn't know where she'd be going after a short stay with her parents in Youngstown.

Eight Mile and Woodward. The border, a ruptured membrane between city and suburb, between before and after. Between Black and white, too, but not all at once. The city had always been divided into discrete neighborhoods, a kind of de facto arrangement of race and ethnicity that had kept things under control, mostly. The gathering pace of white flight to the suburbs didn't change that all at once. But where the city ended was less an imaginary boundary than before and a deeper scar.

Duncan thought a book about a bar like the Fox Hole, the girls who worked there, the men who paid to drink and watch them, might say something about what the city had been and what it was going to become. Except the Fox Hole was the fifth place he had walked into and by that time he wasn't saying a word about writing any damn book. And truth to tell, what Duncan Boothe really wanted was not to be at home without Jennifer. What he really wanted was to be as far as could be managed from Kingsmount Academy without sacrificing his job or, the truer truth, sacrificing his mother's protection from the draft. He told Serge, the manager, that he needed the money. That much was true too. Serge looked at his khaki pants and faded blue Oxford shirt and shook his head.

"You know how to pour drinks."

"Sure."

"Sure," he said, skeptical. "I pay you out of the till," he said. "No taxes and no complaints from you. Got it?"

"Sure."

"Sure," Serge said.

It was the middle of the year and he was trying not to get fired, but not trying very hard. He slept through one class, forgot to show up for another. His lessons were increasingly improvised. He'd spin out rambling musings on books, usually novels he'd read in college, rather than those assigned for a specific period on the rigid school syllabus. Papers he handed back late or with a grade scrawled across the front and few if any comments. He wanted to be almost anywhere other than Kingsmount Academy, where the legacy of his family and the invisible watchfulness of his mother pressed on his chest like a heavy stone, forcing the breath, the life, the wish for life from him. But his dread of being drafted to fight in Vietnam pressed back just as hard and he was frozen. What horrified him wasn't a fear of pain and oblivion or a moral opposition to the war itself—any political outrage had largely departed with Jennifer. But after all his years in a boarding school environment, he just couldn't bear the thought of military life, the inspections and hierarchies, the pandering and the humiliations. Whenever he imagined it, a cloying, clawing sense of suffocation over-whelmed him.

At first the notion had been that most of his research would be complete before school began. Maybe a couple of hours a week after that until he'd gathered enough material. But tending bar at the Fox Hole had gradually become its own addiction. He hardly struggled against it. The mindlessness and the easy familiarity with strangers were an escape from Kingsmount, an escape from himself. One night a week, then two, then four, then five. On his feet five, six hours a night, not thinking, not explaining, pouring beers and cheap champagne, listening to stories, signaling the bouncer (Serge often did double-duty in that role) when one of the girls needed a hand or one of the drinkers needed assistance in paying a tab and making it to the door. He wasn't thinking and he was drinking less himself, when he wasn't home. He still maintained the notion that this was a research project. That a book would come of it eventually. Of course, the notion was purely his own, since he couldn't confess the plan to Natalie and her friends, let alone Serge. And he surely didn't dare spill these beans in the hallowed, vine-covered walls of Kingsmount. Except that he did. He let it slip.

One morning, early, it would have been a Thursday because the school paper had appeared and been distributed in the dorms the night before, he was meeting with the student editorial board to critique this latest issue, column by column, story by story. He'd been appointed faculty advisor the previous year, probably because the headmaster felt it was just desserts for Duncan Boothe's manifold failings as an assistant coach of any sport—soccer, cross country, hockey, even football. By his second year back at Kingsmount he'd escaped those duties entirely because none of the regular coaches would have him.

So it was Thursday morning and it was early, and he was both exhausted and slightly hung-over, not having returned home from the Fox Hole much before the time he should have been rising. He looked a wreck, rushing into the seminar room with (an illegal) mug of coffee. All eight boys were waiting for him, several half-asleep, most nearly as mangy as he, with collars twisted, ties knotted askew, shirttails hanging over belts. Among them sat Michael Rosen, editor of the op-ed page for his senior year.

If he looked no more tidy than the rest, he was alert, awake—judgmental. The boy might as well have been drumming his fingers on the long wood table, as if Mr. Boothe had kept them on pins and needles for hours. Judgmental, and so goddamned earnest. That's what annoyed Mr. Boothe all to hell. Yes, Rosen was more mature than most of the others, smarter too. Yet there was something so ridiculously naïve about him as well, and innocent, and easily shocked. More easily shocked even than Jenny.

"Sorry," Boothe muttered. "I was out late."

Some of them were already spreading the newspaper open on the long table and didn't much care. Others were nodding. Michael was nodding. Somehow Boothe didn't like the import of their nodding. Was this their working assumption about what he did, staying out too late, probably drinking?

"It's a book project I'm working on," he began, startling himself. "I was doing research—basis of all good journalism, right?" He shouldn't have begun. He was yammering now, wanting to justify himself in the eyes of these teenage boys, as if that mattered or were possible.

"What kind of research?" one of them asked.

"I'm undercover, sort of, working in this bar. Down in the city, see? Actually it's a strip joint. I'm going to write about the lives of the people there, the ones that hang out, the ones that, well, work." Now he was confiding in them, hoping to impress them or at least make them believe. And he was watching himself prattle with a kind of paralytic horror, as if he were loping toward a cliff with no hope, no real desire to stop.

Surely now he had their attention.

"Wow," said a couple of them together. "Jeez," from another. Michael didn't say anything at first, but he looked amused or maybe contemptuous.

"Seriously," Boothe said.

"Yeah. Cool." This from Michael at last. "We'll have to come visit when we turn eighteen."

"Then I'd have to kill you," Boothe said, soaring with a kind of rapture and despair, the cliff already far behind, above him.

Several giggled nervously. "Wow," one of them said again. But smiling or impressed or frozen, their faces showed that they weren't sure he was kidding. Neither was he.

It was a year of fires.

He'd been balancing a glass with some melting cubes on his chest. A night off from the bar. The small black-and-white television was flickering silently, but he wasn't really watching it. He was lying on his couch, smoking, a tower of student papers teetering next to him on the floor. Unmarked, yellowing at the edges, they were already three weeks overdue. Duncan's cigarette flicked them to life while he dozed. Yet only because these papers were so close at hand could the flames scorch his fingers and wake him, sort of, before the smoke could kill him. Up he blundered, disoriented, batting and swatting and stumbling, and the little fire became a big fire. Up went the school-owned cottage. Down came the school-owned cottage, and with it the few possessions, including the TV, he still jointly owned with Jennifer. If she ever returned for her share there'd be little cause for argument over who got what.

Almost before the local fire crew had finished extinguishing the last embers of the blaze, Henry Hopkins planted Duncan on the other side of the Kingsmount estate, in a small room that had once been the gardener's quarters in the Lodge. Hopkins seemed to want to get him away from the other faculty and their cottages before further accidents could happen.

Did the headmaster have any sense of the irony? Boothe wondered. He doubted it. Henry Hopkins didn't do irony. But surely had he considered, he might have realized that Duncan Boothe would have spent much of his childhood playing in this same Lodge and roaming its gardens and passageways, even the gardener's room with the gardener's smelly belongings still scattered about. After all, it had been the Boothe family home for six decades until, while Duncan was at Princeton, first his grandmother died and then, more swiftly than mere physical health might have intimated, his grandfather followed. His parents remained in their more modern house on an adjacent property. The Lodge passed as per trust and deed into the hands of the Academy.

Ten months after the riots, nine months after Jennifer went away, eight months after starting at the Fox Hole, the stink of the cottage fire remained lodged deep in his throat and lungs, the acrid rasp of burning wood and linoleum, rubber and pumice and who knew what else from a house in flame. He'd tried hot showers in the gym. He'd tried mouthwash and inhalers. Come the last two evenings at the Fox Hole, he tried heavier doses of bourbon even than usual. His snout had always been too damned sensitive.

Yet after three days the smoke still coated the inner surfaces of his skull. It even seemed to muffle the early morning alarm clock, which only slowly managed to drag him out of dark dreams he was relieved not to recall.

Otherwise, this morning he felt just fine. He was in a remarkably buoyant mood.

No way did he trust that mood. He wasn't that foolish. It was phony. How could someone whose life was totally screwed feel so goddamn perky?

He didn't shower because there was no shower in the tight quarters, just an ancient, rust-stained bathtub in an outhouse. Grabbing the black academic robe that hardly disguised just how soiled and tattered it had become, Duncan hurried across the estate towards the school campus. He tried shaking his head to clear it, but that wasn't a good idea—it spiked the headache that had only begun to retreat and brought on a faint wave of nausea. Even so, the giddiness remained intact.

He was giddy, gleeful, shaky with a kind of joy. Then the diagnosis came to him with a sudden stab of certainty: shell shock. That was it. The insight delighted him. He chuckled and thought about lighting a cigarette. But for once drawing smoke into his throat seemed a bad idea. Well, the last cigarette had been a bad idea too.

As he tromped through the wet grass it occurred to him that his banishment to the Lodge was Henry Hopkins's final warning, the headmaster's way of serving notice that he could drift no farther. That grandson of the founders or not, son of Dorothea Boothe, now President of the Foundation, or not, he Duncan Boothe would be dismissed with the next screw up or failure or dereliction. No doubt—and this he realized now belatedly as well—his mother would have approved both the banishment to the gardener's quarters and the implicit warning, thus drawing one last step closer to fulfilling her own threat to wash her hands of him if he didn't steer a straighter course.

So why was he in such a goddamn good mood?

Shell shock.

Only such a diagnosis could account for it. Wife gone. House gone. Career on the rocks. What else might explain the giddiness, the lack of concern, the lack of despair? He found little satisfaction in being able to diagnose himself. Or in recognizing the abundance of irony here too: teaching at Kingsmount had indeed managed to protect him thus far from the draft. His friends and classmates, the ones who'd already enlisted or been yanked out of their lives, they needed all the pleasantnesses of Vietnam to summon their own versions of shell shock. Those who survived. What a talent!—he could muster such dislocations of sense and spirit while protected by this idyllic estate outside a city that had burned the previous summer.

With these thoughts the giggles gradually dispersed, replaced by a bone-deep weariness. Family pull exhausted, academic excuses exhausted, if Hopkins sacked him he might very well wind up lugging an M-16 through swamp and jungle after all, translated from the flames of a city, a house, to the flames of napalm and cordite.

As if to prove that his high spirits were nothing but phantoms (or more bluntly pathological), the May breeze shredded the last of them, assisted by a dew that soaked the grass and quickly his shoes, by the purple azaleas and the hanging pagoda blossoms on the chestnut trees. By the time he reached the central campus he was miserable once more and thoroughly sorry for himself. Rather than lifting, his headache was thudding with dull throbs. He was too late for breakfast, but he could snag a mug of coffee in the dining hall as he hurried past. Coffee he needed in the worst way.

But there wasn't time—if he hurried, if he sprinted for it, he just might slip through the chapel door at the very tock of eight. (No one, but no one, was allowed in after that fell moment when the heavy door swung shut.) The brief service, like the assembly for announcements after lunch, was one of the school's daily rituals. More than a good faith gesture, Boothe's attendance was expected. No doubt his absence would be strictly noted by the headmaster. But he needed that coffee. Even the quick trot across the quad seemed too much to face without it. And here was the dining hall, the first building he would pass, no one waiting there to slam a door in his face or grimace at his appearance.

Dark and massive, with a high peaked ceiling and hanging lamps, the great chamber might have been modeled on some fantasy of an old mead hall or a medieval English college, except that it was also entirely modern, the brick and stone all in loving repair and very much of a piece. A gaggle of local women was scattered about the long tables. They wore starched aprons and little white hats that looked like ducks floating in their hair. Ignoring the intruder, they were piling dirty cups and plates on huge oval trays or wiping down the wooden surfaces. He shoved through a swinging door into the kitchen and poured coffee from a great cauldron that had been cooking it for hours. Mug in hand, he shoved a shoulder back out into the quad and halted. No reason now to race. Eight o'clock had come and gone. Tock.

Across the way and under the Marquis Hall arch he spied a student standing alone. Duncan felt sour enough to veer in that direction and scold the boy for skipping chapel. But within a few steps he realized it was Michael Rosen. He was smoking, casually, flicking tufts of ash at the brick arch. The impudent gesture annoyed Boothe, as Michael Rosen so often managed to do. He seemed to be flaunting the rules and not caring who witnessed it. Yet they both knew that Rosen's insolence here was an illusion, a pose. As a senior the privilege of smoking was his, as long as he did so outside. (Younger boys would sneak off into the estate at night for their round of fags.)

For his part, Michael gave no sign of surprise that this teacher was truant from chapel. He flicked an ash. Along with the half-dozen other Jews at Kingsmount, he received a special exemption from this particular ritual. The others would be scattered about the school, waiting for class to begin in half an hour. But from Duncan Boothe's perspective,

Rosen seemed to be hovering outside the chapel, exempted but still in some way excluded as well, apparently longing to belong. That's what Duncan had always suspected—that the boy wanted it both ways. Wanted, beyond everything else, to be hugged to the belly of the community just as he was, warts and all, Jew and all. This morning he was wearing blue and green tartan slacks, tassel loafers, a crisp shirt and tie under his navy school blazer. It was all perfect, and not one item seemed quite to fit, like pieces jammed together from different jigsaw puzzles.

"You're mighty turned out for a school day," said Boothe.

The boy shrugged. "No big deal." He tossed his stub behind a bush. "My birthday." Shrugged again.

"Eighteen?" Boothe said. "Big day."

Another shrug.

There was something perverse in his need to extend an awkward conversation that neither of them wanted. "You and your pals going to celebrate?"

Rosen didn't respond. Then he asked, "What do you hear from Jenny?" and glanced at Boothe directly for the first time, his eyes dark and defiant.

Stung, startled, he felt his face flush with anger. He'd never suspected the boy had it in him.

"She know about the fire?"

Not trusting his voice, Boothe shook his head.

They, the two of them, hadn't spoken about Jennifer for nearly the entire academic year. Yet they were both thinking about her the whole time, missing her the whole time. Boothe realized what he should have known: that the boy must have missed her about as much as he did, if in a more uncomplicated way. But there was something new that day to his tone—defiant, razzing. Michael Rosen was taunting him.

Boothe, amused and aggravated, almost laughed aloud. Taunting *him*—letting him have it back for a change, instead of mooning around as he had all these years, like some puppy he'd slapped with a wet newspaper. But rather than laughing, Boothe shook his head again. That dead cigarette butt peeking out from behind the shrub looked pretty good.

For three days now the ash in his mouth had made sense of the year for him. It was satisfying to taste the shape of nightmare—a neat trajectory from fire to fire. But now he realized it was wrong. What shaped the nightmare of his last nine months was the living with Jennifer's absence, so potent that it had become a kind of presence. Yet he denied it, ignored it, refused to wrestle it.

And he was responsible.

There was no denying it. (He shook his head again and the boy stared, wondering but not saying anything more.)

He'd driven her away. Probably because she was the best thing that had ever happened to him and he couldn't bear it.

He'd been missing her with every breath and doing everything under the sun not to know it.

The boy had been missing her too.

What kind of a bond was that between them? Not a happy one. But still.

Here was Michael Rosen in his birthday get-up. Eighteen and insolent. With sideburns and a little fuzz on his lip. The boy had been growing up. So Kingsmount was a success for him after all. And Jennifer's absence had only helped toughen him. It gave him some irony—a good gift. He'd needed the irony.

Boothe wondered whether he'd changed too and the answer came to him: not an iota. Fire to fire, he'd been frozen in misery and self-pity and self-satisfaction. Not a hint of change.

The boy was leaning against the Marquis arch, hands in his pockets, not looking at Boothe any longer. And that's when the last rush of intuition swooped—*he* must have heard from her. Michael must have received a message. A phone call? No, more likely one of her notes with the peculiar o's and a's and q's. Only once here at the end of the year? Or had she been faithful to him throughout the long exile?

Boothe yearned to know and surely the boy was eager to tell him, to confirm the humiliation. But what would this particular knowledge bring him either way? Would it help him change? And he couldn't bring himself to beg.

It was a slow night, a warm night and Natalie was in the middle of a fifteen-minute set, dancing on a raised platform only slightly larger than one of the tabletops on the main floor of the bar. Because the only customer was Harold, a foreman at a nearby steel stamping plant who stopped in at the Fox Hole most every night for a couple of boilermakers, head down and deliberate, Natalie was performing for Desiree and Blossom, the two other girls on duty. They sat at the bar too but were swiveled round to the stage, leaning back, calling out to Natalie, applauding each bump, each grind as the pink see-through blouse made its way to the floor.

Duncan Boothe was tending bar and she might have been dancing for him too with the same playful earnestness as for the other women.

"Yeah, that's what I'm talking about, girl—you a star," cried Desiree.

"Give it to 'em, baby," called Blossom, who was distracted by a flaw she'd only just detected in a long white fingernail.

Natalie was grinning at her friends, working hard for them, a slight sheen of sweat on her face in the bright lights, blue and red and white, beamed from above. But her eyes had a far-away quality too, and Duncan suspected she'd started using again, despite all she'd promised Serge. He knew she'd been sleeping with Serge, but that wouldn't protect her ass. If he found out she was back on the stuff, Serge might beat her up so she couldn't dance or he might just throw her out entirely. Serge wasn't the sentimental type. Either way she'd have trouble feeding her kids, not to mention her habit. And given the recent layoffs, she'd have trouble landing the job she'd once predicted with her father at the Six Mile plant.

The last few months had not been kind to Natalie. Age had swept up on her quickly, with a hardness about her eyes and toughness to her skin, and a weary, wary watchfulness that could slough off in a moment all the way to indifference. In the last month she'd begun wearing a heavy blonde wig while she worked, trying to suggest some connection between her own accent and the bustier claims of a country-western star.

Duncan watched her on this night and was saddened by all of this. His own concern surprised him. And while he was thinking such thoughts he had to admit that any lingering pretense that the Fox Hole would provide a slightly titillating insight into the larger life of a broken city had long since disappeared. Black girls might dance here, but never, ever would Black patrons venture this far north to the very border of the city to see them. For the first few months that Duncan had worked at the bar, the occasional single businessman in a grey suit, or even a clutch of three or four of them, usually already drunk, would stop by. They were raucous in a forced, self-conscious, show-off way, and after a couple more drinks and bets and dares they'd usually try and grope the girls. But here was Serge's great gift—he could handle them, dissuade them, without pissing them off or using the force he could. Usually there'd be an extra tip—plenty generous—tucked into the g-string of the woman involved. But these after-business-dinner parties no longer tumbled through the door. It had been weeks since Duncan laid eyes on any of the solo businessmen who used to drop by either. Now it was only the local workers, guys like Harold, who drank hard, who might watch the girls dance, but resisted every come on and watched their pennies too.

So Duncan had already come to think of this as an evening of surprises. Except he wasn't all that surprised when Michael Rosen walked in the door. It seemed in rhythm with the strange blasts of the universe. The school's ancient red pickup truck sat parked at the curb behind him. Spying it, Duncan wondered how he'd managed to swipe the keys. The boy was resourceful. Duncan silently gave him credit. He was also angry—not surprised, but very angry.

"Hey," said Michael with a nod as he slipped up onto a stool. "I'd like a beer." He held out his license to prove his age.

Boothe said nothing, didn't glance at the card. He held a straight glass to the tap. He set the beer in front of the boy and turned away to rinse some other glasses.

"I warned you I'd come," Michael said to his back. "I thought it'd be fun to see where you work for real."

Boothe didn't respond. He wiped the counter, slid a clean ashtray over to Harold and emptied the butts out of the old one.

"How's the book coming?" said Michael ever so pleasantly.

"Look," said Duncan, rubbing hard at some spot in front of him, "on this turf you're a customer. Nothing else, nothing more. Just drink your damn beer. See what you want to see and then get out. I'll pretend I never saw you."

"Really? That's swell—you'd do me the favor. You won't snitch. Thanks. Yeah, thanks."

"Fuck you," he muttered, turning away again.

And here was Natalie in front of him, coming to the end of her act. She bent over, breasts dangling, to pick up the pink blouse. Desiree and Blossom whistled and clapped. Natalie did a quick curtsey towards them, but already the lights had gone off and she looked weary, vacant, a long shift at an end. The routine was for her to slip away behind a partition to a bathroom in back, put her shirt on, and then return to tease customers into buying drinks. But there were no customers to flirt with and the routine was dead. Stepping awkwardly off the stage in her spike-heels, she stood still for a moment, her shirt waist high, her breasts hanging before her. Fatty tissue.

Duncan wanted to put an arm around Natalie, to wrap the blouse protectively about her shoulders, to sit her down and comfort her.

"Makes sense now," said Michael, "why you'd give Jenny up for this."

*

Serge had them both out the door in about twenty seconds. He wasn't gentle. He didn't have to be. It wouldn't take him long to replace the bartender. The only thing Duncan took with him from the Fox Hole was a bar towel which he pressed to his face to staunch the flow of blood from his nose. He hoped it wasn't broken.

For his part, Michael's bottom lip had split in a dark gash and one eye was already closing behind puffy bruises.

But it was over now. The sudden, furious squall had caught them up, thrown them against each other and spent itself and them. It disappeared as quickly as the initial explosion. Together they walked to the red pickup. Although his own car was parked in the alley, Duncan climbed in the passenger side and rested his head back against the seat. The bleeding eased. Michael got in behind the wheel and leaned his swollen face against the cool metal for the time being.

"Can you make it until morning for the infirmary?" Boothe asked, his voice nasal and muffled.

Michael nodded without lifting his head. "I'll tell them a story. Don't drip any blood in the truck, okay?"

"Right."

Neither of them moved for a little while.

"Sorry," said Michael at last. "That was pretty stupid."

"Don't tell me about stupid."

"Right."

When Boothe climbed down from the old truck and walked to his car, it took the boy several tries to get the engine to catch. Finally, jerkily, he pulled out onto Woodward Avenue. It was after midnight and traffic was light. The red pickup swung across three lanes and headed north. One wheel threw off the angry howl of a bad bearing. The brake lights flashed once and then the boy was gone.

Wild Flowers

Etta Bloch tended her memories. Tended her husband Manny and their son Jake like flowers, though not to grow and blossom—simply to remain fresh and alive in her mind. They were her responsibility, and by her attentions she kept them from wilting, from fading as long as she did.

This was nothing she'd set her mind to at first. How could she not think of her boy, after all—cut off like that at twenty-nine, his face cut up so by the glass and the phone pole that the undertakers could hardly make him decent?

For weeks that was all she could see, his face in the hospital (it had only been a formality for the rescue squad to carry him there) and then, stitched along the great flap that had torn loose along the line of his jaw and up round his ear and just under his eye, in the casket that only she and Manny peeked into to say goodbye.

For weeks afterwards Etta spied her son out of the corner of her eye and everywhere she turned. Always in these quickest of glimpses Jake would be staring back at her out of that poor torn face, sometimes with one of his mischievous grins or about to whistle, (everyone knew him for his whistle—he was a wonderful whistler), sometimes round-eye scared. And there'd be salt on her lips while she was still trying to keep her limbs from shaking, her chest from collapsing. What would Manny do if she collapsed?

Jake's face in the casket was the only thing she allowed herself to forget. Until she could manage to do so, however—and it was a long time—the jagged smile on his cold lips stood between her and the real memories, the ones from when he was a boy especially, and turned them into false dreams.

One morning while she was fixing breakfast, Etta heard Manny sigh above the burbling of the oatmeal pot. "What'd you say?" she called. Funny she should hear it in the kitchen. She thought so then, but he didn't say anything more. If he was thinking about Jake, well, she was curious—he never, ever, spoke about their son, which meant she had to do the talking for them both, or do none at all. On the other hand, she acknowledged with a flick of the ladle, what point was there in knowing what had Manny sighing—it would probably only make those bad memories of hers flare up but good.

With the back of her ladle she shaped the oatmeal into an island, around which he'd pour skim milk. Somehow the thought that she shouldn't have been able to hear him sigh flattened the surprise as she backed through the swinging door and discovered Manny slumped at his place. His cheek was resting on one arm, as if he were stealing a quick nap while she got ready for work at Dr. Wilder's office.

Carefully Etta set the bowl down and hurried back to the phone in the kitchen. She could count on the town's rescue squad arriving in under five minutes, but she knew already that time didn't matter—they could take their time. Returning to the table, she slipped onto her own seat and rested her head on her arm and stared at Manny, who was smiling in his sleep, nothing crooked to his mouth.

It seemed that Sarah Abrams arrived before the rescue squad. Though that wasn't possible, was it? Perhaps Etta had called her too? She didn't have the strength to recall. Her arms and tongue were leaden. She felt heavy, too heavy even to think. For that she was grateful.

While Etta sat dazed in her chair, desperately trying to recall Manny's face, Sarah was puttering about. Arranging things on the phone, picking out Manny's dark suit to take to the funeral home. Sometime after ten, Harry Abrams, Sarah's husband, walked through the screen door—it was as soon as he could close his second-hand furniture shop and hurry on over. Harry was wearing his rumpled corduroy jacket and smelling of pipe smoke. It was Harry who called the rabbi in Richmond.

By afternoon the small clapboard bungalow was buzzing. Gladys Shapiro brought the first load of food—a sponge cake, smoked trout from up on the mountain, hushpuppies— and having seen these provisions safely into the fridge and straightened her wig, Gladys seized a plastic pail and a rag and set to cleaning. No one was paying any attention to Etta, not for the time being, except to set a mug of tea in front of her and to replace it in due course with another.

In the early evening it was Harry again who took her hand. "It's time we went on over," he whispered and drew her up out of her chair. Then they were in Harry's ancient

Studebaker. Then they were at the funeral home, Harry handing her over to Mordecai Smith.

"Thank God he felt nothing," Mordi said.

Etta stared at him blankly.

"Do you want to see him now, before the others arrive?" he asked. "We'll have to close the casket by then."

She shook her head. But he took her hand, coaxed her to sit down in his office for a few moments, and, without asking a second time, led her to a small curtained area in back. He all but shooed her forward to the casket. "I'll leave you for a few minutes—as long as you like, Etta."

Oh, but she fooled him. She walked five paces towards that casket with her eyes closed. Listened to what Mordi said and stood there in the middle of the little room with her eyes closed. She didn't want to see whatever was in the casket. She'd learned her lesson with Jake. She wanted to be able to remember Manny right off, not be blocked by how they'd posed him.

Dressing him, of all things, in that stylish mail-order suit she'd made him buy years before—a suit with a pinstripe, a suit he'd laughed at even though he knew it hurt her feelings, a suit he'd worn a first time to take her out for her birthday, and once again five years later for Jake, and then never again. What use had he for such a suit?

*

Late on this Friday afternoon, like every other business day, Etta drew out the files of Dr. Wilder's scheduled patients for the next day (Saturday a.m. only), ticking a pencil in the upper right hand corner for those who hadn't had their teeth xrayed in two years. She tidied-up a bit for the maid, and double-checked that the water was turned off in the bowls by Dr. Wilder's two chairs. Her coat and scarf off the hanger, a flick to the lights, and she trotted silently in her white shoes down to the street just in time to catch Hoke Perkins' 5:10 Locust Avenue bus.

There wasn't a seat, not at this hour, but Etta wasn't going far, and she squeezed out a place for herself in the aisle between Mr. Klagholz, who owned two Hallmark shops, and Virginia Watley, poor dear, who was having some pretty bad trouble with her gums (she smiled distractedly at Etta, her lips pressed tight together).

The bus cut across the older part of town, skirting Court Square on its way out to the new shopping mall and subdivisions. But it was only down the hill from the old courthouse that Hoke Perkins made a special stop in the middle of the block for Etta—she didn't even have to ring the bell. From the rear door she gave him a quick little wave in his mirror and all but jumped down, eager for her favorite evening of the week.

Smiling to herself, excited, Etta opened the door of the bungalow, stepped across the threshold, and turned up the thermostat—the house was chilly after the long cool day. She wasn't thinking about Manny or Jake. No, no, that wouldn't do, not yet. They'd simply have to wait. She sighed at the thought—it was she who had to wait, and the anticipation, the flirting with the pleasure to come, was delicious.

Instead of cleaning the house on weekends as in the old days, she'd taken to sweeping and washing and polishing on Thursday night with the TV turned up loud. And last night— such a productive evening, so much accomplished—she'd also made a fresh chicken casserole (with a good dollop of sweet German wine) all ready to slip in the oven now. Into the oven it went, and a good dollop of French bath oils she poured as well into the bathtub as it filled with hot, hot water.

She was humming something from the FM channel that Dr. Wilder played in the office all day. It was an old, pretty song, one of those songs by Henry Mancini or someone like that. She was humming as she took off her new uniform—nearly new, anyway. She'd given this style a try since the material was supposed to be easy to clean. But what she'd discovered was that the dress grew awfully hot during the day, and now the collar was already yellowing and they said you shouldn't use bleach on this space-age material.

This was the reward, this the glory as she eased slowly, carefully into the almost-too-hot water. Its surface shimmered with delicate colors from the bath oils that protected her skin, (always prone to drying out and to sprouting patches of psoriasis, especially as the weather grew colder this time of year). And the glint of the water smoothed and disguised the wrinkles, the pouches, the patchwork veins that seemed, almost, to belong to someone else. She closed her eyes and let the heat and steam seep and steep and coddle her.

Catching a glimpse of that sneak Manny, all of twenty-two or three, poking his head in for a look, she wagged a wet finger. "Mmm, mmmnh—not yet, you," she said out loud. But she stretched her legs and back and remembered—not him, not his face yet—how she'd preened and let him look at her lying in the tub like this when she was twenty or twenty-one. That was the first time they'd run away to a motel and the first time he'd seen her or any woman naked and the first time she'd not be afraid to let him see. Look at the twitch in that smile—he was ashamed! Yes, he had been, ashamed and excited.

Greeting the Sabbath bride—that was how Manny's father used to talk about preparing for Friday dinner (her own parents had never bothered much with ceremony), and when Mother Bloch lit the candles on the sideboard Etta felt a thrill at the mysterious glow that extended beyond the flickering light.

Tonight, though, as she drew on a brand new pair of pantyhose and the dress she'd retrieved yesterday from the cleaners, clipped on earrings, and spooned out the casserole with its raisins and winy aroma, she nursed, playfully, a deliberate confusion—yes, she was preparing for the Sabbath bride but, after all, she was the bride herself.

Making one concession to the time, she set two candles on the dinette and lit them quickly without a blessing. And standing, ate the casserole and a stalk of steamed broccoli, and sipped at a healthy dose of sweet wine poured into a juice glass.

The synagogue was walking distance up the hill towards Court Square. The night, however, had turned raw with a gusty wind. Already half a block up the street, Etta halted with a sigh, swung around, and hurried back inside the house to fetch a plastic scarf to protect her hair and a woolen one for her throat.

Near the top of the hill, only a single lamp above the doors of the synagogue lighted the front path. There hadn't been any trouble to speak of in years, but out of habit the small community of Jews in a Southern town didn't like to draw attention to itself. Perhaps that was the reason their century-old redbrick building might easily have been mistaken for a church.

Etta hung back in the shadows across the street, trying not to shiver. It was a sparse crowd tonight—half-a-dozen families, a straggler here and there. Harry and Sarah Abrams appeared, Mordecai Smith hurrying along behind them. The Levys arrived three minutes late as usual, dragging along their boy Philip who was shameless about not brushing his teeth—had already chipped two playing football—and who traveled all the way to Richmond once a week to study with the rabbi for his bar mitzvah.

At last the coast was clear, and Etta scurried across the street and up the steps. Cracking the heavy door open, she slipped inside. Tucked in one corner of the foyer, a narrow flight of wooden stairs led to the gallery, from the days when there were enough Orthodox families for their women to cloister by themselves. Most of the time now the gallery was deserted, except when the choir performed from up there or when, sometimes during the high holidays, there were enough visitors from out of town or children home from school to cause an overflow from the small sanctuary. Or when on Friday evenings Etta hid herself away.

She had flowers to tend. To avoid being caught up in conversation with her friends or having to pretend to follow the service on their terms, she tiptoed up the wooden steps. Truth to tell, she'd never been much of a synagogue goer—that had been left to Manny on the rare occasion when he felt like it, on a Saturday morning or for the Yahrzeit memorials of his parents.

Quietly she slipped onto a bench two rows back from the rail. No one directly below could see her. Only Harry or Mordecai standing way up front on the bimah might be able to, but they'd have to stare hard to make her out in the shadows so high above.

Because tonight was nothing special—no particular holiday or bar mitzvah—the rabbi hadn't driven up from

Richmond. And so, also from long habit, the congregation made do for itself. Men and women took turns reading on the bimah. (The handful of more traditional Jews in town, offended by such innovations, would take their own turn in the morning.)

Etta had smuggled in Manny's old prayerbook, its cover a tattered grey cipher without characters, its pages frayed. Skipping ahead of her friends below, she opened the book where a scrap of paper held her place at the *Kaddish*, the prayer for the dead. Quiet, simple, reassuring, this had always been her favorite part, even before she'd lost her Manny and Jake.

Our help cometh from Him, claimed the lines. *The departed whom we now remember have entered into the peace of life eternal. They still live on earth in the acts of goodness they performed and in the hearts of those who cherish their memory.*

She read the words silently and then again, whispering to make it official and buoy herself in the right mood. And shivered with pleasure. Yes, this was what she'd been waiting for, an incantation that released her thoughts and made them blossom. Here she didn't feel guilty; she was performing a solemn duty, not merely indulging herself. Keeping a finger at the spot, she closed the book in her lap, stretched her legs as far as the benches allowed, and closed her eyes.

Her memories had gathered themselves like delicately pressed flowers in the pages of an ancient volume. Back and forth she fingertipped lightly, catching glimpses of Jake across nearly thirty years, and of Manny young and not so young. A single leaf caught her eye, and off she leapt, chasing a flash of water at a lake high in the mountains where they went swimming. Hadn't the car broken down? Yes, there was Manny in a soaked undershirt awkwardly, hopelessly prying into the guts of his pride-and-joy Buick on the dirt road. Etta put her hand to her mouth and coughed a little giggle into it. Manny tinkered and tinkered and couldn't fix a machine for the life of him.

The sight of the two-tone, turquoise-and-cream automobile scratched up a smell she couldn't identify right off. It was sour and unpleasant, but she couldn't let go until she recalled—that was it, the stale smoke and beer (and moonshine if his buddies could make the right connections) that soaked the front seat of the car and Jake's hair and jacket in the morning after he'd snuck home only a few hours earlier. She grimaced and waved the thought away—that wasn't the sort she wanted, not at all.

Down below in the sanctuary, Sy Rappaport was leading a responsive reading with the twenty-five or thirty worshipers. First his thin, nasal tones would drift up (Sy had moved from Brooklyn fifteen years ago, and from what his accent gave away it might have been yesterday), followed by the smudge of other voices rising and falling and indecipherable.

Manny winked at her. He was wearing his favorite suit, a natty chocolate brown, with suspenders and a red bow tie, all still new, which meant he couldn't have been more than forty. And a felt hat, darker brown, cocked to the side. Her heart winced tight. Wasn't it really back then that Manny had blossomed, right about forty? No longer the shy Jewish boy out of place anywhere beyond his own doorstep in the Southern town; not yet the sad, resigned old man who shouldn't have been old so soon. Here he was winking at her. He swung to show profile, pulling in his belly and touching his nose with a laugh—no way to pull in that schnoz. But what did it matter? he'd demand, elbow in your ribs. You know what a big nose means.

And her heart did ache because she knew what it meant and knew why he'd blossomed back then. Natalie Coles, the wife of a buyer up in Staunton, was making him feel quite the Cavalier. For days after he'd snatched a visit with that little tramp, Manny strutted around, attempting lamely to hide these proud, astonished smiles. (One horrible night they'd all had dinner together; Etta pretending not to know; poor Barney Coles, a kind, enormous radish of a man, really not knowing.)

Etta shook her head to clear away such thoughts. They were spoiling the evening—what could they possibly matter anymore?

Philip Levy, the boy with chipped teeth, was standing on the bimah holding up a silver cup and croaking the blessing on the wine. His breaking voice dangled him helplessly, a classroom specimen of anguished puberty.

Try as she might, Etta couldn't tug free of the sour memories. Tonight they were powerful and insistent. So vivid she could zero in on the smallest detail: the coat button sewn on by other fingers, the smell about him when he snuck home at the end of the day—that musky smell of his own after sex, laced with Natalie's catbox scent. It made her furious. "Come on, honey," Etta said, cooing and tugging him by the wrist. "Aren't you sleepy? I'm sleepy."

"It's not even six o'clock." Triumph still dilated his eyes, though they'd narrowed suddenly with alarm.

"What's that matter?" she said. She pulled and dragged and nudged him into their bedroom. Reaching under his jacket, she snapped his suspenders. But didn't let him take off his clothes. Just yanked his trousers open and hitched up her dress and slipped herself onto him standing by their bed. Oh, and he was aroused, miserable, the smells of the three of them commingling.

And in the balcony of the synagogue she too was miserable and breathing through her mouth. She rubbed knuckles hard into her eyes, over and over, trying to shake herself free. She was embarrassed with herself.

But Jake would help her out. So far tonight she hadn't been paying him enough attention anyway. His eyes, the most beautiful dark eyes when he was a boy—everyone said that's what he got from her and it was true.

First thing in the morning she'd slip into his room in her robe without even turning the light on. He lay curled on his side, and she settled next to him, combing fingers through his hair, rubbing his back to wake him for school. She could feel him wake through her fingers. At last the ten-year-old turned over and looked at her, his face lighted from the doorway, his sleepy eyes dark and deeper than deep, unfilled yet with the distractions of the day. "Do I gotta?" he yawned. But once he was out of bed she could hear him whistling the latest song as he got ready.

Could those girls of his wake him with so much love? she wondered, and then bit her lip. Why was she getting into that? That was all so much later. Jake was still in school, too young, too young for all that.

It was Manny's fault, what went wrong with Jake. He'd been undermining her all along. The two of them, man and boy, took each other's side—and where did that leave her?

"Screw college, if he doesn't want to go away to college," Manny said. "Isn't there plenty for him to do here, if that's what he wants?" Just to spite her, that's why he was saying it. And she wanted to hit him, her fingers sore from twisting and tearing at each other. And Jake standing off to the side, thinking his own thoughts and apparently not even listening to them argue. What kind of example was Manny? Etta was trembling with anger, the taste of salt on her lips for the first time in a long time and she not even wiping at the tears, alone in the gallery.

A car door slammed, waking her. She'd hold her breath waiting, and yes, there, the second door slammed. So he was bringing her home again. But why assume it was the same one? Jake was bringing another, a different one each time.

He made no effort to be quiet entering the house. The girl did, but she was drunk and giggling despite herself and though she was trying to tiptoe it wasn't possible in those heels, them striking the floor like a hammer every second or third step.

Manny hadn't stirred, but Etta knew he was awake beside her, listening. Was this an arrangement he and Jake had come to? Did Jake even bother to close his bedroom door? Because they, she, could hear it all, could hear the clothes hitting the floor, and the groping, the first great squawk of the bed, the moans, the rhythm, the cries in the night. So vivid, so vivid, to the smallest detail she was remembering.

Only dimly was she aware that the service below was ending, the small congregation wending through the aisles and out of the sanctuary. With a sudden harsh click the lights disappeared. And Etta sat in darkness. Only the faint red flicker of a hanging lamp up above the bimah, it was never extinguished, remained and grew brighter, blowing shadows everywhere as her eyes adjusted. It was very quiet now.

Two car doors slammed again, nearly in unison this time, and Jake was strutting up to the house in broad daylight no less, both arms around the cute little girl at his side (Meg Tillich, wasn't it? Who'd been a couple years behind him at school and had gone off to Roanoke to become a beautician) so that the two kept stumbling over each other.

Fresh, potent as a morning after wind and rain, vivid as all the other memories, this particular scene Etta couldn't place. But that suede jacket was a clue—his father had given him that later, after he'd left community college to start selling insurance full-time.

Etta felt confused, disoriented. When she tried to leap ahead the memory became disjointed; she had to walk it through at its own pace. Where am I? she wondered. Where was she to see Jake and this Meg saunter up to her house? Was she watching through a window? Did he not care that she'd see?

The screen door slapped behind them. Jake and Meg didn't halt, didn't hesitate, but stumbled on toward the bedroom. And now Etta could smell the alcohol, the smoke, the girl's not-so-cheap perfume. How dare they? Couldn't they show the slightest decency or respect? *Where am I?*

It must have been a Saturday, because there was Manny sitting in his chair in the living room watching a Braves' game on TV. He was drinking too—beer, despite what it did to his system.

Etta found herself panting, frightened, in the dark balcony of the synagogue. A thousand tiny claws clattered on the roof, driven by a hard wind. From one of her deep coat pockets she dug out a ball of Kleenex and wiped her eyes, blew her nose. That last memory had unnerved her. It was so clear, so real. It frightened her not to remember when it happened. *Silly thing, silly me*, she thought. "Silly," she said softly aloud.

Yet the niggling memory tempted her back to discover where it led. The secret lay crouched waiting for her. She could keep it at bay and concentrate on the sounds and drafts and musty smells of the sanctuary. Or she could leave. She could simply walk away. Surely her responsibility to Manny and Jake extended only so far, and not to any memory like that. Sighing, she blew her nose again. Her fingers were very cold. (This would be a bad winter for her chilblains.)

The sharp hiss of the eggs startled her as they hit the hot skillet. Manny's specialty, with a liberal dash of Tabasco, garlic, black pepper—and the magic touch, fresh ginger. Etta stared at her husband. His very round face was accentuated by the bald dome of his head, grey tufts around the sides. Except they weren't grey. They'd gone quite white. And he'd grown jowly, more jowly than she'd recalled.

From the way he was pursing his lips she could tell that the beer he'd been swigging in front of the TV was disagreeing with him. Gas mainly. "Shouldn't you know better?" she might have whispered aloud. But Manny was attending to the eggs. You couldn't let them grow too hard and dry in the skillet. *Why aren't I making a salad?* Etta wondered. *Why don't I remember any of this, even though I'm remembering it?*

The smell of eggs and spice drew Jake out of his room, buckling his belt and tucking in a clean shirt. That girl, that Meg, was she still in bed or had she somehow snuck out when Etta wasn't looking? Jake was whistling—he was always such a remarkable whistler, whistled any tune note for note after one hearing.

She missed him so, wanted more than all the world simply to hold him, to nestle him in her arms, all that he'd done to disappoint her no matter, absolutely beside the point.

He walked into the kitchen and put the kettle on for coffee. Said something to his old man that Etta missed, couldn't make out. Manny shrugged and replied without looking up. But again she didn't catch what he said. It wasn't that she couldn't hear their voices—she could, oh yes, just the way they'd always sounded, gruff with each other and matter-of-fact—but the sounds were muffled, the edge of the words blurred.

Confused, anguished, she wanted to cry out to them. "Oh," she moaned, knowing she couldn't speak to a memory. "Damn, damn. Damn."

Manny expertly divided the eggs with a spatula and slipped portions onto two plates. The rest he left in the skillet and covered with foil on the stove. He and Jake sat down, and there was a third place at the table with an empty plate. For her? Or for Meg still in the bedroom?

Jake rose to get the coffee, and as he was standing at his father's side, posed to pour, Etta's glance traveled up his arm and to his face and now at last she saw what she should have seen all along, the scar along the line of his jaw and up round his ear and just under his eye, healed, faint, undeniable. And she knew that if he was there like that then she had to be the one who was missing. The empty place was not for her.

The steps down from the gallery were treacherous, dark and steep. She made her way slowly, a hand pressed against the plaster. Once she'd reached the ground, however, the front door presented no problem. Three or four paces directly across the foyer it greeted her fingers, and the bolt turned easily. Of course the old men arriving in the morning would fuss at the carelessness of that casual Friday night crowd, leaving the door unbolted.

The sidewalk seemed to stretch forever down from Court Square. Her feet ached and she was perspiring and she was also chilled to the bone by the time she reached her door. Only for the lock stubbornly to refuse her key. Perhaps it was the wrong key. Perhaps—and the half-second's thought terrified her—she'd come to the wrong house.

No, a thousand signs, the mat, the mezuzah on the doorpost, reassured her at once. It was only her nerves, only her hand trembling a bit. And with that the key slipped home.

Without taking off her coat, Etta went directly into the kitchen and put the kettle on for tea. She sat in the chair where Manny had been sitting—would have been sitting if the memory had ever happened, which it hadn't, except that it had seemed more real than all the others. Warm house or no, she was still trembling lightly like a bird.

A whistle began, low and tentative but swelling rapidly towards a shriek. She glanced at the kettle, an old red thing with a wooden handle, fifteen-year's-worth familiar and yet tonight threatening, foreign, not at all what she'd remembered. Didn't stop her, though—she'd be damned first. Lifted that kettle, poured water into a cup, dipped the tea bag, added milk.

Again she settled in the chair, her coat still on, cowering and refusing to look about. The tea was strong and hot and reassuring. This was all it took. Once she got to bed and to sleep and dreamed some honest dreams everything would be all right.

She realized, suddenly, that she'd left Manny's prayerbook in the gallery. It had been so dark she hadn't been able to check about or notice it lying on the bench beside her. *Too bad*, she decided with a shrug. Why did she care? What use would it be now?

She sipped her tea and felt better, stronger. It had given her a nasty turn, what she'd glimpsed. Shook her to her bones. Manny and Jake—what a pair. They deserved each other. *What a pair of bastards.* They didn't care. Not an iota. Didn't miss her at all, didn't bother to remember her. Nothing. Why should they trouble themselves? That's what they figured. What kind of gratitude was that for all her years of faithfulness?

She sighed, rose, and poured another cup—what did it matter if it kept her up a little while longer? Her legs were aching, and it was good to sit back down.

And she nodded to a further truth that blossomed across the table through the steam and sweet tea and milk. Well, after all, what of it if they were such bastards? Hadn't she suspected it all along, down deep, that Manny and Jake were wild flowers and didn't really need her tending? Oh, they'd tolerate her remembering them, they'd let her fuss. But only because it made her feel better. Which was nice. Certainly none of it was necessary.

Sipping the last of her tea and not wishing to get up or turn out the light, Etta Bloch was feeling better, rather relieved. They must have cared something for her after all.

Of A Different Order

The gang of them, boys mostly, arrived after dark. They drove down in three or four cars—they all at the college have those cars—skidding up into the gravel across the highway. It was November and, like I said, dark already, and Cassie was fixing her dinner in the back wing. So she didn't hear anything much until a couple of them got carried away and starting whooping as the fifteen-foot cross finally tore right up out of the ground where her daddy had anchored it years before and keeled over into the dirt.

By the time their shouts reached her and she rushed out into the night, they'd set to hacking and sawing, trying to tear the tough old thing apart. But it was so huge—bigger even, lying there—so seasoned and sturdy, they couldn't hardly more than scratch it. Cassie threw on the floods. With the lights blinding them, revealing them, those kids scampered back across the road, eight or ten of them she thought later, still whooping, taunting her, hollering about how they'd be back. Maybe to them it was some dangerous game or a bit of nastiness meant to scare her, or maybe it seemed like this great adventure. To her it was no game.

That was when she called me. Or actually, no, it was next day she called. First thing that night she dialed 911. The cops arrived fast enough, but then they just stood around, shuffling, looking at the cross lying dark in the mud. They must have shrugged a lot.

If it had been one of their churches, Nazarene or Baptist or even one of our Adventist communions, you can bet they'd have chased after those kids right up the hill, whatever trouble it might bring back to the town. There was no love lost, for sure, between the police and Ransom College. But confronting the only institution in the county with any real money, well, the local authorities saved that for special occasions.

The point is it wasn't one of theirs. Not calling itself the Deliverance Today Synagogue, it wasn't. A blue and white flag stretched across the long grey siding.

No matter the gigantic cross planted out front. It had this over-size hand, like something out of a comic book, pinned to the wood with a dagger or a stake stabbed right through. So, yes, I suppose it might seem there was plenty of confusion involved, what with a synagogue and a giant cross. But together they'd been part of our landscape so long no one thought much about it. That cross had towered aslant above the highway since old Jeremiah Pratt himself drove it into the hill. Embarrassed, locals were always shaking their heads when reminded.

And then those kids swooped in and stirred everything up.

*

So Cassie Pratt calls me. "Ethan," she says. "I need your help with some wood?"

I knew her voice right off, not that I'd laid eyes on her in eight or nine years. Oh, I'd remembered her from time to time. But I was still wary. What she'd remembered was that I'd spent most of my time in school in the woodworking shop.

"I'm not really doing much of that anymore, Cassie. I'm a massage therapist these days. Just if you didn't know."

"I don't need a massage, Ethan."

"No, I figured that."

"Are you going to come out and give me a hand?"

Naturally, she says that, about lending a hand, and I'm picturing—what else?—that big white mitt pinned to her daddy's cross. Like a punch line I couldn't keep out of my head. I still didn't realize what she was on about over the phone—how she was talking about just that, the cross.

"It's not really a carpenter you're after," I was saying. This is maybe an hour later on the Friday, us standing out front of the Deliverance Today Synagogue. The cross was lying there, or leaning, half-raised on one arm in the mud. Traffic comes shooting by on the Bexley Road only a few feet away.

"What I can see, the wood's still sound," I said. "You just need to replant the whole blessed thing, if that's what you want." I couldn't quite hide my own mixed feelings, but she didn't seem to notice.

"Whatever it takes, Ethan. You've got to set it back up. Make it right again." Her voice was low and stubborn and urgent.

But I look at her and realize explaining is beyond me. I suppose I could have made an excuse or even just walked away.

"Okay," I say with a sigh. "I guess."

So I circle around the fallen cross like it's some great wounded beast. I can't help a grunt, picturing what all this is going to take. "But I can't do anything today," I call across to her. "I've got three appointments coming in this afternoon, back to back. And they're all doctor referrals."

She didn't say anything, not seeing the significance. Truth is, she didn't much resemble the girl I knew in school. It troubled me, saddened me. She'd filled out a good bit. You could see it especially in her throat. Not that it made her look bad—just more, I guess, womanly? Now her dark hair, with a hint of red where the sun was hitting it in the late morning, it was parted in the middle and gathered on the back of her neck. It framed her face oval, like one of those portraits of women, of mothers, from Bible times. No lipstick or rouge or anything, but that didn't make her any the less. Her dress was dark too and dropped down almost to her ankles. Over it she was wearing a big mannish coat. I figured it wouldn't be her husband's—with a husband there'd be no reason to call me. So probably her father's from before.

So then I shrug. "How's tomorrow morning for me to come on back with my brother's tractor?"

Cassie stiffens. She got this look in her eye, anger and outrage all mixed up at me for not knowing better. It was like one of our old teachers—the kind who'd always been scolding *her*—turning on me with a vengeance.

"You know you can't work here on the Sabbath, Ethan," Cassie said severely.

I was jabbing the toe of my boot at the hard mud and shaking my head. "Well, hell, Cassie—I guess it's my Sabbath too. I'm offering it to you."

She shook her head back at me, drawing that heavy coat tighter, like I'd done something worse than curse a bit.

*

I confess I was surprised, her calling me. Okay, and I was
flattered too, even if there was still some resentment. But
after a time I came to see it was only a sign of just how lonely
Cassie Pratt had grown in the years since school. Who else
was she going to call?

Her being Jewish was never the problem. We'd gone all
the way through the Seventh-Day Academy together. Maybe
her old man decided it was a safer bet for her than the local
public school. Maybe it was our two Sabbaths landing on
the same day, a nice kind of overlay.

Jeremiah Pratt. My folks knew him, her father. They'd
grown up with him or near enough. They were all Mount
Pleasant families, going back a hundred years and more. They
didn't *approve* of him, if that's the word. I think my Dad, who
was stout enough Adventist, never could get his head around
the confusion, and he wasn't sure the Pratts could either.

He wasn't so much Jew or Christian, Jeremiah Pratt, but
styling himself after his given name, all fire and fury. That was
the legend. He made local Christians feel, what? Unsure of
themselves? That maybe there was something to his coaxing
the Messiah back to our world by being a better Jew than
the Jews. He did lord it over the other Mount Pleasanters,
and they tolerated him, for the most part. Like some distant
cousin who's gone a bit odd. He passed some years back,
while I was in Florida, after Marybeth left me.

At school Cassie always wore a Star of David at her throat.
Yet she never seemed bothered about all the praying to Jesus
that went on. If I considered it at all I might have figured
she'd pray as much as she was comfortable with. Why be at

a school like ours otherwise, no matter the godlessness of the public ones?

What I'd actually be thinking about, however, was her. With the wavy dark curls back then and greenish-grey eyes, and a smile suggesting she knew all the secrets that mattered. Somewhere along the way she got breasts too and I certainly did notice them.

She never took my noticing seriously. Which only made me feel foolish, all innocent, not dangerous enough. Sometimes I half-expected her just to reach out and muss my hair like I was some tame little puppy.

Jewish or not, attending our Adventist school or not, Cassie Pratt flirted with being a bad girl—as much as anyone could and not be banished. She'd sneak a cigarette out in the trees. Hide a tube of scarlet lipstick in her backpack, even if she could only dab it on once she was outside in the afternoon and wipe it off before she got home.

Pretty tame really, compared to all I've seen since.

In those years I was drifting with other friends like Marybeth, waiting, watching.

And working with wood, of course—I did like that, hanging in the shop with the lathes and saws and drills and sawdust, using my hands.

Senior year, this I remember, we were killing time in a corridor near the main assembly hall. For a little while it was just Cassie and me.

"I'm so ready to be done," she sighs, sliding down against the wall and drawing her knees up against her chest—which she wasn't supposed to do, not in a skirt.

"Yeah?" I say lamely.

"Yeah," she says. "I never wanted to be here." As if we'd been having this conversation all along.

I look at her and nod. "All the Christian stuff?"

She frowns and gives her head a shake. "Oh, we believe in Jesus too. Didn't you know?"

"Your father's all about bringing Him back, right?" I ask to show I got the picture. "When's that supposed to happen?"

"Anytime now, I suppose," she says, as if it's all the same to her.

"Then why are you so ready for this to be over, graduation and all?"

"Oh, God," she says, rolling her eyes at the ceiling. "Could anything in the whole world be more boring?"

It's my turn to shrug, though in truth I was excited that she was sharing with me. "So what are you going to do after?"

"Get away. Far, far away. *Live*," she says fiercely. "I'm going to get away and live."

Apparently no Second Coming was going to interfere. Her fierceness, the certainty, it made me feel inadequate and vague.

It also left me yearning after something, even if that was vague too.

That couldn't have been the last time I saw Cassie. But I don't remember anything after. Certainly not the two of us alone. Because by then I was already together with Marybeth. Most everyone in the academy did have someone.

Not Cassie, come to think of it, though there were always boys around her.

Most of us were paired off along the way. We'd find someone or someone would be found. Graduating, we'd be ready to make our way into the world. That meant getting married, starting the next Adventist generation—all that. For some there might be more schooling as well at the community college in Pataskala or two years at the vocational center. This was all part of the Church's expectations, and our families'. So Marybeth and I sort of came together out of momentum combined with inertia combined with, well, what choice did we have?

Almost as soon as we graduated, though, Marybeth convinced me—I didn't need much convincing—we'd do better delaying long enough to begin service in the army. Which would pay for college or at least more training. Sitting on her parents' sofa, I grasped her point after a moment and, after one or two more, grasped how she meant she'd be the one to enlist. I'd stay in Mount Pleasant until she got posted somewhere livable. Then we'd set up house.

According to Marybeth's letters every week or so, boot camp was just as tough as you'd expect. She'd call me when it was allowed. After three months she finally got a furlough. So I went to meet her at the bus stop south of town, and at last here's the bus and out comes Marybeth wearing fatigues and boots, a duffel slung over her shoulder.

"Ethan, hey," she says, kind of shy and proud all at once.

"Hey," I say and lean in for a kiss. All I get is a glance of cheek, a wedge of duffel. I figured maybe I'd missed the target, being out of practice.

An hour later at her parents' house she set me right. A first surprise comes when she tugs off her camouflage cap—she's buzzed her hair short, down to the nub almost. It makes her face seem round and pink.

Taking a big breath, she grins, really pleased and excited to share the news with me, her best friend forever.

"So, here's the thing," she says all nervous. "It finally got figured out for me. It turns out, Ethan, like I'm a dyke."

I stare at her, confused.

"Lesbian," she says, her exasperation growing. "I'm homosexual, Ethan? *Gay.*"

By then I get it, sure. "You went into the army to discover this?"

She flings her arms out from her sides and grins some more, her cheeks pink and puffed round. I'd never seen her this happy. "So much for don't ask don't tell," she says with a laugh. "Nobody asked and nobody seems to care. Except Doreen, of course—she cares. She's really nice, Ethan. And from Fayetteville? Arkansas? You'll like her."

I nodded.

Some of the guys I knew at the Adventist Academy would be embarrassed, what if their girlfriends—fiancées—decided to be gay. But I don't think that's why I left Mount Pleasant. There just didn't seem any reason to stay. My folks understood. My brother—Daniel—he already had his sight set on a first field, soy and corn and some tractor vegetables, just outside of town.

Unlike small-town Ohio, jobs were almost for the asking in Florida. It only took me a couple of days, once I had a room at the Y, before I was working construction in Lauderdale. All that time in high school shop gave me useful skills.

And another reason too: for a couple of years I'd had this suspicion, this sense of a secret vocation of my own—like Marybeth had hers. If Mount Pleasant was the kind of place where church was first and last and most everything in between, Florida was surely where I'd have the best chance for learning therapeutic massage. (I'd been studying fliers and magazine ads in the vocational center.) Up and down the state they had more schools and certificate programs than any place in the country. So once I got a paycheck or two under my belt, that's what I signed on for. I'd be training after work almost every evening.

It didn't matter there was hardly time to eat or sleep. The talent was something I must have been born to. The kind that feels so natural it's as if you've always been doing it—even if you haven't—and can't imagine not. I was studying anatomy and lymph systems and even some of the eastern philosophies behind one technique or another. Yoga to Reiki to deep breathing and Swedish hot rocks. I almost went on to acupuncture, but that's another story.

When I started working on real people—they paid hardly anything to be guinea pigs—I discovered that once my hands set to kneading a lower back or calf or shoulder there'd be this warm flow surging through my fingers, like a low-level electric buzz almost. It told my hands how to read through skin to tendon and bone. It was like I wasn't thinking, or thinking in a different way. I'd be following the instructor, sure. But my hands were always a step ahead. Pressing here. Easing a sore joint there just so. Grinding loose a gristly knot of muscle. "Oh," the client would groan as I began, and soon, as their bodies eased, released by my touch, the "ah's" would come, and the grateful grunts.

It took me a while to see the bigger picture. Yes, Lauderdale may have been the perfect place for training. But once you've earned the certificate and want to go full-time life got harder. If you worked for a spa or club, they'd pay almost nothing. And if you went freelance, your clients, who were mostly older anyway, sooner or later they'd move into a facility—and that's the end of your access. Or they'd just outright die on you.

There was Mr. Morgenstern, one of the earliest, with a hernia that wouldn't heal and these monstrous, proud tufts of hair sprouting from his ears. He became my friend. He hailed from Shaker Heights, which we thought was a wonderful coincidence, Ohio and all. (Though he'd never heard of Mount Pleasant.)

And Mrs. Levine from Hillsdale, New Jersey—she stayed loyal for years, insisting on riding the community shuttle to our weekly sessions even after her shingles grew so bad that the lightest clothes and even my touch, bliss for her as it had been, became an agony.

Let me tell you, it was hard when they passed.

So yes, naturally. It was Florida and many of my clients were Jews. Not that it even occurred to me at first. To them it made no difference either—me, I might have been from Timbuktu for all they cared. And Hindu, Muslim, or Catholic thrown in for good measure.

Mrs. Levine, who I mentioned. It must have been our very first session I noticed the purplish-blue scar on the inside of her arm. Faded figures—numbers, I realized, trying not to gawp. They were jagged, uneven. Jabbed into her arm by some hand in a rush.

Nothing like the neat little gremlin on Marybeth's shoulder blade.

That must have hurt, was my first thought. Followed in less than a breath by, *Why would she do that?*

One instant more and it struck me, what the tattoo meant. The floor shifted, buckling. No fooling—I grabbed for the side of the cot. All this while, only seconds of course, Mrs.

Levine is waiting, never a complaint. I say nothing, of course, only try and catch hold of myself.

Long ago there'd been a tiny seed, a dry fact planted almost accidentally, who knows when?—some class or stray conversation about a foreign world, a wholly different universe. About people called Jews, same as in the Bible, and what had been done to them. They'd never seemed all that real, even if somehow the Pratts claimed a connection. And then this one glimpse of tattooed numbers on an old woman's wrist. Well, suddenly, that dry seed flared to life and grew and grew some more in my thoughts.

After all, it was Mr. Morgenstern I finally asked, not Mrs. Levine.

"Time to roll over," I said one day, lifting the sheet so he could slowly, painfully twist onto his stomach. I started working his left shoulder.

"Okay if I ask you something?" I said.

We were pretty good friends by this point, Mr. Morgenstern and me. Some days, I'd drive him where he needed, fetching his dry cleaning or to a liquor store that carried a certain slivovitz. After, he'd buy us both a BLT and lemonade.

"Does it make sense to you," I said, "those people who say they've always been Jews but claim they're Christian now too?"

"Hunh?" he mumbled into the cloth.

"Or you know, the other ones—Christians who aren't Jews to begin with but who decide they can choose it and speed up the Second Coming."

He lifts his head and tries looking up at me. "What, now you want to convert?" he asks, as if I've gone crazy on him.

"No," I say. "Of course not." Retreating before his disbelief and, I suppose, my own.

I can't be sure I'd have found myself thinking of Cassie Pratt in Florida if not for my clients. It wasn't like all the time I'd be remembering her anyway. But one thing did come clear to me—the Pratts of Mount Pleasant, Ohio, were Jews of a very different order.

By this time my own folks were getting older too. That weighed on me. Twice a year I'd be driving my truck the 20 hours each way to visit. One time I built a new deck off the side of the kitchen for them. Another, it would be mending the fence or running my dad a ramp over the old front steps. Sometimes Daniel would find time from his fields to help me, but by then he had his own family too, on top of the farm.

It was clear enough to anybody that our folks would only be needing more help. Who was going to do it? Daniel was the best of sons, truly, but I didn't have his responsibilities. And it wasn't as if, after seven, eight years, I so much fancied myself belonging in Florida forever. Hot, muggy weather may be fine in February, but sweating that way all year round just seemed wrong. And there were plenty of pretty girls, sure, but I got tired of taking one or another to the same parties over and over or, more often, snagging an early-bird special on my own, alongside everyone else trying to save a buck.

And then one Saturday I'm killing an afternoon in Riley's, which was really just a shack between my place and the beach. I'm stabbing at a pile of rubbery fried clams that might have been cooked a first time the day before. And suddenly the notion flashes through me—almost as if it *was* those damn clams backing up—not even a decision but a certainty, a realization of where I needed to be. It flushed me hot in the face. Along with all the other reasons—my folks, the weather—it struck me how there'd be a lot less competition for massage in Ohio. I might actually make a living.

There was this nice little rental only blocks from the Adventist Academy. I set up shop, painting soft colors in the living room, pulling down the shades, finding an Asian flute cd at the Dollar Store.

To get the word out I tried my hand at a little promotion. A bit of proselytizing you might say. I'd be strolling from house to house with fliers—it wasn't as if I hadn't grown up with these people. I put ads in the *Mount Pleasant Gazette*. And the Yellow Pages. A sign in the yard.

I might as well been Mormon.

Turns out the good people of Mount Pleasant have this issue with spending money just to make themselves feel better. That would be a moral weakness.

Oh, sure, throw your back out riding a tractor or wrestling a metal sheet in the auto parts depot—right away all that chiropractor mumbo jumbo and subluxation and suddenly you're a true believer. No self-indulgence then, paying for these "adjustments." The back-cracking actually *hurts*—which must make it all right from the Christian point of view. But try and persuade an Adventist or Nazarene about shiatsu or deep tissue massage?

Thank goodness for Dr. Devi and Dr. Kumar, the orthopedists over at the county hospital. They were plenty pleased to have a new therapist in town. Certified no less. From them

I'd get one, maybe two, referrals a week. Knees and shoulders and most anything in between. Our treatments never lasted long, six weeks, a couple months at best. Whatever insurance would cover. You'd think a few clients might keep coming, fork something out of their own wallets, now they know how much good it does them.

At least, over time, the word begins to spread. Two or three professors from up at the college began visiting me for regular sessions. A couple of their librarians became clients as well. Massage did wonders for their stress. Even the Dean of Students—he had such knots in his shoulders and neck—before long he was as loyal a weekly client as old Mr. Morgenstern. They helped keep me afloat.

And Cassie Pratt calls me out of the blue.

When it came to me who's on the phone?—my feelings were . . . complicated.

By then I'd been home nine or ten months already.

"What's their problem?" I ask her, mostly because our silence had begun to feel awkward. This was still on the Friday, the morning after her synagogue had been raided. Since I couldn't simply replant the cross there and then—it was too big for that—Cassie insisted I come in for tea before rushing to those new referrals I was counting on.

"They've some students up at the college now, Jewish ones, you know, who don't think we should be calling ourselves, well, *Jews*," she says, shaking her head. "Like we've got no right at all."

Over my mug I'm looking around and there's this stack of textbooks on a chair. And maybe some twenty prayer books—she's already explained they're for Saturday morning.

Across on a table stand a bunch of little Israel flags in holders. Hebrew letters hang on a canvas sheet on the wall.

What did it mean to be more Jewish than this?

I imagined the look on Otto Morgenstern's face.

Cassie balances her own mug on a wobbly pile of notebooks and sighs. I notice how sleeplessness has smeared bruises under her eyes. She's pale and unhappy. The pretty flirt, the naughty girl, has long since disappeared.

It occurred to me to wonder why Cassie Pratt never fled our town—to *live!*—as she'd sworn she would?

As *I'd* tried to do.

I discovered a hurt, an ache, in my chest that hadn't been there before.

"How long's this been going on?" I ask with a kind of desperation.

"Oh," she says, trying to gather some wisps of hair back into her bun, these fine dark strands flitting free. "Can you imagine? In Daddy's time that college was just pretty much Episcopalian."

She cocked her head just so, a faint flair of the old Cassie. That made my chest ache too.

"A while, I guess," she says. Coming back to my question with a sigh. "Last fall some of their new students looked us up before the High Holidays—we're in the Yellow Pages after all. Why shouldn't we be? Three or four of them just showed up. I tried to welcome them—they *are* welcome." She smiles and there's pain in her smile.

"Maybe it was they didn't notice Daddy's cross out front, right at first? Maybe they saw it but came in anyway. Anyway, suddenly, they do realize. They fly out the door like we're going to eat them alive."

She puts a hand across her eyes and I can tell she's trembling. Me, I'm feeling helpless, frozen.

"Afterward, I'm getting all these nasty phone calls and messages from them and from their parents. And then this actual letter from the Dean's office arrives in the mail. Can she pay me a visit? She wants to find out more about who we are."

She looks at me, pleading. "Well, isn't that what our mission is all about—teaching, sharing the word?" She sets to picking at the blue star on her mug of tea.

"I figured they'd be coming here to mend fences," she says to the mug. "But then these two women deans or something show up and it's all hostile and examining. They made me feel like some crazy animal in a zoo." She waves a hand. "Like here's my own cage."

"Ethan." Suddenly her voice is tight with strain, like she doesn't really mean to be speaking. The words are forcing their way despite her. "What am I going to do?" She glances at me, and now there's a streak of wild in her eye. "It's worse all the time. They're going to keep coming back. Aren't they? Don't they want to drive me away? Or worse? It's like one of those old pogroms."

That was a word I didn't know, but I didn't much like it.

Even so, I couldn't help wondering whether Cassie was maybe a bit off her rocker. Whether this wasn't just a kind of craziness that went way back. I looked at her, feeling a mix of things all swapped together, and I was both sitting very close and watching her from very far away too.

Still, it wasn't like Cassie could count on the local cops and so-called Christians to protect her. Seemed to me we hadn't done a very good job so far.

True to my word, two days later I borrowed Daniel's tractor. (I'd have done it Saturday, Cassie or no, but my little brother wouldn't have that either, good Adventist that he is.) So, Sunday, I'm bouncing down the Bexley Road on this high red tractor, 15 miles an hour flat out and feeling like a fool. Kids honking as they whiz by. It was a keen November, bitter wind sanding at my cheeks. I pulled my faded Reds cap lower over my eyes.

On that long, slow, cold tractor ride it all came surging back, vivid and raw. Me as a boy, how I'd watched and yearned for this strange girl—a Jew, whatever that meant—a bad girl—not really, not much—who might just as well have patted me on the head, mussing my hair like I was a sweet boy—though she never actually laid a hand on me. Whatever. Resentments are resentments. I didn't much fancy being twisted this way and that, humiliated by Cassie Pratt all over again.

Why had she called me? There had to be others.

Hearing her voice, seeing the way she cocked her head, it scraped up a spark all right. And I didn't like feeling I could be kindled so easily.

By the time I made it to her place my nose was dripping snot from the cold and my mood had turned pretty darn sour. I swung the tractor off the highway and up the little hill. I was impatient, vexed with the whole situation, vexed with myself.

For its part the cross was still leaning heavily on one arm. I went ahead and trussed it with a twenty-foot cable. For leverage I wedged a couple of stones at its foot.

Then I'm easing the tractor into gear, hard on the clutch, backing slowly, slowly towards the synagogue. A creak and a groan as the lead goes taut. We're straining, and the cross seems like it's resisting on purpose, like it wants no part of this either.

The cable catches. The cross shifts and shudders.

All at once I'm cold clean through and still sweating hard, knob in my throat.

I picture the massive wooden trunk sliding right over and falling flat. Then where would we be?

I wasn't even aware of Cassie appearing off to one side in her father's heavy coat, arms crossed across her chest like it was colder even than it was.

Did she realize it shouldn't be done this way?

Because I can admit this now, I was acting hasty—lazy's really the truth—and I knew it.

Why was I behaving like this?

To do the job proper I should have re-dug the hole, cleaned it out deep. I'd have chipped off the old cement that anchored it all those years. Poured fresh stone and let it begin to set. Leveraged the whole thing with some measure and care. That's how old Jeremiah would have done it himself. Or my own father for that matter.

Yeah, well, this was good enough. I didn't need to be like them.

I was saying such stuff in my head, sounding like an angry, snot-nosed kid even in my own ears.

Still the lead's straining and I'm backing slowly, hardly moving, inch by inch. No easy feat to rock that tractor just so.

Suddenly, with a snap and creak, the head of the great wooden cross jerks free of the earth. And now it's rising, slow as I can draw it, up toward its full height.

Reaching a certain angle, however—I wasn't expecting this—it seemed to come to itself all at once. An instant's hesitation and its cement boot jags, scraping six inches across the hard mud and plunges down into the jagged hole, into its old setting, planting itself proper. It steadies, it waveres a little—nothing too bad.

I climbed off the tractor and then, realizing the height of the lead fastened over my head, I mounted once more. Carefully, wavering a bit myself, I stood on the seat, and reached up to loose the cable.

It was as I jumped down and my feet hit the ground again that other things seemed to shift in turn. I didn't even know about this stone weighing on my chest all along until, as I took a deep breath, it slipped away entire, leaving me a little wavery once more.

"You got a shovel?" I shouted to Cassie. There was no real need to shout. It came out almost as a laugh, startling me.

The filling in didn't take long. I finished tamping down the dirt and laid a couple of bigger rocks at the base. Not for any particular reason, but they looked good. The old cross had always leaned away from the New Deliverance Synagogue and slightly aslant, almost like a bully over the highway. Restored now, the lean was maybe a tad off to one side. The mitt of a hand was still staked through at the top. (That's when I noticed a rough gouge chipped in its palm. I didn't say anything, just adjusted my cap.)

Despite the cold sweat caking on my chest and neck, I was feeling light.

Cassie came up from behind and slipped her hand into the crook of my elbow. Daniel would be waiting on the return of his tractor. But Sabbath or not, it was a Sunday, and I was in no hurry.

Emergency Run

So, okay, Caroline has done this a thousand times. Or if not, then it seems like it and it's been plenty enough. Sometimes they'll be gone already by the time the emergency squad arrives, and there's nothing she or the team can do. CPR. Defibrillators. The body will jerk and jump and flop back. Nothing.

Others, they look like nothing's wrong at all, them a bit vexed at the fuss or puzzled maybe. Maybe they'll be cradling their left arm like it hurts or is suddenly heavy. What made them decide it was a heart attack and call 911? She wonders that sometimes. Of course, many's the time they're wrong—no attack, just indigestion or the flu.

But this run is tense. Out of sync from the get-go.

Randy Jenkins, their squad leader, has paged her twice in four minutes, even though at the first buzz from the dispatcher she rushed straight away from the old woman whose blood sample she was collecting. (The insurance company won't reimburse for a second visit, but that goes with doing this job.) The damn pager trills again on her belt as she's pulling in next to the squad's ambulance—she can see Randy at the wheel. Then she's up shotgun and no joke from him, no flirt, nothing, (a relief for sure, but also goes to show things are out of whack), and he's already got the vehicle rolling.

Not that there's far to go, just up the road to the Student Health Center. Even on a short run the squad is supposed to use the siren. Randy doesn't bother. But as they wheel into the drive, Caroline thinks it's as if some kind of silent siren has been blowing its head off anyway, a special whistle that has the college students milling around outside, watching, glum and scared. They've only come here so Doc Hazzard could check them out for STD's or asthma or strep.

The nurses and receptionist aren't doing much better. They're flapping themselves about in little circles as the squad skids up on the loose gravel, its lights flashing silent and wild.

As team paramedic, Caroline is swinging out her door before the vehicle has fully stopped, jogging quick but under control onto the porch. Randy and Steve Coady, a student trainee who's been riding in back, will hump the equipment behind her.

Like most every afternoon, Doc has been on duty in the two-and-a-half story clapboard house. He's waiting for them in his office. Subdivided over decades and added onto by happenstance, the health center is a complete hodge-podge of elbowed hallways and improvised partitions.

Caroline realizes—the kind of thing you realize in a rush—she's never actually been in Doc Hazzard's office before. She plunges through the door, and the dark little room is crammed with books and random bits of medical equipment, and maybe a dozen old clocks, some of them with their pendulums happily wagging away. Oh yeah—somewhere she's heard that he collects them. But she's never been in this office before, which strikes her as kind of strange now that she doesn't really have time to think about it.

He's sitting in an old wooden desk chair, gazing towards her and very still, which is also something she can't remember ever seeing, him sitting down. Except maybe in the back of the medic. He's crammed in next to her, hunkering on his haunches and tending to whoever is lying on the gurney. The two of them, him and Caroline, rolling with the sway of the vehicle on its rush toward the county hospital.

"Hey, Doc," Caroline says, all sweetness and light as she wraps the pressure cuff around his arm. "When did this all start?"

"It's nothing," he says. Just as she expects him to say.

"Okay, I hear you." She's working quick, already pumping the cuff tight and reading her watch. "But when did you first notice this nothing?"

He won't look her in the eye, and with his pale blue eyes and his pout and his shock of wild hair, even if it's thin and graying, he might be impersonating an obstinate schoolboy. "Yesterday. It was just stress. It's probably just stress." But the doctor is also gray, his skin clammy, blood pressure low and pulse not what it should be.

"I'll bet you never even called it in, did you? Did Nurse Radcliffe figure it out and make the call?" Caroline's shaking her head and not giving him time to reply. "You ought to know better," she mutters.

"Can you get that thing in here?" she yells. But the gurney won't make it into the cluttered office, so Randy and Steve set the brake and tear the straps loose on the other side of the door.

"You come on now," she orders.

"I don't need this. I can ride with you," he says, not quite whining and not even convincing himself.

She helps him up from the chair, a hand under his elbow, lifting, urging him forward at his own pace. He makes it to the gurney, and he's panting now, and sweat beads are popping on his neck and brow. First he sinks onto the padded seat, then sort of rolls full out. While the boys are strapping him down, chest and legs, Caroline notices him close his eyes, letting go just a little bit, just for a moment.

She fumbles with the buttons on his starched and ironed shirt—she knows there'll be hell to pay if one pops off—so she can put the stethoscope against his chest. The long scar startles her, though at some level she knew it would have to be there, a blue-white rip that's probably more pronounced right now anyway, slicing from the top of his sternum down at an angle across his ribs and into the softer flesh below his belt. Seeing it, she's surprised the wound didn't kill him after all, all those years ago.

And that's when a sudden surge of warmth catches her by surprise, almost a thumping blow to her chest. As if an attack sympathetic to his own has flushed through her. Except it's different. She recognizes it right away and falls back a step, startled, needing to consider or get a better look, while Randy and Steve roll the gurney toward the medic.

She's worked with Jack Hazzard better than nine years now. At first she lived in mortal terror—him brusque and impatient, demanding a perfection that always seemed just beyond the furthest finger-tip-reach of achievable when it came to equipment properly sanitized and stowed, procedures precisely choreographed, and patients triaged, bandaged and, most precious of all, stabilized.

Down time could be just as awkward. Doc Hazzard never made small talk easily, never went out with the crew for a simple beer. Or if he did try and hang out, say in the ready room on a Sunday, maybe football on the big TV and pizza slices passing hand to hand, he'd be restless and stiff, twitching almost.

The E.M.T. training he supervised was tough too, every detail, every drill. But she didn't mind the toughness. It honed her, challenged her.

But early on she was scared, no—*wary*—of him because he seemed, well, so out of place. Almost like he came from a different planet. Look at the way he was about his shirts—the only personal possession he'd fuss over. She knew some of the girls at the laundry, and they'd just roll their eyes. His collars had to be ironed just right. Not too much starch—but they better be crisp. And those precious cuffs. *French* cuffs, for heaven's sake. Who in Ohio did that? Except Caroline knew he didn't actually wear them full out with cufflinks most of the time. Routine and ritual: first thing every work morning, standing in the window of the health center, he pops the little studs out of the cuffs, slips them in his pocket, and folds the sleeves back, once, twice, exactly so.

Once, she'd thought about buying him a set as a thank you, given all he'd done for her. His birthday was coming up—a fact she discovered only by chance from one of his ex-wives, Sandy, who maybe was still married to him at that point. But the only kind they had at Wise Jeweler's on Mulberry Street, cufflinks with little train engines or gold hearts soldered on, they didn't look like the ones he wore, somehow so simple and elegant, and she felt stupid even caught studying them in the glass case like it was for some exam. She bought a nice card instead. Which she suspects he never got around to opening.

But what intimidated her, early on at least, was more than his education (which you'd have to spy in his voice anyway because, unlike every other doctor in the county, diplomas weren't hanging overhead to prove him some kind of blue-ribbon stud) or where he came from or even the damn cufflinks. It was in the bits and pieces she'd pick up through the grapevine, from ex-wife Sandy and others too—stuff anyone else would parade around in stories for the rest of their lives. How he'd been wounded as a medic in Vietnam, for starters. Apparently the healing of that scar across his breast and belly was slow, difficult, never really complete, though he was already in med school by then. Afterwards, he built a practice up in Cleveland. Only to abandon it, no warning, no explanation—Caroline figured that must have been the beginning of the end with Audrey, ex-wife number one.

So why pick Coshocton County? Talk about rhyme, reason, and none of the above. No one has an answer to that one. First, sort of out of the blue, he volunteers to take over the emergency room at County, duty none of the local G.P.'s want to touch. It's always been a low-man-totem-pole rotation. Then, maybe five years later, the college dean begs him to fill in for Dr. Shepard, who's been ministering to students almost since horse-and-buggy days. In his seventies, he'd become a little too eager offering breast exams to the coeds. Dr. Hazzard's responsibilities will last only a few months while they hire someone permanent. Promise.

And then comes the years she knows almost first hand. Did they ever really search for a replacement? Doc Hazzard steps in to the little student health center—almost starting from scratch to where it is today—and unlike the emergency room or his own practice, the duties of college physician give him off-duty time for training the emergency squad. And there's the women's shelter too. And the homeless services, and the county jail. Any local organization with sense enough to ask his help, because he can't, won't, ever say no.

This all is what's puzzled her. Doc Hazzard a mystery, like a foreigner or a strange pet you don't ever understand but get used to. It was who he was, and after a while it just didn't bother her anymore.

She never expected to be doing this anyway. She volunteered to join the squad because that's what Randy was doing after he dropped out of the Nazarene College on the other side of town. It was a way to spend more time with him, because they were together then. Then after a couple of years they weren't together, because Randy had been doing something more than flirt with Rhonda Jean Owens. At least that was the excuse she told both him and herself when she broke it off. But by then she'd already passed the first two levels of E.M.T. certification, and Doc Hazzard was encouraging her, baiting her, daring her through the final rigorous stages of paramedic training. She wasn't about to leave and go back to what her life had been.

When the moment finally arrived, he was the one carrying the long cardboard tube like a baton out into the fire station's parking lot. He motioned for her to climb into their ambulance. "Look at that," he said admiringly. "Do you realize? You just worked some magic, Caroline." He gestured from front to back with a wave of the baton then handed it up to her. Inside was her paramedic certificate. "All you had to do was set foot up there and this squad wagon became a medic.

I think that must mean it's for real." He shook her hand. "I'm proud of you."

She'd felt a rush then too, for sure. Gratitude, pride, not a little disbelief.

*

She jogs out to that same medic just as the boys finish hoisting the gurney up into the back. They turn, waiting for her to scramble in as well. They'll ride up front, this time with both siren and lights at full blast for sure.

But Caroline hesitates. Not so much a hesitation as a hiccup, a double bounce on her toes before she's up and through and the door is swinging shut behind. And she's watching herself tend to him. His eyes are closed again, his breathing shallow, a light pant. She should touch him to check his pulse again and she hesitates, again. His eyes flicker open and he looks up at her.

"Hey," he murmurs. "Last time I was on my back this way, they'd brewed up a whole war around me. I hope there's no fuss like that this time."

The wan little smile he gives her is like a knife, slicing through the muscle of her chest, releasing the warmth and pressure that flooded there only moments ago. Caroline never cries—she's one tough broad, as Randy often boasted, sometimes not a happy boast, but she's come to like the notion—so naturally the tears are already running down her cheeks and dripping off the tip of her nose. When she wipes at them with the back of her hand she makes an almighty mess.

Fortunately, Doc Hazzard's eyes are closed again. And his vitals are stable, so she takes two seconds to wrestle a tissue out of her jeans pocket. Here she is, breaking one rule after another of the hygiene he's been so insistent on while teaching her.

Shit, she's thinking. *Shit, shit, shit.*

No goddamn warning or hint or nothing, just the overwhelming fact and certainty smacking her between the eyes.

Why now? she wonders.

It's horrible.

Not to mention absolutely nuts.

What it's not is anything like that platonic stuff that Randy is always gassing about while trying to get back in her pants. But it's not really hot either—about sex. She doesn't want to sleep with him.

Well, maybe she does, but that's not the point.

It sure as hell isn't maternal.

She just *wants* him. Every little bit and scrap of him.

Caroline never cries and she's thirty-five years old and never been in love, not like this, and she's been so proud of it. Now what the hell is she supposed to do?

Normally, she'd make a clean hand-off at the emergency bay, but this time she's walked the gurney all the way through to the curtained cubicle and helped transfer him up into the hospital bed. No one seems to notice her, not even him. Well, why the hell should he?

Back out at the medic she cooks up a ragged excuse about checking on some one else who's already been admitted. So Randy and Steve make the five-mile run home without her. It's not like she's essential. There are two other paramedics they can call and seven E.M.T.'s.

She just needs some space to calm down. To think.

This isn't life or death, not in any immediate sense. If he's actually suffered a heart attack, it hasn't been catastrophic. They can almost certainly deal with it. She's sure of that. Once they'd got him off the gurney, the doctor on duty had them pushing an I.V. into his arm with the usual cocktail of blood thinner, muscle relaxant, anti-coagulant.

Ahead there may be surgery, of course. Angioplasty or even a bypass. But she knows he's not about to die on her.

Maybe life would be easier if he would.

She shakes her head at that thought and then discovers that the thought has set off a trembling from her legs right up to her throat.

He must be fifty. She figures for a moment. Probably more—closer to sixty.

That doesn't matter either.

Wandering into the waiting room was a bad idea. It's sure as hell no refuge. She'd hoped to slip into a seat in the far corner and let the rush and swirl sweep around her while she calmed down and thought it through and recovered herself. But it's a quiet Tuesday afternoon. She knows too damn many people. Seems like half the folks she's ever rushed here in the wagon are back for some kind of procedure or test. They're all so *grateful*, and have just got to express it.

Not to mention the nurses, the techs, even some of the doctors, ones not convinced they're the second coming.

Everyone figures it's real nice to say hi.

Sometimes, she thinks and not for the first time, living in a small town is a pain in the ass.

*

Steve Coady is still working on the squad wagon when Caroline returns to the station late in the afternoon. He's already emptied the cabinets and storage bins in the back for a thorough washing out. Now he's restocking as she comes in the door. If he's had any classes today—and she knows he's been developing a bad habit of skipping—they'd be over anyway. It's not like he's involved in athletics or a frat. Training as an E.M.T., being part of the emergency squad, has become the center of his social life.

No one else is hanging around. The weekly training session will be tomorrow night, Wednesday, as usual. So once the cleaning is done, all he can do is wait for the next emergency call while playing video games in the rec room.

For the first time in better than six months Caroline wishes she had a smoke. She drops her backpack in a corner and hangs her coat on a peg.

"Hey," she says to him.

"What's up?" Steve glances round at her.

His jeans are riding so low on his hips—and he hardly has hips to begin with—she's not sure what keeps them up. Which proves to her, as if she needs the proof, that there's a decade difference between them. But she likes the look of those plaid jockeys peeking out and the non-hip hips.

"Pretty quiet," she says. *How lame can you get?*

"For sure." He shrugs.

"Listen," she rushes into it and won't hesitate any more and here it comes because otherwise it's never going to happen and she doesn't know how she'll get through the evening on her own and she'd thought about Randy for maybe one-millionth of a second and how he's been angling for it and how Rhonda Jean sure would deserve it, and how she knew she'd enjoy it too, except that he'd be just so damn pleased with himself and she couldn't live with that, and spending the night as per most every other night with one of her girlfriends sure as hell won't do, what with little Stevie unexpectedly waiting right here. "I was on my way, you know, just going to throw some dinner together," she says. "It's just as easy to cook for two. And I think somewhere there's this bottle of wine someone left behind. Anyway. Or are you supposed to do the cafeteria?"

Steve looks at her, trying not to show how astonished and eager he is. "Whatever," he says, a beat too quick to be as cool as he wants it to be. "Sure."

Back in her apartment above the laundromat, she pan-fries a flank steak. Which is a mistake because in about five seconds smoke is billowing up to the ceiling. Naturally the smoke detector sets off in the doorway. Steve climbs on a wobbly chair to yank the battery while she's shoving windows open on both sides of the room. A blast of steam from the dryers below blows through. And they're laughing, howling at the idea of their own crew rushing over here to the rescue. Which is good, the laughing.

By the time they're sitting at the table most of the smoke has cleared and the steaks are damn good. And before the bottle of rioja is quite empty she's leading him back to the small bedroom, letting him think he's the one doing the leading.

The wine has worked its way into her head and she's a smidge high and into this. Nothing delicate or romantic about it—they're both peeling off clothes and clambering towards the unmade bed. The boy has a silver ring in one ear. And a small tattoo, maybe a flower or a dolphin, he's squiggling too much to get a good look it, above his right nipple.

He's trying to be a bad boy, she thinks, *and he's so not. He's just cute.*

And with that thought it starts to go wrong.

He's already on top of her, in too much of a hurry, just like boys his age always used to be, she remembers too well. And she'd like him to go down on her or maybe have a little fun with this. But that's academic anyway because she's thinking now, so already it's too late.

Naturally, it means she's going dry.

"Ow," she gasps, biting her lip, as he pushes into her.

"Huh?" he mumbles, thrusting.

"Nothing. You go ahead."

She's lying back and trying not to let it hurt too much. She's gone from thinking about what a nice boy he is, even if he's a baby, to not even thinking about him at all. It's Doc Hazzard now and only him, and she feels guilty, as if she's being unfaithful.

No, it's worse than guilty—she feels bad, this is what hurts, because she's being unfaithful to herself.

It's him she wants, more than ever, as this nice boy finishes more quickly than he wanted. He's the one feeling guilty, she can tell, as he lies panting on top of her breasts, because he thinks he's disappointed her.

"There, there," she murmurs, running her fingers through his hair to comfort him.

After Steve has retreated to his dorm room—no way she was going to let him stay the night, not that he seemed inclined—Caroline gets dressed again and storms around the apartment, cleaning and rearranging, doing the dishes, stacking her videos and compact discs. Panting and flustered and thoroughly wretched, she undresses again and starts to climb into the shower but thinks better of it and runs the bath, hot as she can stand. Luxury for a midweek evening.

What now? she at last permits herself to wonder as bubbles billow over her breasts and belly. Hijacking the boy wasn't a mistake, at least as far as she's concerned. But it hadn't distracted her the way she hoped. Might as well never have happened. Point is, it sure didn't help with the real problem. Even if Stevie does what boys do and it gets back to Randy, so what?

That thought stops her for an instant. How many years, decades, has it been since she's felt anything like that? Felt *nothing*. Not caring what Randy thinks or says or does—it ought to be liberating, something to toast. If the fact it took her this long weren't so sad.

But none of that matters either. Only Doc Hazzard. He's a dull ache just under her breastbone. Each breath aggravates the bruise.

Oh God, she sighs and inhales a stinging wad of bubbles.

The real problem—he's twenty years older than her. More.

No, it's not that either. It's that he's never noticed her as anything other than a trainee or an apprentice, maybe finally a colleague, even if she's not a doctor. But never a hint that she might mean more than that to him. She doesn't take it personally—she's known him long enough. Through two wives for certain.

Caroline didn't really know Audrey from up in Cleveland. She still visited occasionally when Caroline was first volunteering with the squad. And later, with a gap of three or four years between, there was Sandy. Who Caroline did know and liked a lot, and through Sandy she got to see what the man was like to live with.

He was a saint.

He is a saint.

Saints are hell to live with.

Would he notice her now, if she thrust herself upon him?

Could she live with such a man if he did take notice?

Something else long on her mind: it would seal that deal once and for all. She'd never have kids. She knows from what Sandy once confessed—it was during the divorce, Sandy gabbing blearily after too much chardonnay at a solidarity lunch—that he decided on a vasectomy while he was in med school, before either Audrey or she came along. He didn't want the worry or responsibility of his own children. He was too busy worrying about other peoples'.

Caroline is still creating the list of reasons why it would drive her crazy, living with this man, as a second tub of water cools.

She'd wind up killing him or, more likely, herself.

This little game she's playing helps. It really does.

It's convinced her, totally, that she is beyond help or reason altogether.

In the days that follow she has the feeling she's wading through a kind of dream or dare—that she's testing herself or the limits of a fantasy that can't possibly be real or work out any way she might imagine.

*

Tracking his physical status is easy. Given his importance to their operations, the emergency squad receives regular updates. And the early news is modestly reassuring. The initial attack was relieved quickly—once Doc relented, once Nurse Radcliffe called 911, and once the squad finally got him to emergency. But now the question is how much damage the heart muscle suffered. A CAT scan has been ordered, and of course they're monitoring his vitals.

For the time being Caroline quietly cancels the rest of her life, anything beyond her regular shifts for the squad. She isn't available to run medical checks for insurance companies. Or to administer flu shots at the health department. Or to stand by with her kit in the dark corner of the high school gym during a big basketball game (though that alone costs her seventy-five bucks).

Not that she can muster the courage to visit his bedside. That would be too weird.

From time to time she finds it hard to breathe.

On the fourth day after arriving at Coshocton County Hospital, an impatient Doc Hazzard is scheduled to be shipped up to the Cleveland Clinic for further tests and, most likely, an angioplasty procedure. By rule and insurance regulation he's supposed to travel by ambulance. Like any other private citizen he'll have to go private. (The college township rescue vehicle can't be out of commission for most of a day to ferry him.) Which is exactly what he expects, though over the course of a day and a half he also declares loudly and often to his colleague, Harry Nemitz, who is also now his cardiologist, that none of this is really necessary. Why not let him drive himself the two hours and no one be the wiser? Naturally, reports of this dialogue spread across the small community within a very little while, provoking knowing nods and not a little laughter.

What takes some doing is Caroline calling Vince Clippinger, who owns a private ambulance and also serves as local pest control consultant, and convincing him she might be interested in working some overtime after all. She has a sudden need for the extra pay, and no, she isn't going to explain. He hesitates. Vince has been after to her to come over to the private sector longer than he'd admit out loud. As a good faith gesture, she adds before he can draw that next breath, she'd be willing to ride shotgun up to Cleveland no fee, just to get the lay of the land in his operation.

Doc Hazzard is more annoyed than surprised when she climbs out of the strange vehicle at the hospital entrance and swings the back open for him. He's supposed to be strapped onto the gurney again for safety's sake, but that far he won't go and she's not going to press him. With a hand from her, he steps up into the ambulance, almost as if they're heading off on a regular run. Abandoning her shotgun post in front, Caroline perches on the bench opposite him.

"Ready to roll," she calls to Vince, who's catching a quick smoke by the electric doors with one of the ER nurses.

"How long have you been moonlighting?" Doc asks, once they're on the highway.

She's finding it hard to look at him, partly because the full, deep sweep of her feelings have flooded from her belly into her chest and up into her throat, partly because he doesn't look well, not at all. "Just started," she mumbles, eyes on the gurney between them.

"I'm sure Vince Clippinger pays better than the township can do."

"For sure." She nods vigorously, miserable.

He's wearing his street clothes, khakis, a perfectly ironed, perfectly blue shirt, its cuffs invisible within a windbreaker. But the clothes seem to belong to someone else, his belt cinched tight an extra notch to hold his pants up. His skin is pale, almost bluish, with the papery fineness she's seen in plenty of older people, her own father first among them. And a crease has appeared between his eyes—she's sure it's new. Who knows what caused it? Pain or worry, or something else entirely.

How does she take all this in without looking at him? She wonders at that.

She reaches for a stethoscope and surprises herself with her own impulsiveness. "I want to check you," she says. Not waiting for a response, she comes closer to him and opens the top button of the shirt. She listens to the valves controlling ebb and flow, the pulsing whoosh of a heart. From the corner of her eye glimpses again and recognizes the pale purple-blue scar. Now, an intimate after tending him those few days ago, she knows its secret route across his breast and heart and belly. Oh, that scar. She draws the stethoscope away and averts her eyes as he buttons his shirt.

When Caroline was a young girl, ten, eleven and twelve, she had an occasional dream of discovering that one or the other of her parents had died or gone away for good. Worst was that in all the dream's variations, she never had the chance to say goodbye—no last hug or kiss or acknowledgement of love. It filled her with an aching and desperate sadness that lingered even after she woke. Their actual deaths, within a few months of each other and years later, hadn't been nearly so painful, or painful in a different, stretched out, final kind of way.

The memory of the dream, which blossoms now unbidden for the first time in many years, takes her breath away but gives her courage to glance up and confirm that new crease in Doc's dear and drawn face, the pale blue of his eyes, which have never been so pale before.

And it comes to Caroline, a caustic benediction of the old dream, that Doc Hazzard is going to die. Oh, not now and not in Cleveland, and maybe not for years to come.

Death has never scared Caroline. The *idea* has never plagued her, though she knows that others endure a horror of extinction all their lives. The practical reality, on the other hand, hand in hand with the profession she has chosen, has been inevitable and sad too almost always, and natural in its own way. Why worry or fear it?

Her mother passed away first—there was surprise in that, certainly. A woman never sick, not even sick the day they found her. Time came to wake up and she didn't. It was no surprise, however, when Caroline's father followed his wife those few weeks later. What place on earth did he have without this woman who'd been with him from the small school in the small town and on through his life?

Others have died along the way, inevitably. More than a few while Caroline was tending them. She'd be trying to coax a little flicker of breath, a heartbeat, nursing them hard. Only for what had been life to flutter into coldness, into nothing. Sometimes the paramedic felt frustration at her own impotence. Sometimes, perhaps after a long struggle, where she felt she wasn't wrestling just the body before her but something darker, almost willful—she sensed that, yes she did, and never spoke of it—after a spasm from the heart suggested she might win after all, only for the beat, one-two, one-two, one, to miss the next stroke and subside, then a sudden raw outrage might surge through her. It made her want to wail and pound her fists against the cooling body. To all appearances, however, she was always controlled, always professional.

But now it all feels like a cruel trick, a conspiracy of the universe. Not that she fears her own mortality—that's no more an issue than ever. But why should Doc Hazzard have to die? Not the sound of his heart but the glimpse of the ancient scar has brought the truth home. Only now at this advanced age does the puzzlement arrive for her, when she ought to be too old to think of marriage or children or death. It is a gift of her dreams and of the scar and of the crease between his dear eyes. Ever and forever without end. That's what death is, and he is going to die.

She looks that fact full in the face. And suddenly, gently, something lifts from her and passes away.

She's surprised, feels a little guilty. Why should this be?

She's able to gaze now at Doc as if he can be the one to answer.

"How you feeling?" she asks.

He answers with a shrug. "Never better." Wry, impatient, distant, he sits opposite her, hands between his legs.

She loves this man, that's as true as ever, and admires him, teacher and friend. A protective, possessive kind of love to be sure. She nods slightly to herself, confirming it.

But she's come to a new place. She has been released from a spell as if a fever has broken suddenly and entirely. It's a relief, but a weary, sad relief.

She feels a bit chilly, and lonely too, as if, in some manner, she's been left behind.

Doc Hazzard smiles and notices nothing, knows nothing. How like him, dear man.

Impression and Correspondence

The slide action on the older Vandercook is grinding. He noticed it yesterday. A bearing may have worn itself out of alignment, and that will mean shutting the letterpress down for most of a day to repair. But other than his own finickiness, there's no particular urgency. His other presses can handle the current orders of wedding announcements and party invitations.

But in truth it's a Sunday and he's alone, the presses oddly silent. He's given a rare one-day parole to both college kids who volunteer with him for a pica's worth of academic credit, and to his paid apprentice, barely paid at that, but hoping to use the experience here to apply for a graduate post in Chicago.

Why did he ever agree to a visit? For years now, a decade and more, the rhythms of his life have flowed as smoothly as the presses themselves. Does he resent the intrusion? He could have manufactured an excuse, some reason to put her off. But Dami knows him too well. She'd have seen through any feint.

The well-swept, reinforced floorboards reveal no track of his years weaving among the machines. Today, however, he's moving slowly and without any particular direction, a fraying rag clutched in his hand like a security blanket.

A renaissance in hand printing has confounded and delighted him in recent years. From struggling to attract any business at all—real estate brochures, especially in the spring, and glossy coupons, and always the packets of cheap ads tossed into driveways—his shop has evolved into something of a boutique, offering luxurious handmade papers and bespoke stationery. For a few exacting clients he even offers what might be considered a concierge service: personal printing on demand. The notion wearies him. But he can only acknowledge that this new fashionableness has stemmed the slide of his profession into oblivion.

To the volunteers he's demonstrated how the persuasion of inks can yield a precise flow. The choreography of plates and type produces impressions without flaw. Flawless yet with character, that's what customers desire. Working the letterpress becomes a calibrated dance of plates and inks and human limbs.

But the shop lies silent this afternoon. Something eerie in the lack of racket, even on a Sunday. Uncomfortable, he feels a trickle of sweat on his neck.

She's been vague about her exact arrival. Dami. The person who knows his history and his thoughts and even his fading desires as well anyone in the world—better than anyone else in the world. With pen and paper and plenty of distance between them, not to mention twenty years' practice, he's been able to tell her just about everything that is sayable.

Save the one topic they never broach. But that's ancient history.

And he believes he knows her, different as she is—could there be any two people more different?—about as well.

She doesn't drive, of course. A private car is to fetch her from the airport and head first to the conference hotel. The next stage will last almost an hour, ferrying her out into farmland and wooded hills, all the way to this village.

And yet, after such a journey she's planning to spend only part of the afternoon with him. The car will wait for her. Early this same evening she is scheduled to moderate a panel back at the convention center.

Six months ago an assistant brought Dami's attention to an expensively produced, lavender-tinted card inviting her to speak at a gathering of designers, producers, and media. Most of these queries she declines. But this particular program is being staged only forty-five miles from her old college. She'd examined the card, tapping it with her fingers. Excellent stock, but laser printing cheapens the effect. She flipped it again. She's never once been back.

The inspiration flared brightly, sudden with excitement. But a week passed, even after she'd agreed to attend, before she mustered courage enough to write him with the details.

His hesitation of a day or two before replying revealed perfectly well how the prospect unnerved him. It's as she expected. But it disappointed her too and nearly unnerved her as well.

It's also true that from the instant the prospect of seeing him occurred to her—or from the first stroke of her pen on paper in letting him know—she's worried about her own eagerness. What provoked it? Worse, what other long-dormant feelings might flare up once she arrives? Six hours ago at LaGuardia she'd quailed, a hitch in her step as she boarded the flight—was this trip really prudent?

*

Twice a week, sometimes even more frequently, they have been exchanging letters, he and Damayanti Chatterjee. On milled paper or a notebook page ripped out for the purpose. Usually with ink pens. Though on occasion he'll resort to a drafting pencil at hand or she to some kind of fine-tipped marker. Never, never have they stooped to email or phone texts. With the rest of the world, of course, first Dami and later he learned to send electrons fizzing across distant bright screens.

In handwritten letters they will share an anecdote from early the same morning, or perhaps a more distant memory that has been scratched to the surface. Or they'll sketch an appalling or hilarious character who passes through her life in the city only once or who resurfaces in his smaller orbit day after day.

Early on his chatty letters surprised no one more than himself. He'd never thought himself a man for words, other than setting them in type. Language had always felt clumsy to him.

Early mornings he'll sit with a cup of black coffee. Late evenings he's perched in the back of the shop, a single bulb still burning in the lamp above his shoulder as he composes with a fountain pen nearly as ancient as the old jobbing press.

Sometimes it's merely a quick line or two, jotted in a rush. And occasionally, having earned this intimacy, they share each other's most private thoughts and fears, the irrational worries that strike late at night, the loneliness that can rise like a mist, cloaking, choking a quiet weekend that would otherwise be so welcome.

Like an old married couple (not that he'd allow, ever, his pen to commit *old married couple* to paper) they've even evolved a private short hand. A word, a phrase—that's all it takes to elicit a stifled guffaw on an uptown bus or a snort of laughter outside the village post office.

He's chafing at the prospect of her arrival in his shop.

It's an imposition, isn't it? An intrusion? Hasn't their correspondence been satisfaction enough?

Stopping to wipe at a greasy smudge on a metal flank, he's exasperated. Her pouncing on him this way is nothing less than a violation of their relationship.

No, that's too harsh—he's already shaking his head. He must be fair.

He must slow his breath. Calm himself. Too much time on his own and all this silence—it makes him cranky.

Yes, of course, he's curious as well.

But why must she disturb a perfectly acceptable arrangement?

And it's risky. He tries not to think about the risk.

Does she really suppose there's none?

It was she who wrote the first card. Which surely surprised him when it arrived, a good five years since he'd last laid eyes on her. Pale blue stock, high rag content, no monogram. Just her thoughts on hearing of Monica's passing.

By then he'd been reconciled to never seeing her again. Well—he hadn't, hasn't, not until sometime in the next few minutes.

It was also she, Dami, who years earlier had been first to knock at his door. A sophomore at the small college up the hill, she'd stood on the threshold, she and her friend Katrina. She was wearing a bright, flowing orange-and-grey top and some kind of leggings—later she'd teach him it was salwar kameez—while Katrina, wearing jeans and a sweatshirt, toed one of her flats into the floor.

Might they watch him work the machines? Her voice was musical with its Indian-almost-British accent bestowed by a Catholic girls' school. They were art majors, printers as a matter of fact. But their experience so far had been limited to silk screens and wood blocks. It might be fun to observe a letterpress.

Wiping oil from his hands, he considered them for a moment, them fidgeting awkwardly in the doorway.

It might be fun.

He was on a tight deadline, working late on a job that might cover rent this month. Nor did he feel like performing for these girls. Okay, it was a little flattering. But also more than a little condescending. Students always assumed that doing them a favor ought to be honor enough.

Not quite forty yet, he was also wary of these two young women, so sure of themselves and so much younger than they realized. Katrina was the tall one and lithe, a faintly punkish beauty, her blond hair stylishly jagged, swatches of pink jabbed through it for effect.

Dami was shorter, but not short, her hair very dark with a faintly reddish aura. It occurred to him, though he didn't know how, that she used henna.

She didn't strike him as pretty. That wasn't it.

But it was her eyes. And the set of her mouth. Teeth that weren't perfect.

She'd have to do something about the gauzy vermillion scarf—a dupatta he'd learn—or a press would surely snag it like a noose fitted to her throat.

Somehow that same evening he'd succumbed, allowing them to observe. After a while he grew unaware of their presence, so hard was he concentrating.

Four days later, proving persistent, they appeared once more at his door. Tuesday nights and Saturday mornings, their presence became routine. He'd never thought of himself as a teacher, and it wasn't so much anything he said aloud— speaking seemed awkward or beside the point. They'd watch his hands, the adjusting and coaxing as he brought the presses to life and into the rhythm of a dance. Over time they learned how to operate one machine after another.

One cold Tuesday evening that first winter, sleet was slapping against the windows. Darkness seemed to surround the print shop as if it were remote and solitary, lost on a vast plane, rather than anchored in this village. Surely only an arm's reach away, other shops lay invisible in the impenetrable night.

As he wrestled with a plate that kept wrenching loose, Dami stood at his hip, trying to observe what he was doing, looking to be helpful. At some point she slipped her cool hand onto the back of his neck.

Across the floor, largely blocked from view by the clam-shell press she'd recently mastered, Katrina was stamping out business cards on heavy stock.

At first he was aware of her hand without quite noticing it. And when he did notice, he shivered as if shocked by an exposed circuit. She'd never touched him before. She began kneading muscles stiff from a long day.

"Watch yourself," he croaked under his breath. "That causes trouble."

"Yes, well, it is my trouble as well," she murmured back.

Stepping closer, as if merely to help him with leverage in the guts of the machine, she poked a thumb into the hollow at the top of his spine. He'd no idea she was so strong. The thumb drove hard and home. Without warning, every joint in every limb of his body suddenly opened, flowered, dropped away.

He felt himself dropping too—threw out his right arm and caught himself on the edge of the press though he hadn't moved at all.

They acted as if nothing had happened. Of course, there'd be accidental brushings of hands on the press, couldn't help but be, hips edging past hips, glances that were patient and expectant on her part—she seemed older than he and very wise—and puzzled, longing, unsure on his.

Another night she rapped even as she pushed the door open. It wasn't a Tuesday, and only by chance was he working late. Out of habit he looked past her shoulder for Katrina. Dami, her hair pinned in back with a dark comb, turned the lock. Metal blinds blocked the many windows—too much sunlight might mar paper and ink. She swung round without drawing any closer.

"I am not sure this is possible anymore," she said, looking at him and then down at the floor.

"Okay," he said, his heart dropping. "But I was sort of counting on the two of you helping get the Prescott job out the door."

She raised her head again, her dark eyes narrowed with disbelief and the kind of anger one might feel for a child who ought to know better. "You are sometimes a very stupid man, Tyler Evans," she said.

He flapped his arms against his sides. "What?" he said.

A girl was all she'd been, just shy of 20, and still missing Calcutta and her family. Confused feelings kept her awake in the night. Lonely without Baba and her mother and her sisters. But worse was Tyler Evans. Yes, she ached for him even after they'd begun, when they were together and when they weren't.

And there was no one to tell. She tossed and turned, Katrina snoring and snuffling in the bed across the small room.

After a year and more her friends still didn't suspect. At least she'd always believed they hadn't. Not even Katrina. These college girls couldn't conceive such a thing, not with a man ancient beyond time. *Gross*, they'd have thought, imagining the touch. Perhaps they couldn't imagine. Perhaps, if they *had* known or suspected, it might have mattered. Not any more. Who's to care after all these years?

*

Dami's mother's sister from New Jersey drove her away on a dusty Wednesday afternoon in early June. An hour into the drive she persuaded her aunt to stop for a break and called him from a payphone, weeping. He was glad and also miserable and a little bit relieved. And then he heard no more from her.

Two weeks later he dropped a card into the mail addressed to New Jersey and received no response. After another month he attempted a chatty aerogramme—merely one of her friendly instructors—to the address in Calcutta.

Only five years later was it answered. At a fashion gala in Manhattan she'd found herself shouting back and forth with a charming young man. It was one of those encounters—not only had he attended the same Midwestern college as she, he'd even briefly volunteered at the print shop in town. This was how she learned the news.

The note arrived some months after Monica had slipped away beyond silence. She'd been poorly, he devoting more attention to her care year after year. It happened one evening just after he'd fetched her a small dish of chocolate ice cream. Monica smiled at him. She smiled and sighed with puzzlement at what she spied just behind his shoulder, before sinking back softly into her pillow.

He'd sat by her side, the ice cream puddling in its dish, as he tried to imagine what to do next.

Two days later he began hand-printing the notices.

It was only the heavy linen stock that winged his notice, an orphan among bills and fliers on the floor. This was at the shop, not the house, as if his home were still off limits. Monica's passing had provoked only a handful of cards and messages. Most remained untouched. They lay stacked haphazardly on a small table just inside the cottage door, collecting dust like the rest.

He had work to do. It kept him moving, breathing, not really eating, as if his body were akin to the presses, running on a little oil and grease, no thinking necessary, purpose enough in the labor.

Her note apologized for its tardiness, but only recently had she run into the young man at the fashion gala. She mentioned that she too was married, but with her parents' name. No children yet. And apparently no rancor towards him either.

He imagined her voice, mature and sure of itself, less girlish, but like the handwriting entirely recognizable. The card spoke to him as an old friend, an intimate who needn't mention intimacy. Certainly she was no longer his apprentice.

In a quiet moment after two days, he selected one of the cream-colored note cards from the rack by the register and covered all four sides in his own precise scrawl. He described Mrs. Morganthal, Monica's mother, a withered bully who'd arrived from Worcester without warning, and the brother—Samander, of all preposterous names. They'd coerced him into a memorial service in the small Episcopal chapel where neither he nor Monica had ever set foot. And there was the handful of curious and gossipy souls who'd attended. Eloise Pidgeon, for one, who lived next door. It seemed entirely possible that Monica had given up the ghost simply to escape Mrs. Pidgeon's daily prospecting for tattle. The story required more than a single card as it turned out—he fetched an extra. Both wedged carefully into the envelope.

"Ah," Dami wrote back, "You must tell me more about Eloise Pidgeon. I never fully appreciated your wickedness."

He glances to the bottle of wine he's brought for the occasion and is jarred by what's not alongside. A white-paper packet of smoked salmon—abandoned on the battered stand in his kitchen. Fumbling the shop door open, he hurtles into the street. Past the market and the post office he jogs, a stabbing stitch soon in his side, around the corner of the local bank—once famously robbed by the Dillinger gang—and past the bakery already closed for the day. At last he plunges, breathing hard, through his unlocked back door.

And as foreseen, the carnage lies strewn before him. Beau, his ten-year-old golden, has knocked the salmon, a wedge of stilton, the thick-sliced dark bread—discovered for this occasion at the back of the small grocery—all onto the slate floor. Nosing through the shattered white china, the dog has already consumed the full bounty.

Tyler can only lean on the butcher-block cart, breathing hard. A growing blotch is spreading across his blue chambray shirt ironed a few hours ago. The stitch in his side stabs rhythmically and his right knee aches.

No time to fuss cleaning the mess, Tyler searches for the culprit. Predictably he finds Beau lying wedged in the front room between the reading chair and hearth. The dog looks up, nose anchored to the ground, his eyes liquid with guilt. He offers a single lame thump of his tail.

Another smell seeps through the room, acrid and sour. He traces the stink to a soft pile of vomit, gobs of too-rich salmon and cheese and bread deposited behind the door. Holding his breath, he peers closer. No sign here of blood or shards of crockery—his primary worry has been Beau swallowing some broken dagger.

Behind him the retriever belches largely, snout still low.

"You've done it now," mutters his owner with disgust and affection and irritation too.

Once more Tyler heaves himself heavily out into the street, tardy despite all the extra time he'd allowed. In the afternoon sun he notices a smear of vomit along his sleeve.

"Oh Christ," he mutters. But there's nothing to be done out here. On he jogs heavily, his right knee flaring with pain.

And only now does the strangeness strike him, that Dami is coming to meet him at the cluttered, inhospitable print shop, not his perfectly pleasant, gently neglected cottage. That possibility had never occurred to either of them.

No sign yet of his visitor inside the shop or out, and for this he's grateful.

In a closet stands a small stone sink. He rubs at the streak on his sleeve. But the dark water only broadens the smear. He can only hope it will dry and fade.

Without a mirror Tyler squats by one of the Vandercooks, peering at himself in the metal. It offers only a blurry image, and he's not even sure he wants to know the truth about his hair, about his age, about what he's become. His letters have never lied to her—he's happily shared some of the indignities of aging—but they haven't ventured quite all the truths either.

The bottle of white wine bobs in a yellow tub of ice. He'd remembered to fetch it that morning even while forgetting the cheese and salmon. Two (new) wine glasses sit on the floor. He doesn't want to violate the display before her arrival.

But a fifth of bourbon lies in the bottom drawer of his desk. As a rule he never touches it before nine o'clock. Too much risk he'll injure himself or, worse, mess up a job. But rules are suspended today—aren't they?—and he needs something to take the edge off, to calm his hammering heart.

Out of a dusty stoneware mug drop a broken drafting pencil and several mismatched paperclips. He blows sharply into the mug and pours a finger of whiskey. The mouthful burns as he swallows, a good burn. But then it rises back at him. He coughs and sets the mug down. Coughs again. His eyes are tearing. The whiskey churns in his empty stomach.

A car door slams and he realizes Dami has been set loose upon him. Wiping a hand across his mouth, he hurries out front.

She is already standing in the entrance, smiling brightly but uncertain. A sheer tangerine dupatta is flung around her neck and shoulders as if to tease him, as if she's forgotten the dangers. He knows she hasn't.

"Come in, come in," he cries, a coarse bleat that doesn't sound like him at all.

She steps forward and glances from machine to machine, a quick inventory. There have been many, many changes over twenty years, but nothing that matters, he realizes. It's much the same shop. It's he that's changed.

"I'm in," she says gaily.

Stepping toward him, she sets a shoulder bag down and seizes both his hands. "Tyler Evans," she says, leaning forward to kiss one cheek and then the other. The reek of whiskey is powerful and she tries to hide her recoil. He is greyer than she'd expected, though she'd tried to expect it.

How must she appear to him? she wonders.

For better or worse—and it wasn't any particular decision—they have never exchanged photos. Until this moment it hasn't struck her as odd. But now that they're face to face, who could measure up to visions and versions of themselves from the distant past?

Of course, she's been profiled in many magazines, but none he would ever come across, and not that she would mention.

She smiles, and notices him notice.

She's proud to be no more than a few pounds heavier than as a student—and she was so scrawny then. Her face is lean, perhaps too much so, but she is rounder in the hips, and she sags in places she never sagged before. It is early yet in a battle she cannot win—she knows this and has no intention of ceding the fight. Still, she's in damn good shape for forty-three, with two husbands already in the rearview. Well, one. The other's a matter of paperwork. Tyler knows this part, every detail. Almost. And other men, at parties and along the flanks of fashion runways, they still glance at her left hand. That's a sure sign.

For a moment the sun streams across her face in the doorway. "Come," he urges again, taking her hand. He is unsettled by the powder revealed by the harsh light on her cheeks.

Of course she is quite beautiful—this he expected. More beautiful really than as a girl. But she'd never worn makeup in those days. And he remembers—has always remembered this, whatever else—the astonishing softness of her youth. Her throat and the skin stretching across her cheekbones. The softness above the knee and along her inner thigh. He winces at the memory and tries to shut his mind.

Two folding chairs are arranged expectantly by a window. He's raised the steel blinds and shoved the sash open. Perhaps a breeze will flutter through. All the years in this shop and this window may never have been open before. They sit, the two of them, and lean toward each other.

Gazing at her anxiously, shyly, he confesses. "I had lunch for you—but it's all gone. There's nothing." It's a lament as well as a confession.

She doesn't understand, not that it matters. "I wasn't expecting a meal." She waves the idea away as if it's nothing.

"There's this," he says, lifting the dripping bottle of wine out of the yellow tub and fumbling with the cork. Why hadn't he bought a simpler screw-top?

At least while he's occupied he doesn't have to look directly at her again, this woman. It's Dami and isn't. She's cut her hair short, almost mannish, but with such style there's nothing mannish about it. It's lustrous and dark, with no hint of henna anymore and no grey—he wonders if she colors.

As a college student she'd always belonged to a different world—to a country and culture beyond easy reach. But at this moment he feels it so much more intensely. She's a professional woman from New York. Far, far more distant than the Calcutta of old. So self-assured—just the gesture with her fingers to dismiss his mention of food, as if it were nothing, as if he were merely an old man she'd once been fond of. Not until this instant has he felt old and he resents it.

She studies him without letting on, but she can hardly disguise her dismay. Tyler has let himself go farther than she'd feared. He's pale and grayer, a bit shaggier too, than a man his age ought to be. There's a frailty. Perhaps it's the living alone all this time since his wife died.

It makes her feel younger than she has any right. She doesn't quite shiver. In her New York world this would never be allowed, what with personal trainers and stylists and even a cosmetic doctor as needed.

His letters have never betrayed any sign—they've remained forever full of life and his peculiar humor, his affectionate mocking of Mrs. Pidgeon's fussings and of other neighbors in the village. She loves his letters. And there has always been the never-aging parade of students wandering down from the college as if they are, always, the first bold explorers ever to discover his print shop.

When *she'd* been first.

Had there been others after her? Odd, but she's never considered the possibility. The jab of jealousy surprises then amuses her.

Her letters to him have left so much out, and not just the photos. She's considering it now as if she's never glimpsed this truth before. The exclusions haven't been deliberate. It's just that what she wants to share with him—what he's inspired her to share—has nothing to do with couture or furnishing townhouses or consulting on high-priced lobby art.

He's known about the two husbands of course. Indeed, their correspondence began just about the time Raji came into her life—he provided what seemed never-ending tales to pass on to Tyler. Raji, who helped placate her parents about her self-willed exile from Calcutta, at least until he and then she and then they came to terms with his being gay. (Which explained not so much his own regally good looks as his sense of fashion that may even have surpassed her own—though in his case it blossomed, as he did, into a prissiness that was entirely self-oriented.)

And David. A sweet man. She'd liked him so very much and never really loved him enough.

As if goaded invisibly by such failures, she glances over to the shop's entrance.

One cool morning late in the spring, her graduation looming ever closer, she lay quietly in the faint pre-dawn light. And the truth suddenly revealed itself. How crazily slow she'd been to realize. No, to really grasp it. That there could be only one ending. In a very few weeks she'd truly be leaving her college and this village and him. And in that same flash of insight she also understood that he must have accepted this from the very start.

Somehow Tyler's foresight made him all the more to blame. But it also made her flight from him possible. If he hadn't believed all along that she could have no other choice, if any naïve hope had flickered in his own eyes, how much more terrible it would have been when the time came.

Rising quietly in the dim light, she sneaked out of the dorm, not wanting to wake anyone. She half-trotted down the hill on a gravel path and stopped for coffee and a warm roll at the bakery. She lingered, sipping, on a narrow lane.

At last he strode up a side path from the direction of his cottage. Where of course she'd never been invited. Though she'd studied it a dozen times from a safe distance. Not that Tyler ever knew.

Yes, she did think of him as an older man. But not old. Strong and wise in his way, wise in his hands, but needing her too, her love and her health and her not needing him for anything but himself.

She waited in the shadows, beyond his attention, until he unbolted the shop door, just, and then flung herself at him from behind, shoved him across the threshold, squeezed into nearly the same space and same breath. With her elbow she pushed the door shut behind them. No lights, no sounds.

"Hey," he cried softly in alarm. "What's going on?"

For the space of one more breath she stared up and then fiercely slammed into him again. Confused, he was trying to make sense of what she was up to even as she began pushing herself into him, as if this were already the last time ever.

The flash of recall is so vivid it's on her tongue all these years later, the taste of gravel and dirt and the wet grass of dawn as she hurried down the hill. The confusion on his dear face—oh, the deep ache that look once ignited, coursing through her limbs. And a joy too, and an anguish that made her writhe, all woven together, twisting through her, so she was already laughing with a kind of hysteria as she buried her face into his clean work shirt and smelled the scent of him, a laughter of anguish and joy.

Distracted by the memory's swoop and gazing across the shop to that very door, she brings a hand to her mouth, partly in astonishment, partly to disguise her smile. Returning to the scene has collapsed all time and sense and distance into a single instant. Something of the same anguished laughter swells in her throat once more. She's laughing. Could that have been him? Could that have been *her*?

Puzzled, Tyler is staring at her, and she shakes her head, trying to reassure him. It's the laughter that throws him, but can he see her tears glisten as well?

Because the laughter is all she can offer, a kind of hilarity and dismay at the nothing she's feeling. For years and years she's stayed away, at least in part out of fear at rekindling what had wounded her. But it turns out there's no dangerous spark or smoldering coal banked deep within her. The old love has survived only as memory, a ghost of itself, insubstantial.

Yet she finally admits to herself the counter truth—that she's dreaded this other possibility just as keenly. That instead of prodding embers of an old passion, she might discover, has discovered, only cold ash. Where does that leave her?

As the spasm passes, she draws a deep breath, shakes her head again in apology without explanation, and sips at the cold wine.

If the ache she once felt for him has indeed abandoned her forever, and so be it, she is gladdened to realize how much more deeply she knows and loves this man, old or not old. Aren't they equals beyond age? Age couldn't matter less.

He is a different man entirely as it happens. The soul who has written decades of letters to her, intimate of her own soul.

Why is she laughing at me? *How* can she laugh at me? he wonders.

He doesn't think he can ask this outright, and she seems content not to explain.

He is shabby, this he knows. And there's the smear of vomit or some such, she wouldn't know what, on his sleeve. He hasn't been to New York since before she even knew him. His print shop is merely a dusty relic in the middle of nowhere.

He hates his own thin skin—he knows he is unreasonable. But can't she realize how to her, to her alone in this world, he feels bare and vulnerable? How can she laugh at him? Of all people?

He's thirsty. But the whiskey is still sluicing acid through his gut. He doesn't dare touch the wine.

You are a stupid old man, he thinks.

Of course, she deserves the benefit of the doubt—don't they know each other better than all the world?—and the Dami he knows would never be smug and superior. Not to him.

But she's sitting with that amused smile on her face, looking so smug and superior.

Why is she silent? Not saying a word. Seeming so content.

It's torture for him, the silence. Though he has always thought of himself as a creature of silence. Still she says nothing.

"How long can you stay?" he manages at last, attempting to be gracious.

"Oh," she says with a gay little pout, "only a few minutes more, I'm afraid."

He's glad.

She seems to sense his discomfort. "I'm so happy just to sit here with you for these few minutes, Tyler," she says. "I didn't travel all this way to exchange more *words*. Just to see you again and this shop. We have the rest of our lives for words."

Suddenly he doubts this, fears it's not true. Of all his worries, it never occurred to him that her return might endanger even that.

"Yes," he says, and reaches across the narrow gap between them to pat her lovely arm.

Naming the Stones

A sudden upthrust in his gorge caught him by surprise—a heave of embarrassed laughter—as he stared at the body lying propped in an open casket. Peter Cohen considered the impossible fact before him and another hiccup swelled out of his belly. He muffled it, strangled it back best he could. But this wasn't funny—it struck him as funny, as dizzying—but not funny. The wrong old man lay there indifferent to him. Bald skull covered with a white yarmulke; nose a bony thrust at the heavens even as gravity drew slack jowls earthward; body bundled in an orthodox shroud (would his father have howled or been smugly pleased at Peter's decision on that detail, an impromptu made while selecting the coffin itself?) and impossibly small. No—this wasn't him. There'd been some error, some grotesque mis-shuffle.

Stein the funeral director had discreetly disappeared beyond a heavy curtain, leaving Peter to identify his father—the law required it for bodies arriving from out of state. According to plans choreographed a decade before, the old man had been flown in overnight from Florida—last flight landing ahead of the worst blizzard in fifteen years. Peter himself had arrived out of LaGuardia only an hour earlier.

Already shaking his head *no*, he took a quick step toward the curtain in pursuit of Stein. Peter's mouth twisted in apologetic grimace as if it were up to him to break the news and comfort the professional comforter. Maybe, it struck him, maybe the whole story had been fouled from the start—from the moment the phone startled him awake in Manhattan's pre-dawn twilight. He halted, took a breath, forced himself to edge closer. He peered at the dead man's features and, relieved, was able to shake his head once more. Nothing familiar here, nothing he could attach a name or emotion to.

Surer, calmer, only faintly amused now, he leaned forward to study the stranger. And just below the yarmulke spied a long pale scar circling the scalp. From the ancient day when his father had returned from his hospital not, for once, as surgeon triumphant but as shadow of himself, as convalescent, this welt had been a tell-tale shade of plum, fading over the years but never disappearing entirely. Now it stood out dead white, nearly invisible but still, once noticed, a tell sure as any tattoo. Yet the body remained a stranger: his angry, canny father was long gone.

"Yeah," he said after a few minutes to Stein in the foyer. "That's him."

Three days later, days distended by the blizzard, a caravan of two cars inched and skidded through half-plowed streets, high banks of snow trenching above them on both sides. From the cemetery gates a single lane forged on. It had been miraculously cleared, as if the grave diggers themselves were horrified by the delay beyond all tradition—one day, two days, three—forced by forty-six inches of blowing snow.

Beneath a shaggy white crown the granite slab read, simply, *Cohen*. Peter assumed the grandparents he'd never known slept around its base. Perhaps other members of the family lay hidden here as well, their headstones, flat against the earth, invisible under the snow. He stomped his feet guiltily. A mound of warm brown dirt steamed next to a fresh grave. The naked pit steamed obscenely too.

A fierce gust of wind snatched away the hired rabbi's brief murmurs above the pine casket and threatened to dislodge his black fur hat. Rabbi Hirsch's eyes were streaming in the cold as he clutched at the hat and signaled to Stein's men. Smoothly, silently, a mechanical winch lowered the casket into its grave. Peter stepped forward brusquely and grasped a shovel. The rasp of gravel and dirt shimmied in his hands. He heaved the load towards the pit and was grateful that no sound survived the fall. He passed the shovel to his sister Martha as a trickle of melting snow slid down his ankle.

Ten weeks later the mid-day glare offended him as a cab headed once more toward the cemetery. Flat, harsh even for early spring, the sunlight articulated grass and asphalt with a nakedness that swept nausea along with it. Stray bits paper scudded along in the March wind. Peter might have been a sick child once more, confined to the back seat of his father's car on some long journey, cigarette smoke bluing the universe beyond. Instead, he leaned against the taxi's window and stared at the crop of stones sweeping over a rolling hill as his driver turned in toward the cemetery's administration building.

"As I explained on the phone—and there was no need to make this extra trip, no need at all—we simply cannot add your father's name, Cobb, to the family stone. The Board's policy as well as custom are quite clear, I'm afraid. Of course for his own headstone—for that there's no problem." Rabbi Hirsch, it turned out, was also the part-time administrator of the cemetery. Yet he'd agreed only reluctantly to this new appointment with Peter Cohen. He was younger than Peter remembered and than he sounded on the phone. Facing his visitor across a battered steel desk, the rabbi had a porous black beard and fierce, unexpectedly pale blue eyes. The fur hat of winter he'd abandoned for a small kipa pinned to his hair.

"Last time—the weather, the rush and confusion—the whole thing felt—unfinished. So I needed to come back anyway," Peter said. "To get my bearings." He paused for a moment and tried to meet the gaze of this smug man without losing his temper, without—and he hadn't anticipated this even as a possibility—bursting into tears.

The rabbi only nodded.

"And this *policy* of yours—maybe it's time for the Board to reconsider. Aren't there more and more families in positions like this, with name changing and all?"

Hirsch didn't answer directly. Instead he tapped a manila folder delicately with his fingertips. "You must explain this to me," he said. "I'm afraid I don't understand." He smiled, confidential and slightly mocking, and leaned forward across the desk, hands spread before him. "You are Cohen, yes? Your father's name was Cobb. But your grandfather was Cohen as well, like you. No, I confess, this we don't see so often. The point, Mr. Cohen, is that your father changed his name according to secular regulations, not within the traditions of our community. The family stone represents the family, not an individual. You must see we can't abandon that obligation."

A searing dislike—the first intense feeling Peter had experienced in some while—flared hot in his cheeks and brow. But before he could respond, and he did not feel like responding, justifying himself to this man, Rabbi Hirsch noticed something else in the file before him. His eyebrows shrugged high in still greater wonder.

"This here—*Peter*—is your father's given name. And you are Peter as well? I didn't notice this before. Middle name Hayden. Your's too, if I may guess? So let me see—your father changes his own name and then, when you are born, names you after himself. This is true, yes? Not very Jewish, such egotism. So you were Peter Cobb as well. And you have changed back again? Am I right? Good for you."

"My father did many things that weren't traditional. He had a funny sense of names, of naming." Peter's jaw was very tight. He wasn't used to apologizing for his father and the role didn't suit him.

"Funny. Yes." Hirsch leaned back in his chair and folded his hands across his belly as if he were a much older and portlier man.

*

The night was very late. Even Manhattan slept a restless slumber along this stretch of Madison Avenue, only an occasional cab slicing the wet pavement. The mansion, the jewel, lay dark about him once Peter stepped through the foyer and past a guard at the new security desk. He entered the first of the galleries, a rotunda of plaster and rose marble used as public sanctum by the robber baron who built it. Here he'd received various emissaries, functionaries, who-knew-what more common thieves to do his bidding. As Peter's eyes adjusted quickly to the gloom, for he was practiced at this, only the emergency exit signs provided a faint glow.

This wouldn't take long. It was a moment he'd anticipated, a revelation he'd kept to himself and for himself. In a hidden niche he located the soft green glow of switches and dimmers. He played them nimbly. Like water from a fountain, light gathered and rose, precise, glorious, unobtrusive.

From room to room of the renovated mansion he strode and soon the full spectacle was ablaze.

This was his doing. He was the architect chosen to design this critical aspect of the new gallery and, especially, to display the first of its exhibitions, a retrospective of abstract expressionists that even this indifferent town had breathlessly awaited. And he was the first to see, to really see. The paintings were fire and rage and black fury, blue despair; they exploded and whirled, coaxed to passion by light, his light, an art so perfect it drew no attention to itself but appeared both inevitable and unanswerable.

Pleased and oddly impatient, Peter stalked through the galleries as if searching for something that eluded him moment by moment. Tomorrow at the official opening his work would be acknowledged. But suddenly the thought annoyed him—he had no wish to draw attention to himself. To be named in that fashion struck him as false, as beside the point. The prospect was unpleasant.

As in a courtly ritual, a dance, he carefully retraced his steps through the manor, dimming the hidden sources, and retreated into the dark street.

Janey had been spending night and day in her office at Columbia, pressed with late-semester grading and shepherding one of her acolytes through a doctoral defense. Their two daughters were away, Samantha in college, Rachel at the boarding school she begged for. He missed the three of them with a dull ache and a reluctance to retreat alone to their empty apartment. And a second decision flared unexpectedly—out of nowhere. He stopped short on the pavement and turned his face to the cold flat sky, astonished with himself. For he was going south—this was his inspiration—to Fort Lauderdale, a city he loathed, to visit his father, a man he had also often loathed and who had summoned him.

"I'd like you to do me a favor," the old man said. He spoke as if he'd been mulling it for months, waiting for the right moment, as if preparing for the moment he'd be ready to confront Peter. He might have been grinning at his son, he might have been mocking him—it was hard to tell, what with his teeth soaking in the bathroom and his jowls slack.

Peter had arrived on the Galt Ocean Mile half an hour earlier without calling ahead. It had been five years since he'd seen his father, had spoken to him only as necessary every few months. Even now some trace of what he knew was an adolescent petulance kept him from providing fair warning. Yet his father seemed neither surprised nor put out to find him suitcase in hand at the door. "You'll have to sleep on the couch," was all he'd offered as greeting with a toss of his hand. "I'm not putting Miss Bratinski out of her room," referring to the registered nurse who now lived with him in place of two previous wives and who, Peter assumed, provided some of the same comforts if and when his father was up to it.

Miss Bratinski, however, was nowhere to be seen that afternoon—it was her shift at the local clinic. Old Peter Cobb hadn't actually paid her a salary for years, beyond the roof over her head and groceries for the two of them. When at last he was gone, then, then, she'd receive her reward, her due—this he'd hinted often. His son thought her a fool to believe it. What was left that hadn't gone to the wives? But Peter also suspected that Miss Bratinsky—Edna—was in fact no fool. She had her own reasons for remaining faithful.

"A favor." Young Peter Cobb blew on a spoon of the noodle soup his father had split between them. On the kitchen's small black-and-white, Lawrence Welk was pantomiming enthusiasm for the next act. This alone was full testimony to Peter of how far his wild wicked old father had fallen: *Lawrence Welk*—the kind of half-assimilated clown on whom he'd lavished savage contempt when Lawrence Welk still breathed.

"Yeah. A favor. When have I ever asked you anything?" The old man was querulous but trying to keep calm. His son noticed a tremor in his hand as he spooned soup towards his mouth.

"Okay—so ask."

But Old Peter pursed his lips, glanced slyly at his son, coy now and flirtatious. "You'll think I'm ridiculous. But it's not so much for a dying man to ask his son a favor."

"Since when did you decide you're dying?"

"Okay, okay. I'm just asking is all." He blew out a cheekful of air and gathered himself. "Okay, here it is. See, what I'd like is for you to change your name. That's all." Again he paused, as if surprised his son hadn't yet broken in. "And anyhow, not to something new, but something old. What I'm saying is maybe you could take your grandfather's name back."

"Uh-huh."

"I'm not kidding." Old Peter's fury leaped alive at his son's disbelief. He slapped a hand at the counter.

Peter couldn't quite mask a grin—a cruel grin, honed to wound. His father's bizarre request only bolstered his suspicion that the redemption of Lawrence Welk was symptom of some more profound derangement.

Yet a knot of sudden panic twisted deep in his own belly. The unexpected plea had shaken him, startling a buried reservoir of dread out of proportion to what was, after all, no more than a crazy whim. How could he take it seriously? Take his grandfather's name? No—casually snagging a new name, a new identity, a new wife, a new life had never seemed so simple to him. Peter Cobb, young Peter, had clung teeth clenched to his own life and wife and daughters. He wouldn't let them slip beyond reach the way his old man had.

*

Something wrong rustled through the house. Something restless. That's what Peter believed as a boy. At night, lying awake in his room, he heard its walls, its joints murmur with discontent. Sucking a finger, his sister Martha heard too, eyes wide but saying nothing. When the murmurs grew insistent, she'd slip up into Peter's bed and hold herself tight.

Problem was, no one could put a finger on the problem. His father had been short-tempered with the place since they first moved out here from the city. He'd tried to solve it, over and over again. The original farmhouse gradually swelled to something grander, with fluted columns across a verandah and a new wing of clapboard and fieldstone. But that worked no charm. The house remained restless.

Peter's mother watched all the while. The prospect of fleeing the city had never really enticed her, but she'd gone along with that, as she had her husband's other plans. "He won't be satisfied," she confided to Peter and Martha while assembling sandwiches. Step by step, she was working through the problem for the three of them. "You'll see. They wouldn't let him buy in Bloomfield, so he's trying to make this do. And it won't—it can't."

Rachel Cobb had begun picking at her hands. Behind a kitchen counter that made her seem very small, her gestures futile, she was spooning out mayonnaise while wearing white gloves to stop the picking, to stop the raw flesh from bleeding. Sometimes her gloves showed secret pink.

The twenty-five mile move from the heart of the city had seemed wrenchingly abrupt to the two kids. Yet Peter later realized his father had been making plans for months, fretting and plotting even as he lay between life and death in his own hospital. Meningitis, swooping out of nowhere, had gripped him by the throat, crept into his brain, nearly killed him. Another surgeon, friend and rival from the university, had worked the desperate magic of peeling back scalp and skull to relieve demonic pressures.

When after three months Peter Cobb returned to their apartment building at last, stumbling and abruptly aged, his wife Rachel darted from the driver's seat. She caught her husband, leaning up into him so that he wouldn't have to lean. He wouldn't acknowledge the fact. On the porch the children were watching and waiting, helpless and witness. One step, two step, up towards the foyer of the apartment building, and already he was clutching for breath. Old Peter clasped his wife's arm but wouldn't sit, wouldn't retreat, not until they'd accomplished the journey inside. His skull bristled as its hair grew back in grotesque patches. The long purple welt that circled his scalp terrified the children. His son hung back—and for this felt shame. But Indian Village Apartments was suddenly no longer home—when, how did the boy realize?—and as his father's strength returned over the following weeks the great search for a new one was launched.

Almost as soon as the rambling house on the border between dairy farms and new suburbs was identified and purchased, its transformation commenced. As the work progressed, each stage of it, all was topsy-turvy, hope beyond hope. Wandering with Martha, Peter loved the startling discoveries of new light: green canvas awnings, peeled from the terrace early that first autumn, laid the fieldstone bare to a white assault that sharpened and flattened the world; new valances in the library purred a soft illumination from nowhere.

And when the labors were accomplished, each stage, a grand party was thrown to mark the occasion. Cadillacs and Lincolns spilled along the driveway. Some made the trek from downtown, some swung briefly across Long Lake Road from Bloomfield for evenings under Japanese paper lanterns on the terrace, with smoke and wine and great floods of food. Afterwards, always, within a few weeks the work began again. The house wouldn't be finished. Restless murmurs swelled once more, rustling along the walls late at night.

To pay, Peter Senior cadged work; he stood duty at the hospital morning and night. At home he grew more restless, worn.

"Dad," his son challenged him, twelve years old. "Why'd you buy this house if you hate it?"

Astonished, Peter Senior grinned, but the grin rang sour. "I don't hate it—I'm just not satisfied. Not yet."

The boy shook his head. "Why wouldn't they let us buy a house in Bloomfield?" he demanded.

"Hah!" his father laughed, but it wasn't a laugh, and he tossed a hand. "The pricks. The pricks. So you know about that, do you? They let me cut their wives and daughters. They let me save their fucking lives. But no way do they let a kike live across the street."

"How do they know?"

"How? They find a way of knowing—names only tell you so much." He placed his hand on Peter's head for a moment. His eyes glinted with a sharp brilliance as if he'd been waiting for this, as if he were seeing his boy for the first time in a long time.

And for a little while after this conversation, perhaps it was weeks, perhaps a few months, father and son seemed to lean toward each other. On two separate Sundays they cycled together far out beyond the last fringe of developments and through the endless alfalfa fields, leaving Martha and Mother behind. And they talked. How they talked. Of baseball and love, of the old Tiger ball clubs and of girls at school. Young Peter's heart nearly burst with pride that his old man could keep up, could even press him hard, side by side, holding the fine cadence of the long flat straights.

For his part, Peter's father seemed released from—from what? Some private pain or reserve or restlessness. The boy sensed but never knew for sure. He was content to bask in his father's eagerness to share his thoughts, to try them out on his son. Naturally, inevitably it seemed, they came to talk of God, and Peter Senior confided in the boy that recently a friend had coaxed him into visiting an evangelical church. He cast it as a lark, a kind of anthropological expedition to a strange world—fascinating in its way, so different, such an experience, so foreign. He laughed until the tears came.

About this time work ceased on the house as well, never to begin again. Young Peter believed the restlessness had fled for good. At night no murmurs hummed in the walls.

And so he felt doubly betrayed when it was his father who fled into the night with the wife of an anesthetist. Of course, her church cast her out for such brazen adultery, but together they joined another and were married, once Peter Senior converted.

*

"Plenty of good it did you, changing in the first place," Peter said to his father.

The old man glanced up. He was mashing shrimp between his jaws. It was hard without teeth and he was being stubborn about the teeth, as if deliberately to embarrass the son who was standing them dinner on the seafront. "How the fuck do you know why I did it in the first place," he demanded with a soft belch, not at all surprised that the subject had returned but betraying no satisfaction either.

"You must've told me. Or Mom did. One of those family legends. Anyhow, seems like I've always known. Back when you were getting started—early forties, right?—how else could you avoid your medical practice being limited to the tribe?" Pleased with himself, Peter gazed at his father. His ancient dress shirt had yellowed and frayed at the collar. Only a dirty grey wisp of hair remained of what had been a pale fire red that Martha alone inherited. The doctor's nose was more beaked yet also somehow weaker than in the old days. He'd always been able to pass. Not so his son: darker, slender, he was his mother's heir in that regard.

"Once you were *Cobb* you could all play make-believe," Peter went on. "Cobb opened doors that Cohen slammed shut. Even if they knew and you knew. Not that twenty years later they'd let you buy property in Bloomfield."

"Fuck 'em for that," cawed Old Peter, furious and delighted with the memory. Other diners, mostly elderly too at this early hour, glared from nearby tables. "I'll bet Bloomfield's crawling with kikes now. Plenty of schvartze even? Am I right?" He wagged his head and shoved another shrimp between his gums.

Miss Bratinski pushed her nurse's smile against a napkin. She placed a hand on his arm. "*Dr. Cobb*—be good now."

His son's jaw was tight. He sliced a shrimp in two. Sipped his wine. "Haven't been there. Not since Mom moved away. No reason to go."

"That's not *why* anyway," Old Peter was saying, wagging his fork. "Good as I was, I could've built any practice I wanted. Hell, and I did. When you're rich you want the best—they were begging for me to cut them. So that was never *why*."

"So, then?"

"My brother, too, don't forget. Your Uncle Harry. Got him to do it too. Blackmailed him, since I was the one paying his way through school. Got him away from the old man's *shul*. Made him a doctor instead, a dentist anyway. My sister Gert didn't matter. She'd be getting married, so the name would disappear on its own. And Gert always sided with me."

"Sided with you?"

"Against *him*, the old bastard. Against *him*." Peter Senior banged his fork down hard and glared at his son. And then as suddenly as it had flared his rage blew clear like a puff of smoke from one of the Benson-and-Hedges he still sucked to a nub. The old man's face relaxed, its muscles slackening into a beatific grin, as if he'd only just discovered that he'd left something far behind and was amused.

"I wanted to hurt him and what better way? Steal his name, see—rob him of the future. Well, that's what I wanted, wanted him to know how I felt robbed too. Him content all those years working tool-and-dye. Keeping us poor, keeping my mother poor." His eyes grew teary and his son feared the old man would embarrass them anew by weeping at the table. "Christ, she was a saint. If she had an egg, a single egg, she'd hide it away for me so I'd be strong to study." He belched deeply and considered.

"Tool-and-dye. That was your grandfather. He made lousy money even at that because he wanted to spend all his time in *minion*, praying and being holy, being such a damn good Jew. But I remember"—and again his eyes lit up as this ragged archeology unearthed his own youth—"you know, he loved the work too: that he earned his keep. He'd march in our front door, caked with dirt and grease up his elbows and under his nails, proud and grinning and pious, like he'd just slain Goliath himself. My mother kept a bowl and towel by the door and hot water on the stove, ready to pour when she heard him. Washing his hands—it had to be done just so. Plenty of lather and drama and prayer, and hell to pay if one fucking step landed wrong. Sometimes—years and years later—I'd be scrubbing for surgery and the memory of that sight would rise up in front of me. Him, the self-satisfaction on his face as he dug the grease out from his nails—and I'd *laugh*."

The old man was glaring again, jabbing his fork in the air once more. "You pretty much hated me all these years since I walked out on your mother—didn't you, you little fuck? But how about this: you ever care how I never did what *he* did?

Swore it the day you were born and never laid a hand on you, on any of you. Did I? You ever know that about my so holy old man—your grandfather—with all you think you know?

"It was so I'd study Talmud, be his great scholar. Yeah, he'd take his belt to me. Not because I couldn't or didn't—but because I could, I did! It drove him crazy, the gift came so easy to me. A little game was all it was—and his rabbis were *hot* for me. And he knew I was mocking them, that I didn't care. The better I did and the more the rabbis loved me and the more I mocked and let him know—he'd whip me with that belt. And I'd let him, even when I was as big and bigger than him. I'd let him and I'd jeer him.

"And when I threw it up and went off to Ann Arbor—me fifteen years old and the university opens its arms—I could change my name. Fuck *him*. Hah! That, that was delicious!" He was wheezing now, mouth hanging open, scraps of shrimp still visible. Disgusted, his son was afraid the old man might choke on the mess. Edna Bratinski sat patting his hand.

Peter was battling an anger that surged up and threatened to sweep him away in its dangerous undertow. "So now you decide maybe I should change mine too. Just like that. Just on your whim. Jesus, Pop—I'm *Cobb* for better or worse. You can't erase my life, everything I've created for myself, just to make up for your own mistake."

"Mistake?" The old man's eyes flared. "Who ever said mistake? I'd do it again a thousand times."

"Then what's this all about?" Peter demanded. "Why now—why out of the blue? Something happened I should know about?"

The old man shook his head and seemed to retreat, lips pressed thin, protecting himself.

Peter shrugged without shrugging. "Why not change it back yourself?" he said. "Who'll that hurt? No one any more."

"Exactly. That's it exactly." Old Peter stared directly at his son, fiery and sly once more. "What I do is irrelevant. There's no undoing that matters. But why not you? As a favor?"

"Hell of a favor." He set his jaw. "Look, I'm sorry—but this is nuts. Why are you asking me this?"

"I should explain myself to *you*? It's enough that I'm asking. What, you're going to show how tough you are and defy me like I defied my father? And you're making what point?"

Early next morning, a Sunday, Peter sat drinking instant coffee. Neither his father nor Miss Bratinsky had yet emerged, and he'd pointed his chair carefully towards the broad sweep of the ocean so he wouldn't notice whether they came from two bedrooms or one. He'd long ago accepted his own squeamishness on that count.

The night had been long. Despite the wine with dinner and a couple of late whiskeys, sleep had come reluctantly. Instead, the alcohol sent him rolling, awake, alert, miserable.

He had no clue what his father was after. Did he intend now to disown his son as he had his father? Did he yearn to be sole and self-created and defiant? Was the point to cut himself off from all ties? Or was he seeking to mend a tear in some delicate fabric? Now that his own father was long dead did he mean to extend the trajectory of the family name across the very chasm he'd opened?

Peter's resentment had bled away into the darkness, and these questions filled him with dread and sadness and a yearning to reach towards his father as he hadn't done since those long bike rides thirty years before.

But what unnerved him still more was that he hadn't been able to dismiss the old man's bizarre notion. It niggled in his ear; it set his heart pounding; it formed a grit between his grinding teeth. Peter Cobb he'd been for forty-three years (Jr. abandoned at college), but the sound of it—*Cobb*—the sheath of it, had never felt right. *Cobb* reminded him of maple and birch and willow trees struggling in Michigan's sandy soil, shallow rooted all and fragile, easily toppled. Much of the night, except for three or four hours before a harsh dawn woke him, sun blistering an oily light off the surface of the ocean, he'd been repeating the other name, *Peter Cohen*—his father's name but not his father's name. He'd chanted it a whisper, he'd rolled it on his tongue.

"I've got a flight home this afternoon."

Late in the morning Peter Senior had finally emerged to make toast and weak coffee for himself. He kept his back to his son and seemed not even to hear the announcement. Edna Bratinsky had already hurried away for her shift at the clinic with a hug and quick kiss for their visitor.

"Can't stand the couch, huh? Well, I'm not surprised," said the old man at last, still not turning.

*

"Why should I like the idea? It makes no more sense for you than it did for me when we married—less—and remember, I refused." Janey scowled, bristling at the notion.

Peter shrugged.

"Not that it makes any difference to me," she said, playfully swinging a plastic sack of bagels against his arm as they strolled along Riverside Drive. Both were wearing light jackets in honor of this rare day: a gift of mild December weather—nearly fifty degrees—a chance to steal a few hours back from the long winter still ahead.

"What a fool I'd feel now if I'd taken yours twenty years ago, Peter. And what about the girls? Have you thought about them yet—or told them what you're considering? You can't really expect they'll go along with this, this—" She sighed and turned to him on the brink of a corner.

"Maybe I should have insisted they take my name too. But I was so happy and *sweet* after they were born," she flashed him a naughty smile, dark eyes alight, her narrow face pink with cold, mild or no mild. "They were my gift to you. But how can they possibly choose *Cohen* now, for heavensake? They've never even met their grandfather. And for that matter, it isn't his name anymore either. It'll be bad enough if the retro fashion lasts long enough for them to take their husbands'. And probably just to spite me."

"I don't think we're in imminent danger on that," laughed Peter. He wanted to defuse this struggle with Janey. This wasn't a battle between them. Or shouldn't have been. And he'd never any notion that Samantha and Rachel would follow his lead. The battle was with his father alone, unspoken now and on terrain he didn't know. He sensed the sly old man a step ahead of him, circling, setting his snares.

He'd been back from Florida nearly a week. Yet the seed sown there had already struck deep root. Even as he was gathering up the reins of three lighting projects in various stages of disarray, not to mention fielding phone calls and interviews and fresh solicitations only briefly balked when he failed to show for the gallery opening, the favor his father was begging—more nearly demanding—nagged him morning to night. And he wasn't even sure why.

He hardly yearned for some sublime reconciliation with the old man. No, he felt more like wrestling him to the ground, pinning him hard to the dust once and for all. The image of that—preposterous, preposterous—left him grinning. His father would be spitting up at his son like some barely restrained cobra (where would he stash his false teeth while they grappled?), some old-man-of-the-sea startled and writhing, grasped and never quite vanquished.

By the time they'd reached the front step of their apartment building, Janey tossing him the bagels and leaning forward for a quick kiss before flagging a cab for the run up to Columbia, Peter Cobb had decided that he would be no longer. He waved her off, shrugged, smiled at Mario the doorman.

*

The labyrinth had twisted and turned Peter Cohen, spun him and confused him, stumped him thoroughly. It wasn't that he couldn't find his way out of the cemetery—that was the easy alternative. He could see the cab waiting across by the administration building. But he'd lost all bearings he'd taken from the map on Rabbi Hirsch's wall for the internal lay-out of the grounds. And what memories he possessed from ten weeks earlier—of drifting snow and blankness—did him precious little good. Wandering along the lanes and alleys of the graveyard, he was disoriented and unwilling to retreat to the rabbi's office for help. He was also fighting the urge simply to give up the search, bushwhack toward the cab, and flee to Martha's house in Royal Oak.

There were plenty of Cohens, of course, of Kahns, of Kuhns, theme-and-variations sprinkled among the Levis and Roths and Rosenbergs. He'd hoped to recognize the family stone or its orientation to the road. Nothing seemed familiar. On he soldiered, hands in his pockets, wrestling his own impatience and a gnawing frustration that had swooped out of nowhere. He did not want to be here, didn't feel he belonged, name or no name. There'd be no place for him in this family grove anyway—he and Janey had already made provision for cremation, for wine and good cheer among friends, for seemly scattering later on. His shoes kicked at the gravel. Angry, he sent a small stone skittering along the path.

Angry, he stumbled on the plot. It was the unmarked grave that tipped him off. At a glance he saw that its sod had been carefully knit back in place, but the early spring hadn't yet healed the scars. It was also too early, of course, for a headstone to identify the Peter Cobb who lay there. According to the prescribed rhythms of tradition, that marker would only appear next year when he returned for its unveiling, perhaps bringing the girls along too. And so he recognized the spot and only then glanced for confirmation to the central stone, *Cohen*.

*

"We're losing him," Miss Bratinski had moaned into the phone, trying to sound calm and professional but undone by her own grief. It wasn't six a.m. yet and he wasn't awake and then he was sharply, nakedly awake, up on an elbow in the gray light.

"Is he gone?" he asked.

"We're losing him, I'm losing him," she said again.

"Damn it," he whispered. "Damn it."

"What?" she wept, unable to make him out. "Don't you worry, Peter. All the plans are made. You just get yourself on a flight home."

"Damn him," Peter murmured, though he'd already returned the phone to its hook. Janey was staring up at him, waiting, patient, the love of his life. How could he tell her that the old man had tricked him again? Had managed to win the final round, one quick fall, without his son suspecting it had even begun. Had slipped away free and clear without Peter ever finding a way to say he'd done him his favor.

North Star

The screen door slapped against the wall—it usually did slap—as Amy Frankel rushed into the cabin and grabbed at Miriam's ankle where she was lying, reading a glamour magazine on the upper bunk. Miriam couldn't remember afterward, a lifetime later, whether Amy had shouted anything, any explanation or summons. But it was enough that the skinny, dark girl from St. Louis, her best friend here for three years, should tug at her so urgently. Miriam slipped her butt off the mattress, stepped into her sneakers, and rushed after Amy into the early dusk.

Chief Caleb, the camp's owner and director, must have sent the girl to fetch her bunkmate. In the meantime he'd have lugged the awkward black-and-white television from its shelf in the mess hall and set it on one of the long trestle tables.

"I just got a phone call. You should probably see," the director murmured as she arrived panting. He stood behind her and placed his hand on Miriam's head.

She later recalled the open secret of Chief Caleb sneaking beers and watching TV after lights out. But in all the years they'd been coming to North Star, neither she nor Amy had ever before seen the tube actually flickering alive.

Puzzled, responding as if this were one of those innumerable *tests of character* Chief Caleb was always going on about, Miriam straddled a bench, the television humming slightly on the pine table. It reminded her of the big wooden box her father had left behind in their small den. But at first she had difficulty making out just what the gray smudges on the screen were supposed to be showing.

Creatures with heavy, whipping tales turned out not to be spewing the smoke and flame themselves—that was her initial impression—but were instead battling the fires surging from windows and doorways, engulfing blackened automobiles, gorging across heaps of scattered tires. Even as she watched, however, the great streams of water shooting from their trunks slacked and fell off, the engines to which they were tethered falling back too from thick and thicker smoke, heaves of flame. Dark figures wrestled with the hoses, then stumbled, ducked, fled.

Other shadows flickered along the rooftops or lay in the street, twisted into painful limpness.

"What?" she said, turning her head to Caleb Kaufmann.

He nodded. "This time it's your city," he said, nodding at the picture.

She would not see the moon landing for two more years. But she might have been watching a scene on the moon. So it felt. That first moment or two.

*

Camp North Star was located high in Wisconsin, not far from the border with Michigan's U. P. None of this had ever meant anything, in the topographical sense, to Miriam Peters. Only that each summer she'd travel all this way from the particular neighborhood in a city she otherwise hardly ever left.

First, there'd be a train carrying half a dozen of them to Chicago. In those days no one ever worried about sending these children off on their own, ever doubted that they'd find themselves gathering surely enough as planned in the great cavern of Union Station. They'd heave their duffels on the hard stone floor along with a hundred other kids drawn from across the Jewish Midwest.

Counselors sorted them according to the cabins they'd inhabit, cheered on by the director himself. Caleb Kaufmann's deeply creased face was a moccasin brown even in early summer, as if the leather had truly been tanned ages ago. The old man waded merrily through the crowd, greeting newcomers as well as the many veterans returned to his charge year after year. For identity sake, all wore dark green t-shirts with a white star on the chest, pre-ordered with other necessaries through Marshall Field.

Eventually, they'd board a smaller train to carry on north to Kenosha. Another transfer there, this time onto ancient yellow buses for a long plunge through Wisconsin wilderness, forests of maple and birch, trees with roots designed for the shallow, sandy soil. Pines too, and spruce, great stands of them.

This then was their summer world. A green immensity surrounding Camp North Star, its flag pole and mess hall crowning the hill, a rutted path winding among cabins and then tumbling sharply down to the lake.

*

After watching the oddly muffled scenes of rioting on the television (for half-an-hour? an hour?), Chief Caleb led Miriam across the dirt path to his office. Once he had long-distance on the line he passed the heavy black receiver to her. Another minute passed. Finally the operator returned, unable to make any connection. "I'm sorry," her flat voice reported, "the circuits are all busy."

They waited, staring at the phone as if it might ring of its own accord. Then dialed her mother again. This time only a recording responded: "We are sorry, all circuits are engaged."

"We'll try in the morning," said the old man, giving her a hug. Such things could be done in those days. She let him hug her, liked his smell of sweat and aftershave—familiar, reassuring—but her own arms fell limp and she was thinking about what she'd seen on the TV, trying to understand what it meant.

Only halfway back to the cabin in the dark did she realize that Amy was still at her side. She hadn't said anything, which surely wasn't like her. Miriam took her hand. There must have been enough of a moon above the black trees, because she could make out her face.

After she'd climbed up into her bunk a mosquito began whining and dipping about her ears. She pulled the coarse wool blanket over her head.

Her home was on fire. No—she didn't know that. The *city* was. That much she was sure.

Black people—from what she could make out in the dark nighttime pictures—were fighting cops, heaving bricks and bottles, burning tires in the street, even shooting down at them from windows and rooftops.

Though their backs were mostly to the TV cameras, the police looked angry behind their shields and sticks, they looked scared.

The cops were white. That occurred to her for the first time, though she'd always known it. All the cops milling on the sidewalks were white.

Black and white. Like the TV itself.

Did that mean it was the black neighborhoods burning?

What about the white blocks nearby?

Of course, even then she'd realized it wasn't a matter of black or white that simply. Six or ten blocks might be black. Or they'd be Polish or Italian or a half-block of Jews, or whole stretches just white white, like over in Dearborn. White trash, she'd heard that too about the ones downriver.

Was Jewish the same as white?

Her own experience with kids in school suggested otherwise. Jews hung out with Jews. Or by themselves with their books or violins. Some played baseball every day. Some played with slide rules. Unless from time to time a couple of Polish kids beat up a Jew just to make the point.

With black kids she had very little contact. Not in those days. They weren't in her school. Over by her father's shop, of course, there she'd see them regularly enough. Not that there was much to say. Their turf started three blocks south and west of her mother's house.

She could think the thought—the city was burning, people shooting at each other—and it made a kind of sense, but only the kind of sense last year's civics teacher, Mr. Gephardt, made when he was talking about Vietnam. Something real, okay, but far away. Not *entirely* real. Her city was on fire, but what about her home? What did it mean that she couldn't reach her mother? Where was her father?

Although already the middle of July, the early morning in northern Wisconsin was chilly enough for a sweatshirt, the dirt path cool and damp beneath her sandals as she trudged up toward the mess hall. The sun winked through green branches high above, the sky beyond a pale, pure blue.

I'm at camp, Miriam thought. This is Wisconsin. It is a cool morning, and I will have oatmeal and milk in a bowl with a little brown sugar and it will be just any morning.

"You scared?" Amy called softly, catching up with her, a little breathless. "I'd be."

Miriam looked at her friend and saw her braces and a small splotch of acne on her chin. She shook her head. Not *scared*—that wasn't the right word. It wasn't any single word, but *scared* might be part of it, only part. She shook her head again and then veered away from oatmeal and milk, heading toward the main office instead.

This time the phone rang on the other end. Her mother picked up—Miriam could tell just from the way she breathed before saying a word. And in that single instant her heart beat hard—it soared. She'd been right. It was just another morning. Last night had been a mistake, a dream, unreal.

"It's me," she said.

"Oh, Christ," her mother said. "*Jesus Christ*," she said breathily.

Her daughter figured she'd been weeping.

Then the second thought: no mistake after all. No dream. Just nightmare.

"Are you okay?" Miriam said. "Should I come home?— Can I?"

Dorothy Peters took a deep drag on a cigarette, not even pretending to mask it. "No, not yet. Not now. You're better off there."

Miriam knew she meant safer.

She didn't want to be reminded. She'd already been thinking about how she felt always on the outside looking in. Only this time it was from what seemed half a world away.

Plenty of kids didn't know how to watch. Or didn't want to see. But it's who she was—a kind of curse. That was her suspicion, how she'd always be, watching. She wanted to hug her mother, to bury her face in her father's shirt and smell his warmth. She wanted to be swept up, swept away.

"Where's my father?" She called him that just to slip the barb under her mother's skin. "Is he okay?"

"I don't know, damn it," she said. "How can I know if he doesn't call?" Dorothy Peters paused and took another angry drag.

"Knowing him, he's stayed over there to protect the store. He hasn't called and I can't get through."

For a moment neither of them spoke.

"Most everybody else around here took off right away, on Sunday," she went on. "They're all headed out. Can't blame them." Another pause. "Yeah, and where the hell would *I* go?" She muttered that thought, to herself more than her daughter. "There's been no electric since. Just be glad you're not smelling the smoke."

Miriam nodded, holding the phone to her ear, her jaw tight.

*

On an afternoon like any other a little more than three years earlier, when Miriam was nine years old and already home from school for the day, she spied her father through the front windows. He was parking in the street. She figured something was up—late afternoon was usually when the shop was busiest—and she hoped it meant a treat, a holiday for the two of them. Maybe he'd take her for a drive into the country. She ran and let him in before he could use the key.

Then she looked up into his face and knew that wasn't it.

As usual on a weekday, Eddie Peters was wearing one of the suits he'd inherited from his wife's father. Even though Dorothy had taken it in at the waist and dropped each pant leg two inches, the grey suit sagged and made Eddie seem older, almost someone other than himself. Though his daughter never heard him complain, the suits seemed to weigh on him.

He touched her cheek and moved past, heading into the back of the house.

"Daddy," she'd called.

Eddie Peters ran Rosen's Fine Furniture. He'd taken over when Ben Rosen, his father-in-law, first retired and then, nearly a year later, died. Eddie had already been helping out in the shop anyway, part-time, since before he and Dorothy even met. As far as Miriam ever knew he'd appeared in her grandfather's shop one day like a feather come to light, looking for a job. That's how it had been explained to her. A distillation out of the air itself.

So it seemed natural enough when the time came that Eddie should take over—though later, looking back, Miriam sensed that this development must have slipped up on him, a surprise and a burden he may not have wanted. The ownership papers, it would turn out, featured only Dorothy's name.

Eddie wasn't himself Jewish, but he kept the Rosen above the front door. People, especially the local blacks who were his main clients, they expected their shops to be run by a Jew. So that must have been okay with him, his daughter assumed much later as she was trying to figure it, him, out.

Or maybe it wasn't so okay.

It wasn't just that Ben Rosen had been a Jew. They'd known him thirty-five years and more, some of them. He was local. They didn't expect Rosen's to be open on a Saturday, but come Sunday after church you could always drift by, find your seat on one of the old couches up front, sip on an icy bottle of cola from the cooler.

In truth Rosen's did as brisk a slow business in pawn as swapping used tables or refurbished sofas. Zirconium rings and guitars and even ratty old hairpieces were the prime movers. They'd be laid out in glass cases or on bookshelves to one side of the shop. And if Joe Franklin was hard up for a five spot, Mr. Ben would slip it out of his own pocket so no one would see. If the Morrisseys wanted a bed—needed a bed, aside from what they could pay?—he'd find a way to help them out. Later they would pay if they could pay.

It drove his daughter crazy. And later if her Eddie tried to do the same thing or if he didn't do the same thing, either way it drove her crazy too.

It's not so easy taking over from a saint, even if you're wearing the same suit.

She trailed her father into the back of their house and saw that he'd already flipped open his ancient suitcase on the bed.

"Are we going somewhere?" she asked.

Her father looked up and saw her again. His eyes were red-rimmed raw. "Just me this time, babe. Your mom's throwing me out, isn't she?"

"What does that mean?"

She didn't ask *why*.

"Just what it means." He snapped the case.

Panic growing, she tugged at his shirtsleeve. She felt slow on the uptake, her limbs heavy, her grasp a step behind each step of the way. "When do I see you?"

She discovered just now that this was what she'd always been fearing when her parents quarreled, that he'd be the one to slip away entirely and leave her behind.

He shrugged and turned from her, almost fleeing.

The clenching somewhere deep in her chest tore a hole that never wholly healed.

Where had Dorothy been through all this? Perhaps she'd been right there, watching from the hall, but Miriam had no memory of her presence. The house was so small—she couldn't imagine how her mother could be so invisible. It seemed odd that she hadn't been hovering with acid comments as her husband and daughter walked their scene through.

Maybe they'd arranged it all beforehand, her parents?

But once the storm door clattered at his back they were both, mother and daughter, already in the kitchen. Miriam caught her mother sneaking a cigarette. Twisting her head, Dorothy blew angry smoke out the screen.

A white sleeveless blouse made her seem even taller and thinner than usual, her long throat graceful even as she dealt with the smoke and didn't look at her daughter. Her dark hair was pulled up in a tight bun with wisps flying loose. At nine Miriam already knew how she'd fail her mother. Her complexion was splotchy and half-a-shade paler, and her hair kinked in a way foreign to her mother's. She'd never look this beautiful. For years Dorothy would make a point of letting her daughter know she never *tried* to look beautiful.

"When do I see him?" she asked.

"You'll see him," her mother snapped. "You think this isn't hard on me too?"

*

What did she do during the days that week? Everything she was supposed to, she supposed. There would have been needlecrafts in the morning—stitching tiny beads onto moccasins and small leather pouches. Swimming and dinghy sailing in the afternoon.

Miriam faithfully did all that was required. Yet neither the beading nor the backstroke nor archery later in the day—she'd discovered early on a singular and natural talent for drawing the bow taut, arrow notched in the crook of her jaw, and then the swift release, a spasm of flight toward the center of a target forty and even fifty yards away—nothing truly distracted the worries that hovered about her, that harried her. It wasn't any particular notion or images from the television. Just this knot gathered behind the bone in the middle of her chest.

After dinner, while her friends headed off to watch a John Wayne western in the mess hall, she went directly to Chief Caleb's office. He'd ferried the television over here and set it up on his desk, facing out. He sat with her for a while before heading off to evening duties.

Amy may have been sitting there too.

What about the six or eight other boys and girls who'd traveled together on the Lakeshore Limited to Chicago? Would they not have been there? It may be they drifted in and out. Of course, many of them already lived in the suburbs—Huntington Woods, Grosse Point, Southfield, neighborhoods where Jews were allowed to buy—and that made all the difference.

She listened to the voices, the reporters, men on the street, police chiefs. President Johnson took his turn, something about committing troops. Or was that later? None of the chatter helped her make sense of the flickering pictures.

Twelfth Street and Clairmount. That's what the news people kept repeating. Half a mile tops from her mother's house. Only blocks from Rosen's Fine Furniture.

On the glowing screen: puddles and shiny slick, the great black gashes smeared across walls and gaping windows, trash scudding across sidewalks, cars burned out and bottomed out in the streets—all made for a different city altogether, one she'd never seen, one she didn't recognize.

From a safe distance the television cameras followed ragged fistfuls of looters seething into stores and back out again, sofa cushion on shoulder, washtub hugged like a great belly. Police clustered farther down the block, observers for the most part as well. Or maybe it wasn't the looters they were watching so raptly, since snipers were still in business, roaming along rooftops.

Occasionally a squad charged forward, clubbing anyone in its path.

None of these scenes conjured the city she knew. It all remained strange and alien and distant. Still, Miriam found herself leaning forward, peering hard—hoping for a glimpse of her father.

At last she settled back, struggling almost to breathe, eyes bleary and aching, aware again of her safe exile. The Wisconsin forest stretched about them for miles. For the first time in all these years she felt suffocated, out of place, as if the very dimensions of the camp itself were a childhood garment she'd outgrown.

Meanwhile, the television drama was playing out on the blurry screen. It was a kind of make believe. Yet the smoke was real—her mother testified to that. Miriam imagined it sweeping through the streets and suddenly the stink flared in her nose and mouth too, acrid and rank.

She wanted to flee home right now, retracing the long journey, bus to train to train, and search for Eddie Peters among the ruins of their city.

That night, after taps and lights out, after the other girls in her cabin were asleep and Cara, their counselor, snuck out to join her own friends smoking in the woods or skinny dipping off the docks, Amy climbed up at the end of the bunk and slipped between Miriam and the rough planks of the wall. Miriam turned on her side and put her arm around her friend, as if she were the one needing comfort.

*

Three years earlier Uncle Morty had suggested that Miriam be sent to camp. More important, he offered to pay. Even from far away as Sag Harbor, Long Island, Uncle Morty, her mother's mother's brother, perceived what neither of her warring parents could make out for themselves, that the nine-year-old girl needed to get away from all the unhappiness, if only for a few weeks.

Amy Frankel was assigned to the Chippewa cabin too, and within a few days they had found each other. Amy had neither braces on her teeth nor acne yet. She was small for her age and quiet, a bit nervous. She had a way of picking at her hands.

At home Miriam didn't allow herself the luxury of friends. Early on she'd decided she couldn't afford the distraction of welcoming other people into her life, not if she were going to keep the small constellation of her family from spinning out of control. In that she'd failed, of course, totally, and now here was Amy Frankel from St. Louis.

Amy listened as Miriam confessed her failure with Dorothy and Eddie. In those days divorce was still strange and rare. So to make the swap even Amy confessed too: how her own parents presented a perfect marriage to all the world. But her mother would start with white wine at lunch and never stop until she and the bottles were exhausted, sometimes before dinner, sometimes after. It was up to Amy and her brother to make sure something was ready to eat when her father arrived home. It had better be. Nothing fancy. TV dinners in aluminum trays would do. And then he'd set out in pursuit of his wife, Old Grand Dad a quicker solvent.

For Miriam this friendship was enough. They each returned home in August, and for more than two years they'd been exchanging letters, every week or so. Except, of course, for the eight weeks each summer they spent together in Wisconsin. Miriam never allowed herself to feel lonely at home anymore. To Amy she could tell as much as she needed to tell. Often, in truth, she wouldn't confess all her thoughts in the letter she was writing. It was enough knowing she could.

Sometime in this last year she'd found herself wondering just how real a person the Amy in her head might be, as opposed to the flesh-and-blood Amy Frankel in St. Louis. This she didn't dwell on. When I'm older, she told herself.

On Wednesday night she saw the first tank. It was lumbering along one of the avenues, soldiers jogging just behind for cover. What was strange was that, since she didn't really recognize the black-and-white and broken city anyway, it didn't seem so strange. Hadn't she been seeing plenty of pictures of war beamed from across the world most every night? Her parents each watched the TV news programs faithfully. Fire here, fire there. Tanks.

When she came much later to recount the story, first to friends in college and eventually on several and separate occasions to her own children, this was the image—the great grey tank—that she tried to get them to see. Potent, sufficient, it linked the disorienting moment of war abroad and riots at home. And it evoked, for herself as well as for the others, what seemed for many years the essence of the tale—how she'd been stranded in northern Wisconsin, watching the world change on television, this violent launch to the decades-long decay and abandonment of her city. She tended not to dwell on her parents in these recitals, except to admit that of course she worried, given the uncertainty. How could she not?

This may also have been the moment she first asked herself the why of the riots. What lay behind the explosion of such rage and violence. Yes, she'd already grasped the black and white of the situation. But witnessing the tank tracks rolling, grinding, sweeping over anything blocking or inhabiting the streets, the cannon swiveling from target to target, was when she first sensed a faint inkling of the *why*.

When her father walked out the door that day she feared she might never see him again. Wasn't that what his shrug meant? Her mother's angry, careless silence didn't make it any easier. Miriam had cried despite herself, tears leaking down her cheeks. She hated crying so her mother could see. She knew she was an ugly mess of snot and tears and tangled hair when she cried.

But then, the following Sunday, he arrived to claim her for the day.

For nearly a week she'd silently blamed her mother for chasing him out of her life. Only for Eddie to swing by the house on Sunday, his car washed and shining, almost as if nothing had happened, except everything.

For ten minutes Dorothy had been standing in the front room, well back from the window, snatching quick drags on a cigarette and waiting, it turned out, for him.

Miriam heard the knock and answered the door, no clue. She looked at him. She looked back at her mother. Then, closing the door behind her, she followed him down to the street.

Did he say anything?

She'd been tugged into this strange new dance by the two of them. Once again they'd arranged it all in advance. Not a word to her of course.

The Chevy, robins-egg blue, stood at the curb, listing slightly to the left the way it always did. She went around to open the passenger door. That's when she discovered Betty Armstrong sitting on the bench seat next to her father. Betty was the pretty black woman Miriam had known most all her life, bookkeeper at Rosen's Fine Furniture.

"Hey, Miriam," said Betty with a shy smile. "How you doing?"

"Oh," Miriam said, not meaning to be rude but thinking, thinking. Feeling foolish at her own ignorance. She opened the rear door instead and climbed onto the high seat by herself.

Mostly Sundays it would be from then on. Not that it ever came to feel natural. If she went to his tiny apartment up above the shop, Betty would be there too. So sweet—all the things her mother wasn't—calm and sweet. She might offer Miriam help with math. She taught her how to sew a straight seam, how to make her crusts flaky. Miriam had always liked Betty and now she hated liking Betty. It made her feel like she was in on her father's betrayal, not that she'd have used that word at nine years old.

They didn't go out for walks together, the three of them. Not ever. That occurred to her only later.

She'd bring a book with her, of course—there were always her books. She'd curl on the floor between the bed and the window and enter a world as separate in its way as Wisconsin.

Months and months later she also came to realize that somehow during the week, here and there along the way, Eddie and Dorothy had also been seeing each other. As if they couldn't help themselves. Neither ever confessed to her, though once she knew she could always tell. They would fight or not fight—she could sense that as well—but it had become their secret and they didn't have to tell her and they didn't tell her and that was awful.

Did Betty catch on too? Because a few months later still, maybe a year after Eddie moved out, she wasn't riding along in the Chevy anymore and her clothes had disappeared from the hangers in one corner of the apartment. Though if Miriam came by the shop downstairs on a Tuesday or Friday after school, Betty would still be tending the books at the broken table in back, just by the cola machine.

*

On a summer's day like any other, many years later and in the park of a different city altogether, Miriam was strolling on a path next to a small stream. She lived in an apartment not far from this spot. And as she did from time to time at a certain bend in the river, she slipped off her sandals and stepped into the water. The pebbles on its bed were slick and hard, and the stream was sluicing not-quite-cold water across the top of her feet. A moment or two passed before she caught the faint stink of a fish, and almost instantly spied it, a small one lying at the edge of the brook only a few feet away. She did not move. The sight was in no way troubling. But the smell had already rushed her away, swooping along into a sudden dizzying, disorienting memory.

It was Chief Caleb himself who'd come to fetch her on the Friday morning. She was standing at the edge of the lake—no, she was in the water, wet weeds were swooshing her toes. She smelled the distinct sweet rank of a freshwater lake and maybe a dead fish too.

This scene she hadn't recalled in all the years since, nor had it figured in any of her occasional recountings of the story. It was always the tank she'd remembered. Why was that?

Chief Caleb's jaw was scraped rough and red. She could see it now so clearly, almost feel the coarse stubble on his neck where the razor missed. A few wild tufts of grey hair escaped at the sides of his ball cap. The old man's eyes were rheumy, as if he'd been the one on vigil all night. She felt now a spasm, a pang for him—an ancient affection that breathed into her after so many years.

He was panting from the long chase.

"The phone again?" she said.

"Un-huh," he nodded, hands on his knees.

"Did you see him?" her mother demanded.

Miriam's thought in that instant was that something in her mother had finally cracked from the long strain. That she was seeing things. Or imagining that her Eddie had been spotted on the loose somewhere in Wisconsin. Suspicions of this sort became more common, and with greater cause, in the years ahead. For the moment, however, Miriam didn't know what to say.

"The television, damn it," Dorothy shouted when her daughter failed to grasp her meaning.

The set glowed slowly to life with a display of the weather forecast for northern Wisconsin. She clicked the knob to the right, finding only an episode of *As the World Turns*. But the third and final station from Kenosha was offering national coverage of the riots. She realized that most of the pictures were scenes she'd already studied over and over again the night before.

She settled onto a wooden chair. Her mother would be waiting for her to call back. Watching, she was safe and far away from all the destruction on the screen before her—and it was a kind of torture. She couldn't break away from the glowing grey tube, but it was hard and harder to breathe.

Standing in the small stream those many years later, she had no sense of how long it had been before, suddenly and at last, she spotted him. The camera hesitated on Eddie Peters only for a few seconds—her father just one of the interesting creatures offered by the networks as testimony and entertainment to the world.

In that instant she apparently absorbed this all:

Him leaning against the doorframe. The door itself gone, windows on either side shattered. The shop's interior gaped behind him, blackened and burned out.

Her grandfather's name absent above the entrance. How had that happened? she wondered. Had someone stripped the sign down in fury and resentment, or in a wild rush of joy and mayhem? Or had it simply dissolved in a wash of fire and smoke and water spray?

And then Eddie was gone once more as the cameras shifted to another garish scene and on to sports and local news.

After reporting to her mother that, yes, she too now had seen him, Miriam sat back on the hard chair and waited faithfully. Every little while she changed channels, hoping to catch him by surprise.

Another glimpse came at last—and she was the one startled by its abruptness. The scene was exactly the same, of course. But this time she noticed what was more important than all the rest. It was a weekday, a workday, and Eddie Peters had stripped out of Ben Rosen's old suit. He was leaning in the gaping doorway in dungarees and a shirt, sleeves rolled up. He wasn't smiling. But he looked lighter than air, as if the fire had charred him to a different state of being. The wind might take him in an instant.

"Please," she said, looking up at Caleb Kaufmann. "It's time for me to go home."

With that memory, clear and clean and stark, and no trace of what must have followed over the days and weeks to come, she stepped from the stream in the city park, sandals still in her hand, and wondered where on earth she was supposed to go all these years later.

The Excuse

Joshua she left on the narrow porch of the church and limped heavily down the nave, hunting me out. In her fist she was carrying a tight roll of dirty bills as if it were a lantern probing the darkness. A roughhewn cane in her other hand swung ahead at every second step. Since I'd just emerged from the confessional, she found me easily enough.

"We got to talk," said Madelyn. Her cane poked the air. "You want to go back in there?"

"Only if you've got something to confess," I said. I spread my eyes wide, all innocence, teasing her. This time she was on my own territory and I was delighted.

"Not a thing I ain't proud of—but what I got to say is private," she declared with an arch glance over her shoulder at two outraged Armenian women who'd just finished, one after the other, minutely confessing their weighty sins. Yes, and they certainly did stare back at her, this enormous black woman past sixty, money still clutched in her fist.

"You'd better come back into the vestry," I said, and marched Madelyn away.

She limped into my study on her cane, only to wheel round once we'd crossed the threshold. "You got to go to the police and get old Abramson out," she said impatiently, as if we'd already been through this a dozen times. She shoved the money against my chest, but I fell farther back. "They ain't no rabbi here no more," she insisted, "so you got to get him."

My surprise and good humor at Madelyn's visit had by this time disappeared like so much smoke. Wary, baffled, I needed a moment to grasp what she was on about. "What's your Mr. Abramson done?"

"He took a poke with a gun at one of our boys. Jamie's okay—just dumb. Only kid in the neighborhood dumb enough to get caught with candy bars up his coat by that old man. And then to start teasing and bragging about it and calling Abramson names. The boy ain't even scratched. But the police took Mr. Abramson downtown, maybe for his own good. Anyway, Mr. Priest, now you got to run on down and get him out."

I realized I'd been shaking my head and shaking my head, half in disbelief, half in protest. "You don't need me for that. I hardly know the man. Really, I'd be happy to—but I'm supposed to be hearing confessions all afternoon. Can't one of you take the bail down?"

"Can't, *Father*—he shot at one of our boys," Madelyn said, disgusted with such prevarication. "Now how would that look, us goin' down to rescue him? People talk enough as 'tis."

So what was I to do? Was I supposed to stand firm and refuse her? What kind of choice for a priest is that? Dutifully, Madelyn standing at my shoulder, I telephoned and spoke to a lieutenant at the precinct. Yes, they had Mr. Abramson—

Would I come pick him up? The lieutenant sounded only too glad to hear from me. He figured an eightysome-yearold man might not be entirely comfortable among their other guests.

Much as I hated driving, there was nothing to do but climb into the parish's brown boat of a Chrysler (eight months in this parish and I still hadn't mastered its column shift) and head towards the river.

My reluctance—not to mention surprise that Madelyn should make such a demand—stemmed, you see, from my single previous encounter with her Mr. Abramson. For it had hardly been a pleasant introduction, there in his grocery not three weeks earlier.

Our parish neighborhood—most of the city's older neighborhoods—are honeycombed with these markets. Like hermit crabs, many have adopted the shells of strategically placed old houses, their ground floors hollowed out and then crammed with hedgerows of cans and sacks and shelves. The big supermarket chains won't come into the area, you understand. No profits, they claim; too dangerous; shopping carts snatched all the time.

So groceries have become another bother for my parishioners, the ones who haven't yet moved out to the suburbs. Those who remain are still clustered together within a few blocks each way of St. Stephen's, in row houses where they've lived twenty, thirty years or more. Most of the men, at least those with seniority, have managed to hold onto jobs over at the Six Mile Ford plant. Their wives climb into cars and make suburban pilgrimages for groceries. But the Blacks who live on every side haven't been in this neighborhood so long, don't have the jobs or the cars. The corner markets are for them.

Just about the same time that I was assigned to St. Stephen's, the church youth group joined up with Focus Health, a community organization concerned about the poor nutrition of local babies. Our kids, all twelve of them, were to visit local markets and discover what sorts of formula and baby food were available and at what price, compared to the supermarkets out in the suburbs.

Six or eight of the kids at a time went scouring the neighborhood, checking off markets from a masterlist the Focus Health people had provided. Each Saturday morning they traveled out on foot; what trouble could there be? No trouble at all on the first two trips, aside from scowling men at the cash registers. Come the third Saturday, however, they were challenged by the manager at one grocery. Who you doing this for? he demanded. Father Libberdi, they chose to say. He's a prostitute, the manager said.

"He called you a prostitute," Michael Trgovic, the sixteen-year-old president of the youth group, reported to me later that morning in the vestry. The twelveyearold Geiger twins giggled. I sinned in thought.

Thereafter, on Saturday mornings for a month, I went traipsing along on their rounds. Full November, mind you—wind and sleet hurling in from the river. We'd arrive at a market and be allowed in without much fuss, everyone on good behavior, youth group and management, me huddling as inconspicuously as possible by the coal stove or kerosene heater, smiling. The boys up by the registers were white and cool and tough. The men in charge, the managers, weren't so young or cool. In fact, not a few of them were parishioners, ever so polite to me. (Come next morning I'd be distributing wine and wafers to their wives.)

It didn't take more than a couple of weeks for us to realize that mom and pop had precious little to do with these markets. Or that a fair bit of cash could be turned over, what with a captive clientele and no real competition. Different members of the same small pool of management would circle ahead of us, anticipating the bases we were to touch. It seemed they had one of those master lists too. Here and there the same middle-aged men would turn up, badly shaven, smelling of cologne, impatient and wary, but always polite. "How you doing, Father?" they'd ask.

But then one day, on a street even more narrow and tattered than most, its sidewalk broken and dog-fouled, we came upon Abramson's little market. This one wasn't on the corner but half-way up the block. Neither the tough white boys nor their pudgy Catholic managers were loitering about. It was clear at first glance that this shop had been here a long while—much longer than the others we'd visited. Its shelves, stained now and dusty, had been solidly fashioned long ago out of wood, metal, thick strips of linoleum—whatever had come to hand. I wouldn't care to guess how long some of the cans and jars had stood undisturbed on those shelves.

The stock wasn't all that different from what we'd seen in the other small markets, though across from the Gerbers and Similac that the youth group kids were cataloguing there perched a shelf of dusty memorial candles and a few dwindling jars of matzo balls and gefilte fish. Behind the cash register an old man, Mr. Abramson as it turned out, was teasing into one of the jars with his thumb and forefinger, popping ragged bits of gefilte fish into his mouth. He watched us all the while, his eyes redrimmed raw, his nose red too and cocked furiously in the air as he chewed.

It was me he was watching, though from the corner of his eye, darting it away when I glanced back at him. I'd guessed pretty quickly that the kids knew him. For the first time in all these weeks they were acting guilty rather than selfimportant as they tracked down the clipboard list, marking prices and supplies of baby formula. The Geiger twins stood at a metal rack of comic books, spinning it and studying Spiderman and ignoring the rest of us entirely. When the others had nearly finished, Abramson wiped his hands on a ratty towel and slipped out from behind the register.

"What're you doing?" he asked Michael, wedging in between us.

The boy froze, an awkward grin of nonchalance on his face. He looked young and naughty, caught elbowdeep in mischief.

"It's just a survey of baby supplies," I said to Abramson's back. From time to time on our other stops I'd begun to recite this same litany as a matter of form. The youth group was intent on community service, and the task was indeed worthwhile, and never before in that entire month had the words sounded so stiff, so absurd in my own ears.

Abramson paused one long moment to take it in. "I have been here a long time—I never do nothing to hurt babies," he said to Michael, puzzled and defensive. Then, angry at last, he straightened his back and turned towards me. The effort made him seem even older than I'd been guessing. His eyebrows were wild and furious. "What's wrong with my baby food? Is this what you really want?"

"*You, Priest.* What you want?" came a cry from the door. Pulling herself up the last step, a black woman appeared, her bright purple dress stretched taut beneath a little jacket that hung open despite the cold morning. She swung into the market on her bad hip and cane, an empty plastic shoppingbag brandished in her other hand as she headed towards me. Where Abramson had spoken only to the kids, she addressed only me. "You doin' business here?" she asked, suddenly purring sweet, still panting from her rush up the steps.

I glanced at Michael, Mary, and Loretta, the three oldest members of the youth group, who were sidling farther down the aisle. Michael and Mary looked glum. Loretta's blue eyes brimmed with tears.

"Baby food," said Abramson, suddenly innocent as all the world. But he smiled, and I caught something sly and happy in his eye.

"Baby food?" Madelyn snorted. "Don't he know the little girls here feed they brats from the teat or with sugar water? They ain't smart enough to know to use your baby food."

Now she wheeled on me. (I nearly ducked.) "And the boys who knocks up these little girls? They come right here three times last month. Got old Abramson to contribute to charity. Now you tell me, Priest—why don't they buy baby food with that money? Huh? *Baby food!*"

I wouldn't have blushed if the Geiger twins hadn't started giggling again.

"You Joshua," the woman yelled to the door. A man half her size, gnarled and dark as the tobacco twist he was stuffing quickly into his pocket, poked one foot in. "Spit that outer your mouth now—you got to give the priest and his children a ride home in this cold." Oh, she grinned, Joshua grinned, Abramson sagged, the twins giggled, my face was hot.

So Joshua wedged seven of us into his Oldsmobile for the eight block ride back to St. Stephen's. "She give it to you pretty good?" Joshua chuckled when we were safely away from the curb. "That's okay—my Madelyn does ev'ybody pretty good when she want to." A fresh chaw of tobacco swelled his cheek. He kept the window open far enough to spit.

Three weeks or so later, I returned the favor by dropping Madelyn on the corner of Abramson's market on my way downtown to fetch the old man out of jail. I tried to imagine him taking a shot at one of the neighborhood boys, and wondered how anyone could be so stupid. What kind of real trouble did he want?

Bail turned out to be a formality. They'd drop charges against Abramson in a day or two, the lieutenant explained while I waited for the paperwork to go through and for the prisoner to be released. The boy, Jamie, certainly wouldn't let himself be found, and no one else in the neighborhood was going to testify. The police had brought Abramson in only because he was still waving his pistol—registered and nearly obsolete—when they arrived at the market. They figured he needed a chance to calm down, while some of Jamie's friends could use the few hours without temptation for revenge or a little more play.

The lock on the steel door buzzed angrily and Abramson emerged with a stumble forward onto my arm. Quick as I could, I sat him down on a wooden bench. Other visitors milled through and around us, some sitting on benches while grabbing hold of their childrens' arms or collars. Others rocked on their feet or huddled on the floor. And from the walls as much as from these visitors came the dull stink of stale sweat and beer and urine. Abramson was trembling, drawn into himself yet clutching my sleeve with one hand, as unconscious of me as of a tree limb. His own arm felt brittle, lost in the folds of a frayed overcoat that had probably once fit him.

"I shot a boy," he murmured towards me. But I don't think he recognized Father Libberdi much beyond a vague notion that sometime or other I'd been in his market.

"He's okay," I said. "You missed."

"I shot one of those boys," he repeated, enough color to his voice this time that I realized the old man wasn't sorry so much as amazed, and not a little gleeful.

"You missed." I insisted on it.

But by slow degrees his face darkened as a new thought startled him. He seemed to withdraw farther into himself and the tattered coat. "An excuse," he murmured. "Oh, me—I am so stupid, I do not think." Pausing, he glanced sharply to one side and then the other, but not at me. I was still that tree limb, there only at the margin of his hand and his needs. His eyes were fever bright as he trembled.

"This is their excuse—they have waited for this. An excuse they always wait for. Then they come after us." He was panting. "Those boys, those boys. I let them take what they wantI must let them take what they want. But now they will come after us like they used to because I am such a fool."

Mr. Abramson was very far just then from Father Libberdi and the police station. Yet his fears and daydreams, his confusion of one menacing world with another, irritated me as if chafing a sore I hadn't known was there and couldn't quite locate. My collar felt hot and tight.

Suddenly he was staring at me angrily, demandingly. "So, I have shot one of their boys." Still a defiant glee; still more a fresh anger. Abramson trembled.

"But you *missed*. No one's coming after you," I whispered furiously. I was uneasy, eager to get us away. "Your friend Madelyn sent me with the bail—nothing's changed." I gripped his shoulder in return, shaking him ever so lightly to make him listen.

Again he glanced at me, but in that single moment his eyes had dulled, their luster gone. "Please," he said softly, "take me home. I am very tired."

When we drove up to the market, Madelyn's Joshua was sitting vigil on the front steps. "Bring him on up," he called. "I got to put the old gangster to bed."

Even though I nearly carried him up the stone steps, Abramson was puffing hard by the time we got him into the shop. He lifted a hand to halt the procession before climbing the narrow stairs in back to his bedroom. "Close that door—lock it tight," he murmured to Joshua, arm round his neck. "They have their excuse now."

*

The woman tapped with her cane on the open door of my study. "Let me guess—he's in trouble again," I said. I'd been standing by the desk about to button on my collar and head off on a round of hospital visits. But a dull, oppressive sense of repetition, a sudden image of Madelyn enlisting me time and again to the end of time as a nursemaid for her Mr. Abramson, made my hand fall wearily away. I dropped the collar on the table.

This was maybe ten days since I'd seen her last. She looked weary herself, older than I remembered, perhaps even a bit frail despite her considerable size. The creases in her dark face were cut dry and deep. Not to say she didn't look petulant too.

"No—he ain't in trouble. Not the same way at least," she said with a sigh. She shuffled forward to my favorite reading chair and, loosening her short jacket, settled down heavily into it, her feet out. I swept up my collar again and swung away from the bare expanse of thigh where the woman's dress had ridden up.

"It's his Sabbath tomorrow," she said. "And he wants to pray—say they comin' to get us and we got to be ready." With another sigh of exasperation she tugged the hem of her dress back down. "Lord knows he's right. Them boys gonna come back and keep comin' long as he keeps that shop open. I sure can't stop 'em on my own." She looked at me now as if somehow I were responsible for his stubbornness.

"You know, he don't need that shop no more. He's got money to get by, and him eightyfour years old already. Run from 'em once when he was a boy, he says, so he won't run this time. As if them boys care what he done before they own folks was born." Her voice slowly drifted away towards silence. Madelyn closed her eyes.

My part in the story, the heart of it, you see, lay in that moment, the old woman sprawled there in my study, nearly asleep, her feet splayed before her. For I realized then that the vague uneasiness I'd been feeling all along since her first visit was actually resentment. Resentment deep and heartfelt. I surely resented Madelyn's assumption that because my youth group and I had once transgressed by daring to question Abramson's supply of baby food, I had now to participate in her campaign for the health and safety of one old Jew.

Ah, but that's the easy side of it, such resentment is. All part of a priest's duty. Nothing more easily accepted and borne. This sudden crystallization of what had been a vague discontent into a declared foe made the issue all the more clear cut. That I'd do whatever Madelyn had come to ask was settled as automatically as I now picked up the collar from the desk once more and buttoned it on.

Yet, truth to tell, even as I was buttoning I realized that the teeth of the resentment dug a great deal deeper than that. Deeper than any immediate issue of Abramson's latest troubles or how glad I might be to help.

There aren't any other Jews for them to come after, there's only you, I'd wanted to shout at him in the police station as I shook him by the arm. *Your people left here long ago—there's only you. It's not because you're a Jew the boys come. Only because you're an old man with a little bit of money who's stayed past his time.*

Stubborn, sly, not entirely helpless, the old man might just as easily have clutched at my arm and whispered, *Priest, your people are leaving nowmost of them gone already-what can you do for those who stay? I chose to stay. So you? Your bishop or whatever sends you here. Did you choose to come—do you choose to stay?*

As it was, I'd only shaken Mr. Abramson gently and said nothing. He said he was tired and wanted to go home. And in my own study ten days later, with Madelyn silent before me, I realized how deeply I resented what the old man might have said.

"He got to have a *minyon* for his service," Madelyn said at last without stirring. "Ten men. Us gals don't count, naturally."

"He needs ten Jews," I said.

"So where you gonna find ten Jews around here? You gonna bus 'em all the way from Southfield like they was school kids? No suh, Mr. Priest. You and my others will do fine. If we gettin' ready for the end to come, you ten are good as any."

*

An hour before sundown that next day the sky darkened with clouds and a marrownumbing cold whipped off the river. Yet rather than wrestle with the ancient Chrysler again, I hiked the eight blocks to Abramson's corner market.

As I climbed the front steps, I spotted two of my parishioners among six or seven women, black and white, clustered around the front counter. Madelyn herself was just then carrying two pink dinner candles up the narrow flight of stairs in back, shielding them as best she could from the blast of wind I'd let in. (I decided to leave the pair of candles I'd smuggled out of the vestry in my coat pocket.)

"You come on up," she called back to me.

I hurried along behind her up the stairs and through a doorway. Waggling the candles dangerously in one hand, Madelyn wedged herself through the ten men or more who were already gathered in the small, stale room, and with her other hand set two small plates on a folding stand by the window. Dripping some wax onto the plates, she stuck the candles upright before hurrying out of the room.

Joshua was there, draped in a tattered prayer shawl, a small chaw of tobacco in his cheek. He glanced at me once and then away, an embarrassed grin on his face, refusing to meet my eyes.

Michael, from the youth group, stood off to one side and waved to me. He wore one of his father's caps—everyone had a hat—including his father, Joseph Trgovic, redfaced and heavy hammed, his baseball cap with a patch from a local brewery pushed back on his head. Trgovic saw me, pretended not to, stamped, shuffled as if cold, scowled, and screwed himself up all attention to Abramson.

The old man noticed none of this but inclined closer to the candles. He stood next to the window, bowed slightly as if the wind were pressing at him through the sooty glass. He was wearing the only other prayer shawl and a fedora that must once have been carefully brushed but was now a shiny greenish black. It rode on his ears. He was holding a ragged prayer book close to the candles and peering into the reflected light from the page.

The whole of the cold journey from the vestry I'd been swearing (mildly) into the teeth of the wind that this was going to be pleasant. Community spirit after all. Different people come together in a common effort, sharing an experience long to be recalled as special, meaningful.

All we shared, as it turned out, was an embarrassed awkwardness. We could only stand and watch as Abramson fumbled his way through the prayer book, flipping back and forth and mumbling stray snatches of Hebrew that none of us, not a one, recognized. For that matter, the prayers didn't seem all that familiar to him either. Some came easier than the rest—what he remembered from boyhood no doubt. Even so, Abramson seemed oblivious to the rest of us, unconcerned that we couldn't participate with him.

Why did he want us here? I wondered. Were Blacks, Poles, Italians all Jews so long as they helped look after him? Or didn't even that matter—were we here not to participate after all, but simply to bear witness as he readied himself for what might come?

The old man's skin was as nearly the color of parchment as the leaves he turned, his lips colorless and dry save for a single bubble of spit, his eyes loosely shuttered as a dreamer's. Still, he seemed to me to be wearing that sly, subtle smile that gave nothing away. The deep resentment that was directed not so much at him as at myself flared again. I wished the whole thing would end quickly so I could get away and breathe.

Suddenly, without any warning at all, Abramson caught himself up short and glanced about the crowded room with a puzzled frown, as if he'd forgotten something he couldn't go on without. He rested his book by the candles and hurried across the hall into his bedroom.

Joshua tugged out a rag and spat his tobacco into it. "Ain't nothing we can do long's he keeps the shop," he said as if we knew it already. "If they *do* come and get him, again and again, they ain't nothing we can do." He spat reflectively once more into the rag and tucked it back in his coat pocket.

So sharing something now after all—our helplessness to protect this stubborn old man—we waited silently in the dusk of the candles for him to return.

The moment dragged on. Someone coughed. I smiled at Michael. We were restless and the stirring made the room seem more crowded. At last Joshua slipped out and across the hall. Something about his haste had me darting after him, the others crowding behind me into the bedroom.

The first thing Joshua did was flip on a hanging bulb. There lay Abramson on a broken-backed couch across from the narrow cot, his head to one side, the fedora fallen awry on the floor. He was napping. In his hands he clutched a halfempty bottle of purple wine. He must have come to fetch it for a blessing and had sat on the couch—only for a moment of course (maybe he'd sipped the wine too)—but he'd dozed before remembering to rise again.

He was smiling now like a sleepy child, nothing sly to him, as Joseph Trgovic picked him up gently and eased him onto the bed. Abramson stirred a little. "My shoes," he said, draping his legs over the side for me to unknot the laces and pull the shoes off.

When I came downstairs the others were already passing a pint of whiskey. They were silent and serious about it, chagrined only when I appeared. One of the women tucked it hastily into her coat.

"I might try a taste of that," I said.

She brought it forth again hesitantly. Joseph Trgovic rooted up a plastic cup from behind the counter and handed it to Michael for me, as if being dainty might mitigate the deed. But I stuck the bottle to my mouth and swallowed once, twice, before the taste could stop me cold. It was corn whiskey and raw and I choked, my eyes tearing, and that seemed to make it better for the rest of them. Someone chuckled—probably Joshua again. I took another tentative sip and passed the whiskey on.

That smoothed over the rest of it, the drink did. Not that there was enough whiskey to make much difference, except to make the roots of my teeth ache. Yet, after all, we'd completed in a rough sort of way the ceremony for which Abramson had gone to fetch the wine.

PART TWO:

STEPS
THROUGH
SAND,
THROUGH
FIRE

Children of God

A soccer ball lies in a dusty patch of the maidan. Even with a fresh scuff on one side, the blue panels are bright and the white ones glisten in the rare, sweet dew of the morning. Sandip Kumar, trudging hand-in-hand with his younger sister on one side and his father on the other, stares angrily at the ball. With a quick tug he tries to escape. He wants to kick the ball so hard it will fly out of sight. He knows his family will never allow him to retrieve this ball, never pick it up with his hands even. The sweeper's boy, Ganga, has stolen it, has made it his own, playing with it.

Sandip's father squeezes the boy's fingers tight and hurries his children to the bus stop on the main road outside the Greater Kailash enclave. He doesn't notice the startling green of the short grass and high peepul trees. Early February, and the sky rings a deep blue, no shadow of the murderousness the sun will carry in six weeks. Buzzards have been chased away by flocks of small jade parakeets. Roses and poppy blooms explode. But if Kumar's children miss the school bus he will have to drive them halfway across the city, a nightmare this time of morning.

Kumar hurries his children along too so that he will not give in to temptation and rage, not in front of them, and kick that bloody ball himself. Already this morning his coffee and newspaper have been spoiled because his wife forced him to lecture the second sweeper, Radha. The first time he has ever spoken to her directly. Perhaps the first time he has noticed her particular existence.

"Yesterday the ball was stolen from the boy's room," he said to her angrily but awkwardly. His Hindi is rusty and he suspected she couldn't understand anyway, terrified and barefoot in front of him, trembling, one hand clutching a strand of dirty dupatta in front of her face. Before him she cringed, panting or whining like one of the pariah dogs that also afflict the compound.

His wife could control herself no longer but rushed forward to shriek at the girl. "You have polluted the house, all of it. Shame. Shame. I will throw you in the alley dust where you come from. You will never sweep in GK again. Never. Listen to me—here you sweep bathroom and back hall only. You, we do not want you even to wash dirty clothes. You took the ball. We know you or your boy, this badmash Ganga, one of you stole it." Maya Kumar stood hands on hips, chin thrust forward like an angry wasp.

"Enough," Kumar growled. His wife's anger had annoyed him. It spoiled his coffee and *Hindustan Times*. Such village notions of caste and pollution matter only to her and her mother. But stealing he cannot ignore, and for the neighbors' sake as well he must save face. "One chance more, that is all. You hear? Anything else disappears I will summon the police. I will smile when they break a lathi on your back. And the boy—no more of him, your badmash boy. You understand? He is dirty and smells bad. He is too old to follow you. If I see him again both of you will leave, both." Sighing, he tossed the napkin onto his plate—his wife knew this would mean ill temper for the day—and stormed out to gather the children.

The little terrier bitch, set off by such commotion, was yapping and yapping on the flagstone porch where a leather leash bound her to the iron fence. So nervous was the mali at all the shouting and barking and fury that as he heaved his heavy water bucket from pot to pot on the porch, watering the family's plants, his bare feet slipped on wet stone. The bucket flew into a wall. A small tree capsized. Water tumbled across the porch. The mali slapped helplessly at it. As the flood crept toward the front gate, the terrier's yapping grew fierce and hysterical. Kumar, dragging the children toward the bus, sloshed through the water, shoved the dog aside with half a kick, charged ahead into the narrow street. A subji-wallah was pushing his cart along the pavement, singing his tomatoes and onions, but this Kumar failed to notice as well as he brushed past.

*

One by one, in clusters of two and three, children drift toward the playground on the maidan. They are sleepy still, not too hungry yet. A few wear sweaters or vests discarded by their mothers' employers, but their legs and feet are cold in the damp grass and dirt. For now the playground is theirs. They claim it. The boys see the soccer ball. It belongs to them now too. The others will never want it back. All night they dared leave it here so no one boy will claim it and in the grass it still lies waiting for them. They smile and spit.

Ganga, Radha's son, eyes his trophy but veers away. Flirting close then swerving away. Toying.

They are watching the ball and each other watching the ball and they do not yet notice another boy who is strolling on the pavement with his ayah. The stranger spots the all-but-new ball and tugs free of Reena's fingers. The playground is safe—no cars allowed—and she is bored and sleepy. This boy heads directly to the ball, steps on it lightly and rolls it under his foot. With a sharp stab he kicks it across the grass to the other children who are now staring at him.

Ganga snares the skidding ball with his foot but stares at the ferengyi shyly, uncertainly. He is very beautiful, this visitor, with shaggy hair—shaggier even that Ganga's—hair so white it seems to have no color at all. A color that hurts the eye. And *his* eyes are blue and smiling.

But the smile is also a taunt, open and daring. Ganga sends the ball spinning back, but already the other boy, Daniel Ash, is walking toward him.

The ayah cries after him. "No, no, Danny sir, no—please. These are not children for friends. They are not to play with." Reena dashes forward a few steps—far enough to satisfy her sense of duty—and settles on a bench to watch as necessary.

The other children draw farther away. What does this stranger want? Whatever it may be, will they be beaten? Their eyes are dark and suspicious but glint with flashes of longing too. They retreat across the grass. A small pack of boys hunkers on their heels in a patch of dust near the swing set, ragged brown shawls wrapped around them chin to toe.

Only Ganga does not flee. He wants to flee, to fly away, but the taunting grin of the stranger holds him in place, hardly allows him to breathe.

Daniel dribbles the ball steadily toward the Indian boy. He pushes it right up to Ganga's bare foot.

After a long moment the foreigner draws the ball back with his toe. "Jeez," he says aloud, and with a quick punch sends it spinning away toward the fence. Without another glance at Ganga, he sets off to explore the playground. Ganga trails along behind. The servant children scatter away before him, then cluster once more like another flock of small parakeets, this a drab, ragged band.

The swings are lashed together. Only later in the afternoon will the large padlock be removed. But Daniel grabs the bar of a red whirl-around, dented along the rim, and trots in the dusty rut. The whirl-around spins reluctantly, then faster and faster. His head tilts back, his white hair flying, eyes closed, smiling dreamily. The whirl-around tilts too, slightly askew like a top that has never quite managed to topple. Daniel leaps onto it and for a few rotations the whirl-around carries him.

Grinning mischievously, he waves at Ganga. "Come on!" he cries. The other boy hesitates but doesn't need to know the words, then runs and leaps onto the metal. Daniel pushes again with his left foot, driving them both faster and faster. Off he jumps, catches himself, and continues to push the whirl-around with both hands as it flies by.

Still aboard, Ganga holds tight, his face revealing nothing. But he's scared. Not of the whirl-around. Long master of this toy, he can fly clear whenever he wishes. But the ferengyi boy—Ganga is drawn to him and afraid of him. He recognizes mischief and power. The boy has snatched the ball from him as easily as he himself crept after his mother into a house yesterday and smuggled it free—soiling it forever—from Sandip Kumar.

*

By five o'clock the afternoon is cooling once more. The morning's children disappear like smoke from the maidan. They have retreated to the safety of the alleys and the tight fists of shacks that gird GK like a coarse rind of some desert fruit. Only Daniel Ash wanders slowly across the grass, dribbling the soccer ball in boredom. He insisted that Reena bring him here again after a nap in the afternoon heat. Both his parents are working, but they haven't yet found a private Indian school that will admit him this late in the year.

From the mouth of an alley behind the small temple, cloaked by shadows, Ganga sits and watches.

Soon other children appear still wearing school uniforms, drifting in from all sides, loud, bursting with laughter, claiming the playground as their own, girls curled tight in conversation, boys jostling each other and tossing cricket balls from hand to hand. Servants release the swings. The see-saw is unlocked too.

None of the children will give away the secret right off, but all have noticed the blond stranger. Like a breeze, whispers spread the word through GK before most of them have even reached the fence. Shyly, they study him from the corners of their eyes.

Of them he seems oblivious—worse, he is indifferent. The ball alone occupies him. Bored, irritated, he scuffs it into the hard-packed dirt near the pavement. In fact Daniel is very well aware of the others, aware they are watching him, whispering about him. Why does everyone here *notice* him? Everywhere his parents have dragged him, to offices and shops and homes of their friends, people grin at Daniel, they stare at him and pinch and squeeze, offer candies, will never, never leave him alone or stop watching.

Sandip Kumar is among the last to arrive, and he strides directly up to Daniel. The other children fall silent in astonishment. This is not the Sandip they know, a quiet, sulky boy who pouts and stares at the rest of them. But Sandip and Daniel have already met—their families have spent an evening in the same room—because the Ash family is renting the house next to the Kumars. It belonged to Sandip's grandparents, but not long ago his Babu died and Grandmother moved in with them, sealing herself in a white sari alone on the upper floor.

"That's my ball," he says with a shrug, hands in the pockets of his navy-blue shorts.

"Yeah?" says Daniel with a shrug of his own. With the outside of his foot he nudges it indifferently toward him. Sandip hesitates.

"Sandip, no, no—you mustn't," scolds his sister who has been eyeing them enviously. Uma makes a face. But she replaces it at once with a flirtatious grin for the blond boy who now lives next door.

"You can have it," Sandip says with a sigh. "I'm not allowed to anymore."

"How come?" says Daniel with fresh interest.

"They stole it from my room, one of them did, and Papa will not allow me to touch it."

Daniel says nothing but he taps the ball again toward Sandip. Perhaps he hasn't understood. Perhaps it's a challenge, a test.

Sandip is tempted. Beaten and bruised, the ball still draws him. But he knows Uma is watching and will happily report to Papa. But why, he wonders, can this American play with the ball so easily? Will he get in trouble? Will this mean that now they will not be able to play with him, that he too has been soiled by the contact? Must he go through a cleansing at the temple?

Even as the thought occurs to him he knows that none of this will happen, that touching the ball makes no difference for the American. The rules are different. This boy can be polluted and it will not matter. Papa is too pleased to have the money for rent. And more: renting to an American family, all but having them live in your own house, this brings glory that thrills his mother and sister. The rules are different and he resents it.

Daniel senses something of this as well. With that mischievous smile he picks the ball up in his hands, tosses it spinning high in the air and catches it. He punts it, high again, higher and higher, until it lands in the grass twenty yards away, children scattering away from its reach. The boy hiding behind the temple rises off his haunches, tempted to dart out and capture the ball again.

"*Ganga.*" His mother hisses from behind, slaps at his head, catches him by the ear. He casts one last glance at the ferengyi and then the pain from his mother's clutch whips him deeper into the alley.

Next morning, as Daniel is heading through the back hallway from his bedroom, a heavy booming blow strikes the metal door onto the alley. His mother fumbles to unbolt and unlock the door, and tugs it open for Radha, who comes to sweep the bathroom and this hallway as part of the arrangement with the Kumars. She leaves her plastic sandals on the stone threshold and pads into the hall. Already the small, wiry woman is chattering endlessly to Daniel's mother who, because of her professional studies, speaks Hindi. Daniel, hardly noticing, glimpses the Indian boy from yesterday morning squatting patiently on his haunches in the alley, a ragged brown shawl drawn tight around him against the cold, as the door swings shut once more. Not for a moment does Daniel doubt that the boy is waiting and watching for him.

He hurries into the family living room and shoves one spoonful after another of American Corn Flakes and milk into his mouth. Reena, the ayah, hovers at his shoulder, making a show of such attention for the boy's parents as they rush about, dressing and snatching up papers and briefcases in preparation for work. Soon they have departed and Reena's attentions too have wandered.

Daniel slips away into the back hall once more. Reena, having switched on the small TV to a Hindi movie, will assume he has gone to the toilet or into his bedroom. Radha is scrubbing the stone floor of the bath, and Daniel quietly sneaks past. The heavy door is bolted again but not locked. Carefully, stealthily, he swings the bolt up and pushes it forward. The door creaks open. He draws it shut behind him, and suddenly he is surrounded by high walls and barbed wire and packed dirt ruts, a separate world hidden behind Greater Kailash. Two paces away the Indian boy is watching him. He hasn't moved. He isn't smiling. Daniel, fighting not to shiver in the cold, hunkers down next to the boy and doesn't smile either.

A fire of twigs and dung flickers a few yards away. An old man is warming himself, lean shanks thrust nearly into the kindling. Daniel nods at it. Ganga hesitates, but the other rises and heads to the small blaze. The smoke is heavy, the air hard to breathe, but a dull warmth does hover close. Daniel squats. The old man, chewing toothlessly at something invisible, eyes him but doesn't move or speak.

Soon Daniel has soaked enough warmth or grown used to the chill and he rises. Without a sound, Ganga sets off and Daniel follows him deeper into the maze. They turn a corner, two, coming upon other fires scattered here and there. Each bend of walls and dust is all but identical. Disoriented, Daniel coughs, looks back, sees nothing familiar or singular. A heavy cloud of coarse smoke leans on everything. He has no idea where the Indian boy is leading him, what there is to show, but he eagerly follows as if to discover some potent secret he will never find on his own.

Ganga has no particular destination in mind. All he yearned for this morning was a glimpse of the white-haired ferengyi boy—he never expected him to enter his world, couldn't even dare hope it.

Together they wander past a cluster of shacks backed against a concrete wall that bends in an arc for a hundred paces. On the other side is a sewer trench. In this cold weather the stench is muted, cloaked by the ever-present smoke. Each hut is patched together out of mud and cardboard and scraps of corrugated tin, including the one where Ganga and his mother live. He wonders whether the ferengyi boy will sense anything, will want to see. But Daniel is watching everything carefully without seeing, without sensing, and Ganga suddenly does not want to draw him into the darkness of their hut, to show him they have nothing to offer, not even chai, with his mother off working at this hour. He's imagined sharing his secret treasure of pins and pens, half-smoked cigarettes and the tiny glass bottles he's collected, one way or another, and hides in a box tucked behind a mat at the wall. But now he realizes this too is impossible.

A peacock hen screeches invisibly, startling Daniel. He trots around the corner and discovers several birds scratching in the dust, pecking at a small roost of garbage dropped next to an anonymous door. A male spreads its wings and lifts heavily to a rooftop overhead. Delighted, Daniel waves to his friend. Ganga follows but doesn't understand what the ferengyi is upset about.

Ahead on the path he spies two of his friends hunched intently. He almost pats the stranger's arm but hasn't the courage, doesn't know what the response will be. Will he be beaten for risking a touch? Phlegm gathers in his throat at the thought, and he spits heavily at a wall. But Daniel has spotted the other boys too. He tugs at Ganga's thin shawl, (Ganga grins to be answered so quickly, a thrill shooting through him, but the other boy doesn't notice), and they hurry to find out what in the dust is worthy of such attention.

Ganga's friends are squatting on their heels, one wearing a blue sweater-vest with a wide gash at the shoulder. The other's brown shawl, identical to Ganga's, is wound tightly about his shoulders and knees. Only his dark eyes move. They are quick and alert. Beneath them, a butterfly swatch of pink skin, a birthmark or scar, stretches from cheek to cheek across his nose as if the top layer has been seared away.

Blue sweater has a stick. He jabs it into the jowl of the pariah dog which isn't quite dead at their feet. It twitches, muscles pricking involuntarily. Its eyes are crusted shut. Scabs cover much of its lean gray body.

Daniel watches, horrified and slightly sick to his stomach, fascinated. Again blue sweater stabs with indifferent cruelty. No twitch this time, no sigh, nothing. Between one torment and the next, death has worked its transformation. No pretense remains that what lies before them is anything more than loosely gathered sticks covered by a stained rag.

For the first time the boy with the butterfly mask moves, a hand appearing from beneath his shawl to grab one of the dog's hind legs. Without a word or sound, he rises and sets off down the alley, dragging the carcass behind him with some matter-of-fact purpose that is all mystery to Daniel. Blue sweater follows lackadaisically.

Ganga watches his guest, uncertain. Daniel is uncertain too—he is sickened and excited all at once. He knows he has witnessed something as ordinary as the dust and smoke about them, and yet it is disturbing, thrilling. He would like to see more, but he doesn't know what and he doesn't know how to ask. He turns his eyes to the other boy, who wags his head from side to side reassuringly, imploringly.

Still unable to fathom the stranger's reaction or desires, Ganga sets off down another alley. Without warning they emerge abruptly behind the temple and onto the small maidan of Greater Kailash. The subji-wallah brushes past Daniel, pushing his wooden cart on the cracked pavement toward the next row of houses. His tomatoes, eggplants, and onions glisten purple and red and green in the morning light.

Startled, Daniel feels more disoriented than in the maze of alleys. Haven't they wandered leagues and eons from this life? Can reappearing be so easy?

Ganga has reclaimed the blue and white soccer ball. Its sheen is fading, but he feels they are on safe ground once more, as if the familiarity of yesterday's game reestablishes the harmony of the universe. The ball scuds toward the blond boy. Soon Daniel will return to his house where Reena will shriek and sob and say never a word to his parents about his disappearance, her terrible failure. This he counts on already.

*

By the middle of the afternoon Sandip Kumar's mother has already heard the tale, and the moment he returns from school she sets upon him with a flurry of outrage and dire warnings. He grimaces as he drinks his cup of milk, listening to her all the while, his dark eyes narrowed to sullen slits, his head drooping.

Before he even reaches the playground he spies the American boy besieged, nearly overwhelmed by the children of GK. Shy hesitation has disappeared today. The girls, all of them wearing western skirts, are coyly holding hands with each other and offering this visitor sweets. Their brothers race about, kicking the blue and white soccer ball as if they're innocent of its history. Yet for all their flailing and shouting, they never stray far—without ever quite looking at him, they hope to lure the American boy into their game.

Sandip's fists clench in the pockets of his shorts. "You mustn't play with those servant children," he shouts glumly.

Daniel stares at him. "Why not?"

"You just mustn't. They're dirty, they cheat and steal."

The ball skids close by and Daniel's foot snares it. He picks the ball up and shoves it at Sandip. In that instant Sandip sees that the boy's blue eyes have flared with hate. Regret and longing fill his throat and turn swiftly to bile, to ashes. He can hate too, and the surge of it releases him. Sandip lets the ball drop to the ground, but kicks it cleanly to Vijay Singh and joins the game. The American runs as well, swept up in the shouts and passing and tumbles in grass and dust, the hatred a secret pact between the two.

As dusk gathers, as mothers and servants call the children to dinner, as Uma gives up trying to tug Sandip away, as Reena goes to fetch Daniel's father to order his boy home in turn, for a long, oddly quiet moment only the two of them are left on the darkened maidan. Sandip says nothing, makes no gesture. He stoops to pick up the ball and bears it closer to the other's face. As Daniel watches, wary, the Indian boy pulls a small clasp knife from his pocket. With a quick thrust he stabs the leather and the ball sighs. Sandip rips hard with the blade, widening the gash into a nasty grin. He flings the suddenly heavy, lifeless ball toward the alley behind the temple. It thuds with a half-hearted bounce and lies still. Daniel says nothing. Chilled to the bone, he turns away and trudges home. The evening has suddenly grown too dark to make out whether anyone else has seen.

Already Daniel and his parents have grown used to the startling variety and volume of sounds rising in the narrow streets of Greater Kailash, the car horns and cries of beggars and peacocks and always more horn blasts. Yet the wailing and raging shouts that wake them early next morning are too alarming, too close at hand to ignore. Daniel's father tugs the front door open, but it is Daniel who slips out first and peers through the fence that separates them from the Kumars. All there is bedlam. Uma is sitting on the stone porch weeping. Maya Kumar shrieks and wails, her hair loose, hysterical. Sandip stands brooding and sour as he watches his father angrily saw with a kitchen knife at a leather strap. Someone has wound it around the top of their iron fence. It is stretched tight—this is why Kumar must struggle to get a clear angle with the blade—around the throat of their terrier. Its limp body hangs five feet above the flagstones, tongue swollen, eyes abulge at nothing.

Daniel's father, a step slower in recognition, stiffens abruptly and roughly tugs his son away from the fence, herding him back into the house they are renting. Much as he and his wife have wanted their son to experience the real

India, not some sanitized version created for tourists and diplomats, he hopes to protect the boy from such sights as this. But Daniel, sensing his father's impulse, knows it is too late. Two days have sped him along, forced him like a winter flower. He is much older now, unshockable he thinks, almost a different person. He nearly pats his father on the arm—he imagines doing it—to reassure him.

The day is long and quiet. Daniel's parents have delayed going to work. The incident next door, nothing so horrible in itself really, has upset their equilibrium. Daniel hears them making plans at the small dining table. Perhaps the Embassy School is the best option after all. Political friends can use their influence to find or create a place for him there even at this late date. Reena trails after him throughout the house. She will hardly let him out of her sight this morning, especially with her employers at home. No Hindi movies for her today.

No thumping on the alley door either. This morning Radha never arrives to sweep. When Sara Ash inquires next door—she has wanted to go anyway, to offer sympathy and any help—Maya Kumar tells her (in Hindi because she remains shaken, nervous, on the verge of tears and rage) that Radha has disappeared, that she's probably returned to her village for some festival or family matter. They will find another sweeper.

When Sara passes the news on to Daniel—also that Uma and Sandip have been kept home from school as well, perhaps they can play later in the day—his heart sinks. His friend will have gone with his mother. Yet it occurs to him that returning to their village is perhaps a wise course. He nods to himself. The momentum of desire and violence that gathered so quickly and now has broken like a powerful wave across three families scares him.

"He is the one, your *friend*," Sandip says bitterly. "He tortured our little dog to death. No doubt of it."

Daniel doesn't reply. What can he say?

The two boys are trudging across the maidan, brought here by mother and ayah as if this is their hearts' desire and worth any sacrifice. Middle of the afternoon: the playground is deserted, one universe of children already fled, the other not yet arrived. Before they are aware of it the two almost tread on the sunken shell of the soccer ball. It remains where it landed the day before. But the ripped leather has quickly turned gray and stiff, as if before long it will disappear into the soil in the natural course of life and death. The two of them veer abruptly aside.

Walking with the American so close, almost hand in hand, Sandip is aflame with longing and anger. He wanted to be friends with this strange boy, to run his hands through the golden-white hair. He would have shown him secrets and been rewarded with friendship. But Daniel Ash has rejected him for Radha's son—untouchable, wild, dirty—a thief he will become or a badmash altogether.

What did the two of them do while he was in school? What had the devil boy shown him? Sandip pictures the brown hands and long fingers caressing the soccer ball, *his* soccer ball, and a cold rage sweeps over him again—a sour triumph too as he remembers gutting the ball with his knife. He wishes, yes, he could stab this golden boy, hurt him, open his flesh so he will sigh like the ball and bleed into the earth. So caught up in the fury and the vision is Sandip that he trembles invisibly. His teeth are chattering. He glances at Daniel Ash, afraid the give-away clatter may be audible. But the American boy is caught up in his own thoughts, hearing nothing—which only enrages Sandip still more.

Reluctantly they arrive at the whirl-around. Neither puts a hand on the bar to spin and bring it to life, no matter that the adults wish them to play. They stand in the dust, staring awkwardly at the tilted, dusty toy, their heads bowed, as if joined in close accord. Suddenly both glance up, sensing something, startled, as if a high whistle pierces the air, one only they can hear. Together they spy a flash of cloth in the mouth of the alley behind the little temple, a blur of browns. Daniel's eyes open wide. Sandip's darken. His fists tighten in the pockets of his shorts.

But no one appears. The two boys linger on the maidan as the other GK children arrive after school to shout and run and play, into lingering twilight, resisting the first calls for dinner. At last, still together, they drift toward their side-by-side houses. They have hardly spoken in these several hours, and yet, taste of tarnished metal on their tongues, they have communed after all: resentments and angers ache into clenched teeth. They understand each other now.

Daniel is restless. He paces through the small hallways of the house, his face hot, his feet cold. After a dinner of eggplant, rice, and chapatis prepared by Reena, which he hardly touches, his mother asks him several times what is wrong. His father finally snaps at him when Daniel knocks a small wooden Ganesh onto the floor. What can he say? How can he explain? It's impossible. "I'm sorry," he murmurs under his breath and retreats to his room. "Get some sleep," his dad calls after him. "You've got school tomorrow. You obviously need it."

Daniel hears a light tapping at the door and his heart leaps. He slips on his bathroom sandals and races out of his room. But it is the front door that Reena has already tugged open, so he knows it will not be Ganga. To his surprise, Sandip peers in, gesturing to him as if Reena is not even there. This time Daniel thinks to grab the shawl his mother bought him, and reluctantly, curious, follows him out into the chilly morning.

Without a word, hardly bothering to notice him, Sandip leads quickly on. He turns a corner and then another, and suddenly they are in the alley. Daniel is surprised by how well the wealthy boy seems to know the alley world, how confident and comfortable he appears, as if the Kumars own it too. He glances over his shoulder just in time to see Radha bang on a heavy door which opens to admit her. It may be the Kumars' or some other house entirely, but clearly she has not fled to her village after all. She kicks her plastic sandals into the entryway and bangs the door shut behind her.

Already Daniel is lost once more and disoriented. He must put his faith in Sandip—this he doesn't like. The sun hasn't risen high enough to peek over walls in this maze, and the smoke from countless small fires is thick and acrid. Daniel's eyes sting.

With the muted stink of a sewer as marker, he recognizes a long sagging stone wall. Ahead in the dust two boys are squatting intently over something. He can't be sure they are the same two he saw when Ganga was his guide, not until he makes out a ripped blue vest. The other's brown shawl hides everything but his eyes and a butterfly scar, pink across his cheeks. To their side a small fire of twigs and dung smokes a dull blaze. Between them in the dust lies another collapsed bundle.

Daniel knows at once, knows bone deep before he can even make it out distinctly, though crumpled on the ground Ganga is hardly a greater bag of broken sticks than the dying dog. Clumps of hair have been torn from his scalp. He eyes are swollen shut and his lips are bleeding. He is panting lightly, each breath wracking him. Instead of gouging with a stick, the two other boys have brought water and are clumsily bathing his face with a scrap of cloth. They glare fiercely at Daniel when he draws close, as if he is somehow to blame.

He stops short, sickened, angry. Is this my fault? he wonders.

Furious, he spins round, ready to fight, to lash out with fists, to bite and kick and shout. But Sandip has already abandoned him. He is striding away quickly, hands driven deep in the pockets of his shorts, his shoulders hunched. Two older boys, teenagers who work for Kumar, have fallen in behind Sandip, slouching along like trained dogs. In another moment all three have disappeared.

Awash in anger and regret and dismay, Daniel is breathing hard, close to tears. Even if he wanted to follow it is too late.

The chill of the morning cools him, chills him, and he hugs himself. The labyrinth resists his gaze. He is not sure whether to go right or left or keep true ahead. Once more he has the feeling that he's aged in only a few hours. Yet he also feels alone, more alone than ever before. Not scared. No. Sadder, lonely, but not scared. There will be no explaining this to his parents. Not what happened, but how it's changed him. Will they even notice, since it's all inside, that he's not the same boy?

The first step lies before him, through the dust and smoke of the Greater Kailash alleys, to find his way home.

Mistaken Identity

The sleepy sack of a man was waggling a strip of card-board with her name on it as passengers wearily surged through the arrivals gate at Gandhi International Airport. Only now did Vera Kahn first suspect that perhaps, after all, she'd made a mistake by accepting this invitation. Next to the driver, a U.S.I.S. bureaucrat—he could be nothing else—was craning his neck and failing entirely to see her as she approached. Ludicrously, he was still trying to spy something, someone else, over her shoulder even as she dropped a heavy bag nearly on his toes.

"I'm Vera Kahn," she said with hardly any smile at all.

His pale eyes registered the problem in a series of stages he did his best to mask despite the very late hour. "I'm sorry?" he managed first, belatedly.

"Kahn. Vera Kahn. I'm your poet."

The poor man, straw-haired and tie limp—Vera was glad he made sympathy so difficult—struggled not to say the obvious: that there must be some mistake. There *had* been a mistake. She was very well aware of it. She wasn't about to let him off the hook.

"Are we waiting for someone else," she asked, "or can we go? I'm pretty well shot."

"Right—okay. But can I see some ID first? You know, security's sake. It's standard procedure over here." Although he looked miserable and confused, struggling to maintain his official good cheer, not to mention his authority, Vera was impressed that he'd managed to improvise the lie at this hour. She handed him her passport.

He studied her photo. "Right. Okay!" he shouted more cheerfully to conceal his greater dismay. "Shankar, let's get a move on." With a nod, the driver shooed away a scatter of boys eager to help and, reaching for the bag himself, let her name drop to the floor where it joined a ragged swirl of scraps even now being swept away as travelers and greeters, officials and porters and pickpockets dispersed into the Delhi night.

The air felt less tropical, less exotic than she'd expected as they emerged from the airport. It was plenty warm—laden with a muggy haze and wood smoke and the less acrid stink of burning cow dung. Vera felt a stab of disappointment. The irritability and disaffection she'd hoped would somehow magically lift on arrival in the East was instead merely chafing into a raw, weary restlessness.

"I'm Walter Tyson," said the American official more genially as he directed her toward a small red car parked in a reserved space. "I've read your work." Then he stopped lamely once more, doubting his own truthfulness.

"That's so thoughtful of you," said Vera Kahn and left it at that as she climbed into the back of the Maruti. She knew he hadn't read her poetry, either the one book from a good press or the couple of smaller chapbooks she'd all but paid for herself. Not that the lie was intentional this time. No doubt he'd read, more or less out of a sense of duty—whose idea had it been to extend this invitation?—some selection from the poetry of Veera Kahn, a Black woman of almost precisely her own age who taught, not at the small Catholic college in southern California and not with the glorious view overlooking the ocean (this one of the few satisfactions of the common misunderstanding), but a few miles inland at the much larger school by the same name, but with a U.C. in front. It used to be that Vera would imagine the two of them getting together and giggling over drinks about their ongoing entanglements. But Veera had made it clear on the occasions when they did meet, usually by accident or confusion or someone else's sense of jolly fun, that she wasn't interested in playing pals. Never did she let on how *she* came saddled with such a name, Kahn. Being confused with a now middle-aged white woman of little fame could have done Veera's own career no particular good.

For twelve years, on the other hand, Vera had felt shadowed by the other woman's celebrity. Every professional charm coming her way—engagements to read, solicitations for new work, even the occasional call for a date by some friend of a friend—increasingly seemed tainted by this confusion of identity. She knew it wasn't true. Not entirely. But she'd grown used to spying similar symptoms of mistrust, disappointment, resignation that had flitted across Walter Tyson's brow. It hadn't grown easier. It had grown harder, especially of late.

So what should arrive on her desk in mid-August but an invitation from the United States Information Service to spend two weeks on a reading tour in India? Only eight weeks warning. Someone even more prominent than Vera's near namesake must have canceled on them, not quite at the last minute. U.S.I.S. Delhi scrambled. Hence, no doubt, the sloppy research, the mistake. She'd had to scramble too, bargaining with colleagues to cover her classes, with students to water her plants and feed her cats.

That look had been in the Dean's eyes too when she requested permission—he'd grown used to such confusions between Vera and Veera. Not that he'd complain or admonish her: he was perfectly thrilled for the sake of the college reputation. Still, that knowing smile on his face. She ignored it, she loathed it, any doubt about the wisdom of taking the United States Information Service up on its offer, honest mistake or not, eased itself from her thoughts.

Five hours sleep was all she could manage that first night, and Vera rose, woozy and disoriented. She was sniffling too. Apparently, a cold had stowed away for the journey. Most of the hotel's other guests had already breakfasted by the time she appeared in the dining room. Its tightly sealed windows overlooked the bright bustle of Connaught Circus—and shielded her from it. She'd been so eager, yet now she lacked the courage to venture immediately into the mayhem. Cranky, annoyed with herself, she sipped at a second cup of tepid coffee. Perhaps she'd been expecting too much of India, or of herself. She didn't want to be disappointed.

Oh, bullshit, she thought, pushing the cup away and staring out at a street of swarming scooter taxis, of buses spewing swathes of dark smoke, of pedestrians and peddlers and darting children with shoeshine kits, all wrestling for advantage. Only a faint but constant bray of horns seeped through the windows.

A little past one in the afternoon, Walter Tyson appeared, freshly shaven and shirted, his face lacking any trace of the suspicion and discouragement it had betrayed a few hours earlier. No doubt he and the U.S.I.S. staff had already made some calls. They'd discovered their own mistake. Like it or not, intended or not, it was Vera Kahn they'd invited, not Veera. And Vera had taken them up on it. Here she was, and at least she was a poet too. Perhaps some careful political calibration about race or fame, or both, had been vexed. No solving it now. A later program could be altered. Crossing the lobby, he smiled at her with an enthusiasm that went with the job. His face was pinkly tanned and round, faintly boyish. Vera smiled back.

But it wasn't so easy as that, of course. Tyson drove her to the American Center to meet the staff and check out the room where she'd be giving a first reading that same evening. With each of the senior officers, even with the librarian who'd already hidden away the copies of Veera's books specially ordered for the occasion and who, without question, had spent the morning trying to discover whether a single copy of Vera's book existed on the subcontinent, she spied or imagined spying in their eyes the smoke of disappointment that she was only she. They probably also suspected her complicity in the matter. Her anger flared. One young cultural liaison, lips glossy with color, hair in a careful bun, nearly got herself slapped.

What right, Vera forced herself to acknowledge, sagging a bit, had she to claim any innocence at all?

"Can I sneak away from here for a while?" she whispered to Tyson, tugging at his sleeve in a hallway.

"No problem," he said, apparently relieved to be asked so little.

She hadn't really intended that he escort her, but on the other hand she had no clue where to go or how to get there. He seemed well accustomed to the task. "Let's swing you through some of the national monuments," he offered as they climbed into the Maruti, "mostly built by the Brits. Then we can try the Old City—you'll like that."

She wanted to be filled with wonder and exhilaration. Yet the broad avenues and Edwardian monuments of New Delhi only soured Vera's mood still further. India Gate, the Parliament buildings, cracking pavement and peeling paint, waves of stench and billowing heat, a welt of mosquito bites just behind her knee, Tyson's enthusiasm, all nagged and niggled her into a raging petulance she hadn't felt since adolescence. She was aware of it and ashamed and unable to govern her own mood. Gritting her teeth, she nodded at each banality the man offered with a wave of his hand.

Slowly the car began tacking toward the north. They passed a railway station, teeming with solitary men wearing only strips of cotton wrapped around their waists, families besieged by bundles, and young Americans weighed down by enormous backpacks. The streets narrowed, traffic slowed, boys tapped on the car's fenders as they slid past. Vera's nerves were taut with exasperation. She struggled not to shriek at Tyson, demanding that he return her to the hotel, where at least it would be cooler and she could take a shower.

Around another corner they finally made out the cause of this particular tie-up—a dozen tree trunks had slipped their chains and tumbled from a long flatbed truck. How could such a huge truck be allowed in this part of the city, on streets as narrow as these? Scooter taxis and cars were inching up one by one onto the ragged sidewalk and crawling around the blockade. And suddenly Vera realized what she was seeing, as if until this moment she'd been unable to recognize or make sense of it: an elephant heaving one of the logs off the ground and back onto the lorry. A scrawny boy perched just behind its ears tapped the animal's attention towards another piece of lumber straddling the road. It wrapped its trunk around the near end of the log, hoisting it at an angle and leaning it against the bed of the truck. Then, using the edge of the truck as fulcrum, the elephant deftly grasped the bottom end of the log and swung it up and over with a last, delicate thump. Dust and exertion were smudging the elaborate pink flowers chalked across the elephant's flanks.

"Probably on its way to a wedding," Tyson said. "The mahout figures he can pick up a few rupees from the truck driver."

Vera nodded. That's what blind-sided her—the apparent ordinariness of such a sight. Her heart thumped hard in her chest. Her throat swelled. Joy—there was no better word for what swept over her, so glad was she to be right here, right now, watching this elephant at its task. How long had it been since she'd experienced such joy? Tears welling in her eyes, she felt amazement as much at her own reaction as at the scene before her. Such violent swings were entirely unlike her. In an instant she'd been wrenched from raw misery to this wonder, this elation. Joy, yes, but harsh too. She sniffed and blew into a tissue, hoping to disguise her emotions. Again Tyson glanced at her. She wouldn't face him.

By the time they reached Old Delhi's web of narrow streets, she'd regained her composure. They parked the car and made their way by foot through thick crowds. As they penetrated deeper, buildings were leaning towards each other above their heads like trees in an ancient forest. Yet this strange world all seemed distant, as if she were still peering through a window. It was the wooly congestion in her head and a haze of fatigue and jet-lag—everything seemed pushed beyond arm's reach.

Old men in pajamas and skullcaps gathered in stalls and tea shops. Women, mostly wearing scarves over their heads or with full chadors hiding their faces and limbs, scurried by with infants in tow or picked at plastic shoes or soap trays or children's t-shirts hanging from a wire frame. Young men hovered about Vera and Walter Tyson, shoving packs of handkerchiefs and small chess-sets at their faces. Jeeringly persistent, the pack of boys flitted along through the winding lanes, darting forward, trying again and again. Tyson flicked his hand, shooing them, and pressed forward. "This is the best walk to the Red Fort," he cried over his shoulder.

The boys circled and swooped, calling out to her in a sing-song chant. "Buy this, sweet lady. It's good for you! I make it nothing for you, no money at all. A gift from my heart. Buy, sweet lady." She couldn't quite make out all the words. The boys were pressing closer. The sing-song danced about her head, mocking, crude, taunting, obscene. The boys were laughing, leering.

Suddenly a hand groped hard at her buttock and she jerked in pain. From another direction fingers jabbed one of her breasts, pinching for its nipple. Other hands snatched at her shoulder bag.

"Stop," she shouted. Was there any sound? Did anyone hear? The grabbing, pawing, clutching spun her around.

"Help!" she shrieked, flailing out, her hands balled in tight, child-like fists.

The boys scattered in a single gleeful instant as Tyson waded towards her, and he was hurrying her back the other way, back towards the car, and he was saying something or asking something, but she couldn't really hear in the clotted silence all about them now. Tyson was apologetic and courteous, yet he couldn't quite mask his impatience too, as if she were making a lot out of nothing. She was furious with him, furious at those boys. Yet, curiously, the anger seemed distant too, almost beyond reach, and she wasn't weeping in the car: she was sniffling and blowing into her tissue, that was all.

*

"It's a terrific turnout," whispered the woman with her hair in a bun, Bridgit, the one Vera had wanted to smack earlier. She seemed sincerely pleased that the room was better than two-thirds full as the two of them peeked through the doors. Both were aware that they owed the crowd of middle-class Indians, expatriate Americans, and local academics to a grave misunderstanding, but neither was going to mention it.

This moment was worse even than confronting Tyson at the airport—only now did Vera feel truly a fraud. Nervous, irritable, she strode to the podium. The small auditorium might have been on any college campus in America, the kind of place she'd given dozens of readings in her career. She had nothing to be ashamed of. She was sweating despite the air conditioning.

"Good evening," she said brightly. "I'm honored by the invitation to read to you, and I'm delighted you've turned up to hear." A few people applauded politely, unaware of anything amiss. Vera smiled bravely past confused looks and harsh whispers from others.

Once she plunged into the first poem, however, the audience settled and so did her nerves. Now she was on home territory at last. She relaxed and read well. Once or twice, glancing up, she spotted a face here, eyes there, a pensive smile, listeners who were with her. Such delicate connections were all she sought from any public reading.

Earlier in the day she'd tabbed the selections she'd read from her book and a new manuscript. Yet the pages were in fact mere prompts—as always she was reciting from memory. And she had the odd sensation that she was observing her own work from something like the distance she'd been seeing Delhi since her arrival. The poems were hers, yet separate too. They pleased her. Their workmanship, their sensibility and insight, the knowledge they demonstrated of the craft, all of this pleased her. What more did she have to say than she was sharing this evening?

That question startled her for a moment, and she stumbled, reciting a line twice. Was this enough? she wondered. Did this mean she'd finally matured as a poet—or that she was finished as one? The prospect suddenly seemed unclear, unnerving, the footing of her career treacherous.

For forty minutes she held the audience and then ceased, smiling, sipping at a glass of water. A long, pleasant moment passed as both she and they took stock. No better evidence of success than such silence. Could anyone from U.S.I.S. complain now? The applause when it broke was warm, dissolving only slowly into a fluster of people rising, chattering, making their way up the aisles. Among those who ventured forward to thank her, a woman in a gold and crimson sari waited her turn. "It was delightful—a wonderful treat," she said, proffering Veera's book for an autograph, despite the back cover photo of a noticeably different woman than the one who'd been reading on this podium.

*

No American official was stationed in Jaipur to welcome Vera as she descended from the train into a blast of desert heat and scalding sun. Instead, an Indian in grey trousers, blue shirt, and a short black tie hurried up to her on the platform. Someone at the American Center in Delhi must have tipped him off about whom not to expect.

"You are Miss Vera Kahn? The poet?" he said. He seemed uncertain about whether to shake her hand. "I am Dr. Kanthan, head of the English literature department. We are so very delighted you have made this arduous journey to grace us with a reading. It is the event of the year for our students. They are so very, very excited."

"I am too," she said, and allowed him to lead her toward a car. She welcomed the dry heat and cleaner air of Rajasthan—though the congestion in her head and chest stubbornly refused to clear away. The train's first-class compartment had been sealed tight for the entire journey, its air conditioning oppressive and only partially effective. She much preferred this, even though sweat was already prickling along her arms and legs.

No one had mentioned any plan or particular schedule, but she was rather surprised that Dr. Kanthan drove directly to a small bungalow which, she soon gathered, was a guest house. Without switching off the car, he stepped out and pulled her bag from the back seat. "The remainder of today is for you to rest and perhaps to visit something of our most beautiful city," he said. "Tomorrow morning, 9 a.m. bright and early I will fetch you here to the university. It will be a grand treat no doubt." With a little wave of his hand, he was back in the driver's seat and pulling away.

For three days Vera had yearned for some freedom, for some time alone, unshepherded by Tyson or anyone else.

But now that Kanthan had so unceremoniously abandoned her on the hot asphalt, she wasn't so eager to be on her own.

Her room was spartan but adequate, with a heavy A/C unit in the wall. Black scorch marks around its plug made her nervous. She'd sleep later without it running. In the meanwhile, she had no intention of remaining cooped up here. Strolling once more out onto the road, she spotted several bicycle-rickshaws huddling in a patch of shade a hundred yards away. A dark-skinned old man with a turban and no shirt was cleaning his teeth with a twig. He spat and looked up at her as she approached. "City?" she said. He nodded.

The rickshaw gathered speed enough to bathe Vera's face in a dry breeze. The old man pumped slowly from one leg to another, standing, his legs young and thin and powerful in their rhythm. As they passed through an ornate wooden gate into the city he glanced over his shoulder at her. "Go," she said with a smile and waved him on.

Through the streets and sprawling market they wove, sometimes quickly, often slowed to a walk. A bright pastel pink wash covered almost all of Jaipur's buildings as if defying the surrounding blankness of desert and grey dust. Likewise, the Rajasthanis themselves dressed with a far greater exuberance than people in Delhi—scarves of orange and flaming red, scarlet cotton shifts and leggings.

Spying one woman, no youngster but with beautiful dark eyes, a persimmon duppatta over shoulders and head, walking two children by the hand, Vera careened with a fresh surge of joy. She'd never been anywhere so beautiful, so full of life that was strange to her and yet palpably real—ordinary even in its strangeness. She was also keenly aware that she could only hover outside, riding a rickshaw like any tourist, and watch.

Along an avenue stretched the stalls of spice merchants with their careful heaps of cardamom, stalks of ginger, bright orange mountains of other spices and seeds. Swaying around a corner, she found herself sweeping among the silversmiths. Trays of bangles and earrings, rows of goblets and cups. In the back of larger shops Vera could make out young men working the metal, tapping with mallets, etching with an instrument that looked like a razor.

"That's what Andrew would love." The thought startled her. It had been months and months since she'd thought of her former husband. But it came to her now that *he* was the one who'd always hankered to visit India—a desire that seemed extravagant and childish to her when they were young. Northern Italy, perhaps, if he insisted on traveling. Jamaica if it had to be exotic. Wasn't it enough they managed to steal a few days together in bed in New York, a city where the publishers had him chained? India—they could have their pick of East 6th Street take-away, hauling the cartons and little cups of chutney right into their tangled nest of sheets. Or if he stole out to California every few months, why shouldn't that count?

She wondered, possibly for the first time, whether she should have taken his name after all. He'd shrugged, said it didn't matter. Had it mattered? Over time, a continent apart, they'd forgotten each other or failed to keep up with the stiffer, more mysterious adults they were becoming. Vera looked about her. Andrew would love Jaipur.

Every few minutes the rickshaw-wallah glanced back for directions. He seemed increasingly suspicious—his trade was to ferry riders from one place to a specific destination. Such casual touring as this made him uncomfortable. Finally, in the middle of a square, he climbed off the bike. Without

quite looking at her, he held out a hand. "You pay now. I eat."
He scooped his fingers at his mouth to help her understand.

For a moment she considered exploring the city by foot.
But she still felt a bit light-headed from the deep-rooted
cold in her chest. "No," she said, shaking her head. "Take
me back, please—I will pay you." The old man shrugged as
if he'd merely been seeking this reassurance and mounted
his cycle once more.

More quickly now they whizzed through the streets, up
an alley and out a different gate into Jaipur's more modern
precincts. Disorientation soon dizzied Vera. Vaguely uncomfortable, she had no sense of their direction. Had the old
man understood her?

Several ancient buses were jammed haphazardly into a
lot. Some stood empty, waiting for future assignment, one
or two abandoned entirely. Others, arriving or departing,
overflowed with passengers squatting on the roof with bags
and parcels or clinging to doors and window bars.

Hardly slowing, the rickshaw-wallah swung wide around
a corner and peddled along a narrow lane, past a row of low
derelict buildings. Scabby trees covered in dust threw a paltry
shade here. It wasn't cool, but the sudden escape from the
sun seemed to silence a harsh and terrible sound that had
been ringing in her ears.

In the sand along this lane dark bundles lay scattered.
She couldn't quite make them out. Large and small, they'd
been dropped casually in odd contortions. Off to the side, a
stick collapsed in the dust. Vera turned her head toward it.
And still it took a moment as she was being driven past to
realize it was a leg that had fallen. Above the haunch lolled
the uncovered head of a young woman, jaw slack, eyes naked
and blank and unfocused. Now Vera could translate: men,

women, children, sprawling motionless, sparsely covered in scraps and rags. Their entire absence of movement was horrible, testimony to an equal absence of hope or purpose. What had brought them here? What were they waiting for? Were they waiting for anything?

Rage at the deception flooded through her—the beggars in Delhi had been toying with her after all. Those young mothers holding infants and banging on car windows near Connaught Circus wore bangles on their arms. Those babes had flesh on their bones.

Not the sordid shapes lying here in the sand. She spied a shoulder—a small boy's shoulder—no more than socket and bone. These shadows made no appeal. Indifferent in their lethargy, they didn't notice this stranger rolling past. Had they called out she might have flung her bag, her ring, the clothes she wore. Instead, she sat frozen and horrified.

The rickshaw-wallah took no more notice than he had with earlier marvels on this improvised tour. Shade and convenience were his only purpose in fetching his passenger along this particular route.

But the vision of such casual detritus pummeled her. The exhilaration she'd been feeling only moments before disappeared like smoke in a sudden gale. Tourist, she'd already been borne safely past, the only trace a sickness in her belly, a spot on her soul.

Bright and early as promised, Dr. Kanthan fetched her from the guesthouse. She'd taken a simple dinner in her room and then spent the hot night tossing with dreams she couldn't recall.

Rajasthan University stretched across a large swathe of desert, its concrete subsiding in reddish sand and ragged patches of wild grass. Kanthan led her first to his own office where the eight other members of the English department were already gathered. The one woman among them rose and stepped towards her. "Dr. Shukla," said Kanthan.

"We are so happy you have come to visit us," she said. Her hair was pulled taut. A streak of henna marked its severe part. Vera had seen looks before like the one Dr. Shukla offered her. Senor women in American universities shared it. They'd broken the bastions first; they'd made a place for themselves, suffered what had to be endured, compromised too deeply in order to survive, and would brook no latecomers, wanted no sisters or sympathy. Their claim was too precious. "Please, you will take a cup of tea with us before your talk?" she asked. And handed her a cup, a saucer of sugar biscuits. Vera didn't dare refuse.

She'd been asked by U.S.I.S. to prepare a lecture for occasions such as this, and so a few minutes later she entered a large bare room packed with at least three hundred students. Perhaps thirty-five chairs were reserved for faculty and administrators, all but swallowed by the crowd. Most students sat on the floor. At the front of the room a bare wooden desk and chair perched with cold authority on a platform. But Vera couldn't bring herself to sit in that chair. Giggles exploded and were shushed as she propped herself on the edge of the desk. "I'm more comfortable this way," she said with a smile, hoping to win them over. She coughed, wishing she could clear her lungs even for a moment.

Certainly the students were smiling and eager, willing to accept anything this visitor might offer. "My talk today," she said slowly and clearly, "is called The Best of Times, The Worst of Times: the contemporary literary scene in America." She glanced up from her paper and saw them eagerly nodding, these hundreds of young people. They were gazing so intently. Without warning, a surge of dread swept through her, leaving ash in her mouth. Bone deep she knew, only now when it was too late for anything but to soldier on, that this was the wrong talk for the wrong audience. She'd intended it as a light introduction to American themes and authors, with diplomatic bows to Rushdie, Desai, Roy—Indian writers who'd been fashionable of late. But the students before her had no clue what she was talking about, not enough context to imagine a context. And she could tell from their eyes, gazing at her with fascination as though she were an exotic creature babbling some strange gibberish, that they could hardly understand the sounds she was making. It wasn't that they didn't speak English: their English wasn't hers but a language whose sounds were trained to a different clef altogether. Sitting amidst department colleagues jotting diligent notes, Dr. Shukla stared up with a grim triumph at her helplessness.

When Vera finished—she ceased speaking somewhere in the middle of the talk, middle of a thought, middle of a phrase—a ripple of polite applause passed quickly. But then, to her amazement, the students surged towards her. "Miss Vera," a brash boy cried out, "please sign for me." He thrust a pen at her. Laughing at the joke, she autographed a scrap of paper. "Miss Vera," crowed two or three girls side by side and giggling with excitement. They too pushed pens at her.

"Miss Vera, Miss Vera," swirled calls from all sides. A throng of dozens seethed towards her. "Miss Vera!" shouted another boy. "Sign this book—*please*—you must!" She found herself backing away, herded towards a wall. No one came to her aid. No sign of the faculty. It seemed Kanthan had abandoned her once more. Arms flailed about the celebrity, all waving pens and markers and pencils. Someone's pad struck her accidentally, dislodging her glasses. She clutched at them.

She was shaking her head, waving her hands, chagrined at the adoration of this mob. Besieged on all sides, still she could recognize the scene as ludicrous. "You don't want this from me," she kept saying over and over. "I'm just a teacher, a poet."

It was clear that at some level they all knew this, but it didn't matter. She was American. She'd been brought to see them and for them to see. When had they ever been visited by someone from beyond Rajasthan—when would they ever again? She was signing note pads and the frayed covers of textbooks, shirts and even bare arms and hands, all thrust demandingly into the path of a pen. The students kept pushing forward with desire but without intent. They'd pinned her against the wall and still they pressed tighter. It was hard to breathe. Just a little panic giggled in her throat.

"Miss Vera, Miss Veera, Veera." The sounds grew confused in her ears. Whose name were they calling? Even here the mocking pursued her. "Veera!"

*

"How you holding up?" asked Walter Tyson, reaching to give her a hand off the train at the Delhi station.

She shrugged because the answer wasn't easy. How could she explain the buffeting her own ambitions had subjected her to? His glance quickly took in the dark shadows around her eyes, the loss of flesh along her jaw and throat—his sudden concern a more reliable gauge than the mirror in her bag.

"We can slow all this down if you need. The symposium in Simla can manage without you—and you're supposed to be having some fun too. How about I arrange someone to run you to Agra for the Taj Mahal?"

"No. Thanks." She shook her head and didn't cough. "I kind of like the working just now. I'll go back to being pure tourist at the end." She didn't want to confess that lingering in Delhi seemed impossible—she needed to keep moving. She also didn't want to let on quite how pleased she was to see him. Oh, she was confident she could manage on her own, but a lift to the hotel was certainly easier this way.

"Okay," he said. "Better get some sleep then. It's an early start tomorrow. Train's at 4:30."

"Can I get a taxi at that hour?"

"No need. I'll pick you up on the way. Didn't I mention the symposium's my baby?—months and months getting the arrangements settled. So this leg of your tour we'll be traveling together."

It was only after they'd sleepily switched trains at Kalka that the sky lightened enough for the world to gradually grow visible. They'd begun to climb now, and the air was fresh and cooler. In the lingering darkness of the mountain train's old-fashioned compartment, thick stands of pines seemed to cluster close to the rails like a ragged blanket. But the trees fell away along with the darkness of night, and as they moved from hills into the first smaller mountains of Himachal Pradesh she was surprised by long vistas of naked reddish and yellow rock. No telling whether the train had already crept above the tree line, or whether men had long ago scraped these slopes bare of stumps and brush and soil.

The rails stretched where the mountains allowed, not blasting their way through but clinging to each bend, sometimes dipping, sometimes climbing sharply, always searching for the next pass, dragging the train higher. Long ago during an undergraduate history course Vera had happened to read about the summer capital of the Raj—a quiet retreat in the distant skirts of the Himalayas where the British sought relief from the furnace of May and June. Her distant studies hadn't prepared her for this: a jagged landscape of high peaks and blasted ridges. How desperate for relief the British must have been to carve this railway all the way toward Simla, seven-thousand feet high and misleadingly called a hill station.

Walter Tyson's small pair of binoculars perched on a shelf by the window. Looking up from the book in his lap as the train jolted sharply around a bend or soared for an instant at another crest, he'd gallantly offer them to her first. Twice, and then again, she couldn't bring herself to say no, delighted by the rock and sky. She studied the landscape and she found herself, rather as a surprise, studying her companion.

"Any must-sees in Simla?" she asked for the sake of hearing his voice again—she hadn't really bothered to listen to it before.

"Not much beyond the mountains themselves, as far as I know," he answered with a smile over the rims of his reading glasses. "There's the old Viceroy's palace, of course, and a famous monkey temple too—supposed to be worth the walk."

Vera nodded. Whatever adventures she might have conjured for herself in the frantic weeks between the mistaken invitation arriving and her own departure, some wild sexual fling hadn't figured among them. Oh, well, perhaps at the margins, as a never entirely not-present hope or possibility of possibility. Middle age had brought her some relief from the humiliating urges of youth, a relief ratified daily by the young men, the *boys*, in her writing and literature classes who gazed at her or through her as if she weren't entirely visible. Nor did the harried, pallid men in her department cause her pulse to race with any dangerous temptation.

Relief from urges. She shook her head now and immediately glanced up to see whether Tyson had noticed—she didn't want him thinking her any crazier than he might already suspect. Relief came at a price: a withering, a numbness on the tongue that wine and poems in small magazines and nights out with her sister never entirely chased away. If she hadn't come to India looking for a fling, no doubt somewhere in the impulsive deception lurked a desire to fly free from that lingering taste of mortality for a few weeks at least.

Walter Tyson. She smiled at the thought, deciding him a kind man, with his granny glasses perched at the end of his nose, with his slight paunch, and the prissy way he rolled his cuffs back with such care, once, twice. Ever since his initial shock at the airport, denying she might be who she claimed, he'd been quite thoughtful. Could there be any more to it than professional responsibility? She wasn't sure. She doubted it. It didn't matter.

Maybe if she could ever shake this heavy cold in her lungs and the light-headedness dogging her, maybe then it could matter.

Simla clung to a long, sweeping ridge in terraces of markets and brightly colored houses and shacks. Like a haphazard bookshelf, these terraces were articulated along three or four narrow streets, one stacked above another. As Walter Tyson and Vera Kahn emerged from the station, she was surprised by a cloud of diesel exhaust and soot hanging low about their heads. Traffic was snarled worse than Delhi, trucks too big for the streets wedged growling one against the other.

"Are you up for a short hike?" shouted Tyson in her ear. "A porter can fetch our bags, and the hotel should be walkable."

"Absolutely," she cried back.

The station sat at the bottom of the town. They set off at an easy stroll. Yet even before they'd begun to climb towards the next street she was feeling the altitude, panting heavily. She tugged at his shirt.

Distracted or daydreaming, he was startled at her touch and immediately abashed. "Sorry—sorry. Do you need to stop for a minute? Should I grab a taxi after all?"

She shook her head. "No. I'll be fine." The acrid smoke hovering in the air stung her eyes and throat and congested lungs.

Tugging out his binoculars as if he'd just noticed something, Tyson pretended to study the rather limited view west and south, the landscape through which the train had passed, giving her another moment or two. When they set off again it was at a more leisurely pace, and she could manage it, just.

The hotel was new and pleasant, not very fancy. That suited her fine. The scholars and teachers who'd been invited from across northern India to a symposium for which one Vera or another's visit was the instigating opportunity hadn't yet arrived. Dinner was scheduled as the first official function. And lunch wouldn't be served for another two hours. Despite the cough she tried to sneak away into a handkerchief—the altitude no doubt—she was restless. She wanted to see something of the town, the mountains. "Care to explore a little bit?" she asked Walter in the lobby after the porter delivered bags to their rooms.

"Oh damn, I can't right now—after lunch, for sure?" he said, looking disappointed. "I'm meeting the hotel manager about preparations for the next two days."

His straw-colored hair, thinning to be sure, still fell with a hint of boyish wildness. She was quite pleased at his reaction and smiled at him in a way she hadn't yet—hadn't in years—and headed off with a little wave in any case. She didn't want to waste what was left of the morning.

After a couple of easy switch-backs, Vera found herself on a road gradually rising. At one twist in the pavement, just below the mall, a sign marked the spot beyond which Indians weren't allowed to trespass during the days of the Raj. All about her, of course, Indians were strolling, pushing, hawking souvenirs. The only creatures not allowed beyond this marker any longer were cars and other motor vehicles. Their absence made Simla's mall, a spine of macadam along the top of the ridge, quite pleasant. The stinging cloud of soot and smoke remained trapped in the terraces below. Up here the air was fresh and even chilly, with a quick snap of wind.

Other colonial vestiges remained intact. A small stone theatre where, according to the plaque, amateur performances of Shakespeare had once been staged, now offered Hindi films and touring concerts. Banks and other looming gray-stone edifices mimicked the architecture of other distant precincts in a vanished empire. Yet at a peak in the road, next to mounted telescopes where for ten rupees one could get a clear shot to the north, a large bust of Indira Gandhi commanded the city.

But what a disappointment: the Himalayas themselves were shrouded in haze. Looking out across long valleys and lesser peaks, Vera could make out nothing beyond. The haze didn't appear terribly thick—the day's light simply seemed to fall short before it could reach the great mountains. Even plunking coins into a telescope yielded nothing.

Frustrated, she strolled farther along the mall. Narrowing gradually and climbing again, it soon turned into a lane running past private residences with high gates and bungalows guarded by lounging men in khaki and berets. At one bend in the road a fresh fit of coughing brought Vera to a halt. When it finally passed she was left with a blossoming headache. She nearly turned back in despair. But just above her head and nearly hidden by the branch of a tree—only by chance, only right here should she notice—a faded monkey urged her with all six arms to keep climbing. Intrigued by the sign, as though the message were hers alone, and unwilling to skulk back to the hotel so early, headache or not, she remembered Walter mentioning a temple.

She expected to discover it over the next rise, but nothing lay waiting for her but another sloping bend in the path— pavement had disappeared a hundred yards back. A first smudge of dirty snow appeared at the base of a pine. Other travelers were picking their way up from the town as well, she now noticed. Mostly young Indian couples attired in silken shawls and well-polished black shoes, they wore the shy, eager grins of newlyweds. Apparently a visit to Hanuman's shrine offered an auspicious beginning. So be it—she welcomed the company, the occasional conspiratorial smiles thrown to her by young brides. And, guiltily, she also wished she'd waited for Walter Tyson's company.

She was panting again, straining for the thin air. At home, treadmills and twice-a-week aerobics kept her in decent enough shape. She brushed away a glaze of sweat from her lip. If these young couples could manage the climb in saris and stiff shoes and suit coats, she could too, middle-aged westerner or not.

Any pretense of a casual stroll had long since disappeared. The slope had grown steeper, more treacherous. Rough hewn steps had been hacked into the rock, but these were slick with old ice. Beside them a gully of packed mud and scattered stones offered better footholds.

Gradually a prickly sensation of being watched put Vera on edge. Sharply she snapped her head to the side, then again up into the trees, trying to catch a glimpse of the spy. Out of the corner of her eye she noticed the dull brown rock twitch alive—a monkey swung by one arm from a tree branch and dropped to the ground. Once recognized, dozens appeared out of the thin soil, young ones darting and tumbling over each other, older, much larger monkeys staring at the human visitors, appraising them with hostile indifference. As patches of snow along the route became more frequent so did the monkeys.

Forewarned, many of the newlyweds had packed along popcorn balls as offerings. Once these were tugged into the open, the monkeys approached more boldly, screeching and demanding their due. One young bride fumbled with a paper bag of loose popcorn. She giggled nervously. Her husband, embarrassed by such behavior, stood stiffly beside her and pretended not to notice. A great gray male ambled toward the girl with its hand outstretched, impatient and querulous. She struggled not to drop the bag, clutching it against her chest, trying to extract a handful. A few grains splattered to the ground. Too proud to scrabble for stray kernels, the angry monkey hopped forward and with a scolding shriek snatched the bag from her hand. The girl shrieked too. Popcorn peppered about her feet. Her husband strode silently, furiously away.

As the peak in this ridge finally drew close, a pack of teenage boys seemed to emerge from the rock as well. They hovered about a large clearing. "You need a guide, Miss," one boy announced with a shout to Vera. Thirteen or fourteen, he was cocky and very handsome, with long lashes and delicate dark skin and a clove cigarette dangling from his mouth. Dramatically, he tossed it into a mound of snow. She couldn't hear the hiss. She shook her head.

"I'm okay," she said.

"Miss, you need a guide for the temple."

Again she shook her head and trudged forward, yearning only to reach the damn temple so she could tag it accomplished, catch her breath, and begin the hike down to the hotel. Could she make it back in time for lunch? The question occurred to her, and suddenly she was ravenous.

A blow slammed her head and shoulders from behind. Vera staggered forward, startled, terrified, trying not to fall. An attack? One of the boys? A heavy weight was riding on her back. Lurching, hunched over, she struggled to keep her balance. Something rubbed past her ear. A small hand was reaching from behind her head. It clasped angrily at her eyes, closing on her glasses and snatching them away. Eerie and disorienting, the moment froze her. The monkey leapt from her shoulders and scurried away.

Monkeys were screeching, boys were shouting. The one who'd offered his services—for bodily protection, she now understood, as much as for guidance into the temple's mysteries—raced after the animal. Vera was already picturing her appearance at the seminar. How foolish she would look staring vaguely out at the Indian scholars, attempting to recite her talk on the worst of times from memory.

Fuzzy shapes were scrambling higher off the path. The boy halted for an instant at the top of a boulder to hurl a chunk of ice at the monkey, then leapt in pursuit once more. Vera couldn't make out just when it happened, but the animal must have surrendered at last, flinging its trophy away. Because abruptly the boy was back, shoving the glasses into her hands.

"Here, good lady. I save them for you," he declared proudly.

"This deserves a big reward," another voice suggested helpfully at her elbow.

The lenses were smeared, the frame wrenched awry at one corner as she tried to re-establish the glasses on her head, hands trembling.

"You must do something for him," offered still another advisor.

Vera was aware of tourist couples watching. Gratitude, relief, embarrassment flooded her with warmth. She shoved a hand into her pocket and tugged out something more than a hundred rupees. Hardly equal to her relief, yet far beyond what the rescue warranted, she knew. Wouldn't the others despise her being such easy prey? The boy didn't hesitate, didn't wait for her to consider, but sealed her generosity by pulling the bills from her hand with a cry of "Thank you, dear lady," and a whoop of glee. In another instant Vera was abandoned, boys and monkeys and tourists vanishing with the conclusion of this particular show. What cut of the loot had the monkey earned? she wondered.

Ahead and through a thick stand of trees, she glimpsed the gray bulk of Hanuman's temple perched on a rounded knob. Shaken by the attack and its abrupt reversal, she felt no yearning to delve any further. Her mouth was dry. She coughed and coughed again, harsh and deep, a fit that doubled her over and wouldn't let her snatch a breath. At last it eased. Hesitant, teary, afraid of triggering another attack, she limped to the far side of the clearing's bare rock and snow. She needed to gather herself before braving the descent into town. And casually looked up.

Startled, Vera fell back a step as if she'd been physically struck once more. Distant and impossibly close and impossibly massive, the Himalayas loomed high above the world. No trace of haze protected her any longer. Glasses damaged or not, she made out sun striking rock, shadow caressing snow with a clarity that snatched the last air from her lungs. Earlier, on the mall in Simla, haze erasing all sight, she'd tried to imagine just where on the horizon these mountains might scratch the sky. Here and now, her vision restored, the Himalayas towered above any such human measure.

Yet this view wasn't exotic. It wasn't alien. It simply was, with a certainty of overwhelming fact. Had she been chasing illumination on this journey? No illumination here, beyond the sun striking the mountains themselves. Each stage of her journey so far, each powerful jolt that jerked her between joy and despair, might have been in preparation for this moment, softening her up so she could see. She saw, yes, and she had no idea what to make of it. Poetry failed to soar from her soul as it might have done when she was younger. Barren, spent, her spirit cowered before the ordinariness of the rock before her eyes and beneath her feet. She felt able to see and she felt small and alone and afraid.

*

She was aware that Walter Tyson had summoned a doctor. She was grateful to him, wished she could tell him so, accepted the fact she couldn't.

"It is altitude sickness. No doubt about it," the young doctor was saying. She felt the distant stab of an injection. "With any luck this will do the trick for her, quite quickly no doubt."

She felt very bad that the seminar would be disrupted and Walter put to more trouble. Well, surely they could carry on without her. She wasn't whom they'd been expecting anyway.

"It is a puzzle to me. No, if it doesn't work already, another dose will be without effect and as well may be dangerous."

The side of the bed sagged and Vera opened her eyes. Walter Tyson was leaning on an arm, studying her closely. Startled to find her gazing up at him, he drew back. She tried to smile. He lay his hand on her arm—she could feel it.

"Should I get a med-evac helicopter up from Delhi?"

She wasn't sure which of them he was asking.

"I think it is a bug I don't know," the young doctor was saying. "It may be one she brought with her."

As she approached the edge of waking, she sensed a light in the room and a larger darkness beyond it. A jumble of quiet voices. Were they close by? Where was she? she wondered, without opening her eyes. She wasn't sure yet, wasn't quite awake. Those voices—were they her parents?

For a terrifying moment she wasn't sure quite where she was, quite who she was. She was sick—that much she knew. Her face felt hot, her throat parched. But still she wouldn't open her eyes. It seemed far too great a challenge. She wasn't ready. The only certain fact was her own awareness. She took that in. She was she and the rest of the universe, small or large, was not she. It lay outside, beyond her closed eyes. Terrified and determined—with all her soul and all her might she'd cling. Teeth clenched, she wrestled to hold her own.

The electric light in the room had been switched off but, coming to herself, Vera saw a grayish light leaking in from beyond the windows. Dawn or dusk, she couldn't tell. Walter Tyson was sitting, arms on knees, in a chair by the window. Realizing she'd awakened, he rose and drew close. His face was dark with shadow and with concern.

"The copter's already landed, but the ridge wouldn't let them get very close. We're waiting for an ambulance to come ferry us up to the mall."

She wanted to smile at him again, at Walter Tyson, but she was weak—when had she ever felt so weak, her body and her head and even the muscles of her jaw so heavy. And yet she also felt light, terribly light, as if the faintest puff of breeze might sweep her away entirely.

"I'm sorry about all this," she whispered, surprising them both.

"Don't be," he said and touched her arm again. She wished he'd keep his hand on her arm. Just a little while. "It was our mistake, not yours. I should have done my homework better before sending an invitation."

A giggle—did she have the strength for a giggle? "Not that, silly man. You'd have liked my talk." Exhausted, she couldn't say any more.

Tyson snorted, laughing for them both. "One damn talk? You can recite it for me later. Once we get you to the East-West Hospital in Delhi. It's their copter." Prattling on, he was sounding worried again.

Vera guessed the journey back down, even by helicopter, would be all she could manage. Thirsty, she glanced to a side table and, understanding, Walter Tyson brought a cup of water to her lips.

Americaland

This was the first moment he'd felt outright alarm. Oh, there'd been intense feelings aplenty since arriving in India—awe certainly, delight too, and no few instances of disgust—but it was only sitting in this small dim room surrounded by eleven ladies in bright saris that he'd sensed such open hostility.

"What do you intend to offer our students?" asked Mrs. Sharma, the department chair. She gestured for a servant to pour tea.

Overhead a ceiling fan turned slowly, as if to acknowledge the heat rather than relieve it.

Matthew Saunders, sweating and uncomfortable, wondered if the question were some kind of trick. "As we discussed in the correspondence . . . ."

"*We* were not privy to any such correspondence," snapped Mrs. Kapoor, who was sitting at the other side of the circle, wrapped in purple and gold. "*We* only learned of your appointment yesterday when the faculty reconvened for the new term."

He nodded, feeling foolish, yet unable to provide a better response on the spot. He considered tasting the tea in order to temporize, to distract his antagonists. But the chamber was already stifling and hot tea could only make things worse. A drop of sweat gathered dramatically at the tip of his chin and, before he could swipe it away, dove in full view of his audience toward his lap.

Though swathed in their lavishly flowing saris, the ladies of the English department seemed perfectly at ease, save for their open annoyance at having this male thrust upon them.

Dr. Indra Banerji, president of Lady O.D.C. College, had informed him earlier that same morning that he would be the first man ever to serve in the faculty ranks of her elite institution. She had made it sound an honor and privilege. Only now did he grasp the equal measure of peril.

"It's not really an appointment per se," Saunders replied in the direction of Mrs. Kapoor. "As a Fulbright lecturer, I have been assigned here for only six months. And as for what classes I might offer, Dr. Banerji suggested I go with my specialty—postcolonial literature."

Several of the women glanced skeptically at each other.

"Yes, the principal has a habit of arranging these unexpected treats for us," said Mrs. Sharma at his side. "They enhance the stature of the college, I am sure. But she does not necessarily consider what the needs of our department or our students may actually be."

Saunders pictured the footlocker he'd lugged along from the other side of the world. Heavy, unwieldy, it contained novels, textbooks, critical studies that he'd intended to bequeath to students in his classes. He'd assumed such fashionable texts would not be readily available here—that they would be a welcome gift. It had not occurred to him that they might be unnecessary altogether.

His shirt stuck to his skin. Sweat was dripping from his hair. He'd grown desperately parched. He reached for the small cup on the table. Remarkably, two swallows of milky tea helped almost at once, slaking his thirst and even cooling his skin.

Only a few heartbeats later, however, he was all but overwhelmed by a different, urgent need.

"Excuse me," he whispered to Mrs. Sharma. "May I use a restroom?"

She looked at him blankly.

"A lavatory?" he said.

Other members of the department rustled with their own consternation.

"I'm afraid the faculty toilet is for women only," Mrs. Sharma explained.

"Male servants generally make use of the alley," offered Mrs. Kapoor with a vague wave of her hand.

Saunders took her meaning at once, but he was becoming desperate enough to consider the suggestion.

"Come." Mrs. Sharma gestured with brisk inspiration.

She led him down a flight of stone steps to the principal's office. "I'm sure Dr. Banerji will not mind," she said, ushering him toward the private washroom.

"Oh, well, that's just *Americaland*, isn't it? No one ever actually goes there."

With simple disdain Priya Parvati had thus dismissed the idea of visiting the embassy compound. This was several months earlier, Matthew reading aloud to her on the phone from his small cottage in Ohio. According to the letter he was holding, it seemed that as Fulbright Lecturer he'd be granted access to the US Embassy's commissary, the pool, other such amenities.

Final plans for their separate and joint sabbaticals were just then coming into focus. Priya was to join him a month after his arrival. To all but her parents they would present themselves as husband and wife, since living openly together under any other arrangement would still, even in this day and age, be considered unacceptable.

Saunders, now on his own in the city, was certain that once Priya did join him, arriving at about the same time as the cooling monsoons, he would be able to resist Americaland's allure. For the time being, however, he did not even try. Its comforts beckoned.

He emerged through the college gates after the initial interview with his new colleagues—*welcome* didn't seem the word to characterize the exchange. On the main thoroughfare, taxis beat motionlessly against the thick river of other cars and busses, of bullock carts, bicycle rickshaws, peddlers with their flowers, their packs of playing cards, various portraits of gods and Bollywood stars. Over all there hovered a great cloud of dust and heat and blaring horns.

An impulse struck him. Saunders rather delighted in its recklessness. He'd never really been one given to recklessness. But what else could one call snaring a tricycle-scooter on the fly? Before he'd even fully alighted on the seat the scooter-wallah flung it toward the first intersection.

The air was scorching, but having it blown full in the face was better than sitting still in the immense and dusty oven of the city.

Traffic lights blinked their signals but the scooter-wallah flew without notice or pause. Busses too he ignored. Their riders were leaning far out of windows, clinging to door rails as the behemoths swayed heavily down the avenues. The scooter wove between them and around, sometimes aimed in the dead center of the highway, then swerving hard and running along its verge, and on into the next eddy of vehicles.

Matthew Saunders gave himself up to death, accepting it as both imminent and certain. All fear was thereby skimmed from him. He felt giddy and light.

When at last he dismounted in the diplomatic quarter of the city and paid the scooter-wallah something equal to a month's wages, Matthew Saunders, Senior Fulbright Fellow, was windblown and filthy. Abashed, he tucked in his shirt and pushed fingers through his hair before marching to the main gate of the embassy, precious pass held out before him.

Americaland. Yes, once he'd crossed through the passage it really did feel that way, as if into a different universe altogether. Everything glittered, bright and clean, calm and quiet. Orderly. Just the sight of the Olympic-sized swimming pool, families cavorting in the afternoon sun, refreshed and revived his spirit. He'd certainly take a swim himself later, before returning to his spartan flat with some groceries from the commissary.

The bar was dim and cool. At this early hour only one or two other souls sat by themselves in its pleasant gloom. CNN was blaring just a little too loudly from a TV above the bar, but even that was welcome. He signaled for a tall gin and tonic, and then a second, moisture gathering ever so delicately on the outside of its glass that was, ever so quickly, emptied.

Saunders felt he was coming to himself.

His watch read five p.m. He tried the arithmetic, and then double-checked with the bartender. Yes, six-thirty at home. A.M. Though he'd yet to figure out how the extra half-hour came into the equation—no doubt some long-ago incident of superlative historical note. All that mattered, however, was telephoning Priya for their agreed-upon weekly chat.

"You're in that place, aren't you?" she said by way of affectionate greeting.

Why not, *Oh darling, I've missed you so dreadfully?* he wondered. Then he acknowledged silently that any such dialogue belonged to a different relationship entirely.

"Well, yes," he replied. "But it's much easier to make the call from here. I'm not sure where else I could even manage it."

"It's just so, well, *colonial.*"

He sighed and traced a finger through the condensation on his glass. "Once you're here, you'll never have to see it—I promise. And I won't have any desire. Not for this."

Priya was his soul-mate. So she'd told him and so he believed. Though at thirty-five he was, he knew perfectly well, rather long in the tooth for the discovery of one's first true soul-mate. That recognition only made him the more grateful.

They didn't teach in the same department, thank heavens. No, she'd attended his panel at a Modern Language convention and sought him out in the scrum afterwards, eager to explain the manifold ways in which his understanding of post-colonial literary theory in general and of Indian culture in particular were simplistic, out of date, and hinted at a paternalistic condescension. He'd lifted both hands in a gesture seeking truce if not offering surrender. And because she taught at a smaller and slightly less prestigious college, because he was eight years older and tenured and already had a published book in the hamper, because of her eyes, he chose not to be wounded by her assault.

Two years later they were alternating weekends, as often as possible, between small town and big city. They'd arrange months in advance to attend the same scholarly conferences. Finally, they were each applying for sabbatical in India, he on a Fulbright, she with an NEH grant to perform research in a dusty government archive. Only in the final stages of planning did they realize that the academic year at Lady O.D.C. College commenced in early August, a full month before Priya's visa allowed her to arrive.

The next morning he set out early for the college. Mr. Singh, the ever-present taxi-wallah at the corner outside his apartment building, seemed to have anticipated the need. He had the door open to his car when Saunders emerged and this would become their invariable routine.

When he arrived once more at the college,, few of his new colleagues were yet to be seen around the grounds or hallways. The full heat of the day had not descended either. Despite the dust and dead-kiln smell that shrouded the courtyard and gardens, as if the rains had abandoned them forever, he acknowledged that Lady O.D.C. College was spare and lovely.

One of the male servants showed him his classroom. Large fans spun slowly in the ceiling. Girls began to flush into the room in small groups, though one and all of them stopped and stared when they saw him, then with giggles and averted eyes took their places among rows facing a wooden platform with table and chair.

Matthew waited until the room was full before mounting the platform. He was used to a more informal environment—he'd have his American students drag their chairs into a circle or join them at a single seminar table. This arrangement struck him as awkward and unnatural. He considered leaning against the table, but there wasn't enough space. Grey and rickety, it seemed unlikely to bear his weight. Reluctantly, he settled on the chair, and looked out over fifty pairs of eyes dark as Priya's.

"Good morning," he said.

"Good morning, Professor Saunders," they shouted in chorus.

Much of the night he'd spent awake in his small flat, the single air conditioning unit groaning feebly and perspiring a steady leak down the wall, as he prepped a lecture on *Jane Eyre*. This would have been a challenge in any event, since the Nineteenth Century British Novel lay far outside his usual classes. That he hadn't read Bronte's novel himself since sophomore year in college didn't make it easier. On the other hand, he'd discovered long ago that teaching a text he knew only casually was more straightforward than trying to make a sensible argument about one with which he'd wrestled years upon years. The better he knew a novel, the more it would baffle and bully him with nuance and with contradiction.

*

After class, Saunders made his way upstairs to the staff lounge, an open-air chamber shaded by great Peepul trees outside the windows. Fans induced a semblance of breeze across faded couches and chairs. He claimed a space off to one side and ordered a cup of tea from yet another male servant. This fellow smiled conspiratorially and refused the 50 paisa that Matthew offered in payment.

He was content—truly—sitting by himself with *The Hindustan Times* when Mrs. Sharma and Mrs. Kapoor settled onto ottoman cushions across the same table.

"And how did your lecture go today?" asked Mrs. Sharma. She was a plump woman well advanced into her sixties, her graying hair parted in the middle with a streak of vermillion powder. The bindi above her eyes was a teardrop of dark gold today. What this change signified—yesterday's round dot had been bright red—he had no clue. This was how he felt about India in general after his first week—a constant bombardment of signals for which he lacked any crib.

What he did make out, however, was that somehow his status had assumed a different slant in the hours since yesterday's interview. No longer was he an outright intruder. Instead, Mrs. Sharma's manner (if not so clearly the faintly puckered frown on Mrs. Kapoor's face) suggested that he was to be treated from here on as a young and naïve apprentice, adopted by the ladies of the faculty as they might a foundling. With this as well, and very much to his surprise, he was entirely content.

"But I thought your parents lived in Gurgaon. That you'd be taking me to meet them for Diwali."

He heard Priya sigh on the other end of the line.

"Okay," she said. "I'm sorry, Matthew. Truly, I am. But the simple truth is I lied to you." She sounded brisk and almost matter-of-fact.

He knew her—they were soul-mates—this meant she was being defensive, trying to hide powerful emotions.

Outside the embassy compound a long rolling boom of thunder announced the start of that afternoon's heavy rains. The monsoon had come late this year, vanquishing at last the dry, withering heat. Now Americaland served as refuge while the downpour lasted.

"Don't you see?" she said. "If I'd told you all along they live in Newark, you would make such a big deal about meeting them before now. You, you'd insist on playing the proper suitor or bridegroom or something equally ridiculous."

He could see her dismissing the absurdity with a wave of her hand.

"Oh my god," she said, as if just now considering the image anew and finding it freshly impossible, unthinkable.

"Okay," he said, though he had no idea what was okay.

"Mummy's taken a bad turn. Her blood pressure is spiking high, and the doctors can't find anything. Daddy is beside himself. He can't possibly deal. *She's* always been the one to take care of illnesses."

"I understand, Darling. But what does it mean?"

Another sigh, this one longer, leading nowhere. "It means I've postponed my sabbatical until next year. The dean has been very understanding."

"Ah," he said.

*

Gita and Anjana, two of Matthew Saunders' favorite students, third years, came originally from the south, one from Madras, one from Kerala. Since neither had family in Delhi, they were among the girls who lived in the hostel on the grounds of the college. After class one day in late October they invited Professor Saunders to join them for Diwali celebrations.

He paused, books and papers gathered in his arms. The mention of Diwali had caused a pang, but there was no way to explain, nothing to be done. "I'd like that," he said.

Somehow, and he'd never quite confronted his own feelings, the absurdity of what he'd planned and hoped, he'd maintained a secret fiction that Priya would yet appear. Odd though he knew it to be, they had continued to speak once a week as if nothing had happened, though all their conversations seemed unanchored to any particular world in which they might actually live. This allowed him to believe, never breathing the thought aloud, that surely her plans would swing again by shear force of desire. She would join him in time for the Indian holidays. She would come to him here in her city and she would take him to visit her parents in Gurgaon.

Except of course that they were in Newark, not Gurgaon. How much of all she'd told him had been made of such untruths?

It seemed the invitation from his students had lanced the little fiction swiftly, cleanly. Not even a twinge of pain or suck of breath troubled him as it disappeared, however. That's all that startled him. It cleared his gaze.

By early evening the city had grown strangely subdued in anticipation of the Diwali festivities. In his several months acquaintance, Saunders had never seen the streets so empty, so quiet.

A heavy dusk had begun to settle as he arrived back at the small campus. As per their routine, Mr. Singh halted the taxi outside the college gates, which had been closed already, earlier than usual. Firecrackers popped loudly in surrounding streets and alleys. Bottle rockets whizzed invisibly through the air. But this all felt distant and unthreatening.

The guard with a bad hip recognized Saunders and saluted him with good humor. Limping, he dragged one heavy frame of the gate far enough for the American to slip through. Inside the college grounds, the dirt paths were lined with red earthenware bowls, alight with oil and floating wicks. As he approached the hostel it too was alight, every window, every flat surface blazing with lamps and candles.

The front door swung open at his approach. Formidable as ever, Mrs. Kapoor seemed to have been waiting for him. Senior housemother and warden, she also lived in the hostel, though in a separate apartment.

"Oh, Doctor Saunders, we are so pleased you've come," she said, startling him with a pat on the arm. By the standards of the last few months, this was an astonishing display of intimacy. "It's good of you to show this special attention to our pupils. They're terribly excited. Yes, yes, come this way," she commanded tartly, ushering him through the hallways. She walked briskly to the small dining hall and delivered him to the waiting girls before disappearing back into her own flat.

Gita and Anjana came up to him demurely, repressing their obvious excitement, and each bowed, hands pressed together.

"Sir, welcome," said Anjana.

"Welcome, Sir," said Gita.

He'd bought a bouquet of roses and carnations in the local market that afternoon but hadn't thought to separate it. Awkwardly he offered it to the space between the two young women and they each put a hand out. Then he returned the bow as best he could, fingers touching his forehead, smiling but solemn.

The girls were dressed in their best attire. Long silken scarves of purple and pink, green and salmon, floated about their throats. At one end of a long table in the commissary they'd carefully arranged plates and cutlery for the three of them. Other girls looked on with mirth and excitement.

They directed him to a stool at the head of the table. Saunders allowed them to serve.

"Go ahead," he said. "Now it's your turn."

"No, Sir, no," said Gita, shaking her head.

Anjana laughed. "You must go first. It's the proper way."

They'd set fork, spoon, and knife, along with a paper napkin at his place, and he hesitated, considering the different modes of addressing the food heaped on his plate. If Priya were here, she'd make clear with a simple gesture that he should use the utensils like the westerner he was. At last he picked up a nan, tore it, and scooped rice and dal into his mouth. This too made all the girls laugh.

Some while later and sleepy after so much food, Saunders was wondering if it might be possible to slip away before dessert without offending his hosts. As conversation continued, he eyed the syrupy balls of gulab jamun sitting in large serving bowls. At that very moment, however, and without apparent plan or cause, Diwali erupted in its immensity. Saunders didn't quite notice, at least not consciously, the first rolling thunder that passed in a wave over the city. He was trying vainly to shout the end of a sentence, something about *Silas Marner*, to Gita, who was sitting only inches away.

But the next explosion lurched him right off his stool. Staggering, he stared out into the night through an open balustrade. The slum that leaned against the college's outer wall seemed to have launched a terrible assault. This great boom was followed by another greater still that rang in his ears, rang in his kidneys.

Yet these initial blasts served only to announce a more general barrage. The firecrackers he'd heard earlier had been a trickery, nothing more than a mild carbonation to the atmosphere in anticipation of this greater assault. Soon individual explosions lost all definition within the steady welter of deep, thudding blows.

The sound pummeled him. Shock and awe overwhelmed him. He had never thought himself a coward, but only the sight of thirty girls gathered in the open windows of the dining hall, gazing out into the invisible maelstrom with excitement and perfect ease, kept him from seeking shelter under the trestle tables. What would Priya have done? For once he couldn't imagine.

As a special treat, Anjana's uncle had secured them a box of sparklers for the holiday. Mrs. Kapoor had granted permission as well. Each wand was a good three feet in length, its sparkles less sparks than flashing flames akin to tiny blades. Matthew feared for the girls' clothes, their fingers, their eyes.

Then, ever the generous host, Gita proffered one to him.

Smiling warily, he accepted the wand as if it were one of the cobras swaying atop baskets in the narrow streets. "Thanks," he mimed as she lit it. The sparkler tingled, vibrating, sparks dancing as he waved it at arm's length. Just as it sputtered out, a bone-jarring blast from the alley jolted the dying stick from his fingers.

And still and on and forever it seemed, the deafening, pounding roar of explosions continued, pulsing through the city, joining all its citizens beneath a crashing wave beyond mere sound.

Professor Saunders had intended to share the holiday meal with his students. He'd thus be storing up another cultural experience to share with Priya by phone—even if she were in Newark with her ailing mother, not Gurgaon—or carry safely to the flat for later savor, transcribing the memory carefully into his moleskin journal. By eleven o'clock, his lectures ready for the next day, he'd have been safely abed.

Instead, no alternative offered itself other than to endure the celebration of Ram's great victory over Ravana, the vanquishing of darkness by the forces of light, all while trying to conceal from Anjana, Gita, and the other girls his own dismay at the onslaught.

It was after midnight when he finally emerged from the grounds of Lady O.D.C. College. Mr. Singh had long since returned home. No other taxis or scooters were to be found. He had no choice but to return and tap at Mrs. Kapoor's door. She seemed neither surprised nor satisfied with his plight. Rather, she motioned him to sit while she telephoned a servant to come round with the ancient college vehicle, a grey Ambassador with curtains in the windows, usually reserved for ceremonial occasions.

The old car glided through empty streets. A heavy pall of coarse smoke hung in the air. The city was peaceful, the kind of peace that might come after panic had chased all its denizens into exile, into traceless oblivion. No sign of life or movement appeared in a place that usually teemed with a vast surplus of both. Despite the acrid stink of smoke and gunpowder, Matthew kept the window open at his side. He needed what air his lungs could find. His ears were ringing. His chest felt hollow and battered.

In the morning, Delhi had been restored to itself. Matthew emerged from his apartment block, showered and fragile. His hearing still seemed muddled. The morning light shone more weakly than before, more watery, as if it had modulated to a different key. He wasn't sure whether this was his imagination or a first suggestion of the winter approaching in what was, after all, a city built in the desert.

Something seemed changed in him too, though change was perhaps too grand a word. He couldn't quite put his finger on the feeling. Perhaps he'd been modulated to a new key as well. That was the distant ringing in his ears, as if he'd been struck upon the skull, vibrating now to a single note that belonged to a strange new chord.

Mr. Singh the taxi-wallah awaited his appearance as on every other school day. His car was freshly washed, its rear door open by the curb. Matthew climbed into the taxi and acknowledged that, however he felt, this was just another day. According to habit, after his teaching duties and a conference or two with students, no doubt he'd make his way across the city to the embassy, to Americaland, for the weekly call to Priya. Unusually, however, Americaland seemed entirely unnecessary and unbeckoning this morning, as distant in its way as Priya, as Newark, eight-thousand miles away.

Steps Through Sand, Through Fire

When the silver headdress slipped again over Gerald Knapper's eyes, causing him finally to lose the balance he'd been struggling to maintain for nearly an hour and plummet from the high white horse—an ill-tempered and ill-treated brute—and into the red Indian dust, the jarring pain in his left shoulder jolted the breath right out of him. He flailed, wrestling against the clenched muscle of his own chest. His eyes widened in despair and fear as he choked. At last, at last, the spasm loosened, allowing him a gasp, a short breath, a flicker of tears. He lay panting, feeling relief and gratitude above all. The worst of the humiliation was surely behind him now.

Even through that first flash of pain and of loose grit slamming into his teeth and nose, he'd heard the ragged cry of merriment from twenty-five boys and men, most of them hired for the occasion. They were his retinue, what had to pass for his family, his friends. Blowing reedy horns, beating cymbals, they accepted his embarrassing tumble as merely another inevitable event in the ceremony. (But certainly also as yet another gaffe by this ludicrous American, a pale, middle-aged man whom they could mock even as they cheered him as hero, the conquering bridegroom.)

"Respected sir," said one old man with an extravagant mustache, gray and coarse as rhino tusks twisting off to either side of his lean jaw. Roughly shoving his large, gnarled hands under Gerald's arms, he hoisted him to his feet. In an instant the others had set upon him as well, patting the dust from his suit, punching at him to demonstrate his own well being, and shoving the silver helmet back across his brow.

Thus was he planted, sagging but upright, before Ravi Singh, the man about to become his brother-in-law. Ravi wore a casually restrained smile. "Hard luck. No need to worry," said the younger man. His speech was just as perfect though slightly more clipped than his sister's. After college at St. Stephen's in Delhi, Ravi had spent two years in London and Cambridge, whereas Sita had gone to the States. His accent was no more British, however, than hers was American—they spoke the Indian-rooted English of Delhi's new princelings, at home anywhere on the globe.

Gerald sensed not only Ravi's vague amusement but his disdain as well. And for the first time in nearly a month he realized a truth that had been veiled before—that he was in some sort of struggle with this young man, that they were wrestling in the shadow behind word and deed and even his own conscious intention. But this wasn't what he cared about. It wasn't why he was here. He was too old to waste any emotional force on this younger man, the brother of his bride. Patting at the dust on his linen suit, Gerald was perfectly willing to grin and shrug in disarming acknowledgment of the ludicrous spectacle he presented.

No dust dared soil Ravi Singh's double-breasted blazer, nor his tasseled loafers, nor the polished nails on the hand he flicked at the small mob. Instantly, as if the American were no more than a rather rumpled puppet, they heaved him once more atop the garlanded white horse that had already carried him better than a mile from Ravi's house. Hands bolstered him aloft so that he could clutch the headdress in place. Rampant and in artificial triumph, Gerald rode a last few yards towards the high painted gates of the wedding pavilion. It had been erected in the shadows of a nameless emperor's monument, and Gerald assumed that the staging of a private wedding in these otherwise public gardens in the heart of Delhi was one mark of the family's influence.

All evening he'd struggled against a late arrival. It was the one failure, the one mark of bad grace that he dreaded. Hundreds of elaborate crimson invitations had been launched into the world, clearly announcing 6 p.m. as the start of festivities. But the horse hadn't appeared at Ravi's door until nearly seven, and then the procession scudded so slowly through the streets, what with the cheering and braying of horns and the clapping of hand and drum, not to mention his own precarious mount, that at times they seemed to be drifting in hapless ebb rather than toward his Sita. Now, finally, having survived his fall, Gerald prodded his steed through the twenty-foot papier-mâché arch festooned with auspicious marigolds. To a last ragged cheer from his distracted cohort—they were already peering towards handouts of wedding food and additional gifts of coin—Gerald Knapper, the groom, did arrive.

No one noticed. A spare spatter of guests who'd come early in order to slip away to other affairs were milling about rather vaguely, attentive only to passing trays of food and drink, greeting each other with caws and kisses. No sign anywhere of Sita or her parents. Once again Gerald felt he'd gone wrong, that he should have known better, that even as he was dismounting he'd stumbled another wrong step in a dance whose proper rhythm eluded him.

Most of his retinue had abandoned him at the scaffolding just inside the ornate movie-set gate. Surprised, alone, he glanced back and saw plastic jugs splashing something clear, no doubt something potent, into their mugs and cupped palms. This, plus handfuls of rupees doled out earlier and hope of more to come, kept a few of these hired friends faithful to their horns and drums, welcoming guests as they appeared. For a long moment, staggering a bit now that he was off the horse, shorn of his make-believe troupe, still balancing Sita and Ravi's great-grandfather's silver helmet, metal tassels and all, on his head, Gerald felt as disoriented as at any moment since arriving in India. He was also struck by his apparent invisibility, given that the elaborate pageant only beginning to gather momentum was in honor of his wedding.

A constellation of enormous tents stretched away to all sides. Carpets large and small were strewn across the dirt and dust and grass, elegant Persian designs next to coir mats and wide strips of green plastic turf.

Not for the first time, Gerald regretted failing to persuade Sita to marry him in Columbus. Larry Tomsich, a friend of many years and local magistrate, would have performed the task simply and tastefully. A few friends in attendance. Perhaps even one of his children might have deigned to come—they'd have thought him merely foolish then, rather than out-and-out crazy. But Sita held fast. She couldn't do such a thing to her parents. Though he sensed even from half a world away that given her age—past eighteen, past twenty-five, even past thirty and fled to America—the family had all but abandoned hope of any proper marriage for her.

Thinking of Sita flooded him with joy like a schoolboy and a first crush. Without warning, it swept over him and rooted him in this moment, this place, glad for the incense in the air, the dust, even the distant waft of burning cow dung in the February night. He loved her with a passion that he'd thought long extinguished. Over nearly a year of dinners and gallery visits and chaste strolls along the Scioto River—and then, finally, when he'd nearly crashed against the limits of what he could endure, the not so chaste retreat into her modest TA-funded apartment at the university, (never, not yet, not until after this marriage, into the far from modest house in Upper Arlington that he'd shared with his wife Margot)—she'd brought him alive again. For this he was willing to travel anywhere, undergo any ordeal, even a wedding like this.

As Gerald stood gazing into the hazy evening, Sita appeared as if conjured by his thoughts from out of the incense and smoke. Her mother in a plum-colored sari on one arm, father on the other, she came gliding toward him, transformed, and Gerald was frightened. This was his first glimpse of her all day. Her eyes were dark with kohl, their lids the blue of a bird. A single diamond stud pierced her nostril. Her own sari was wound tight about her and yet seemed to be flowing all at once, an infinitely fine fabric of gold embroidery on crimson with a single loop covering the back of her head and neck. Her long dark hair was pulled back tight from her face. Looking up from under at him, she might have been ten years younger. She might have been a stranger.

Perhaps she spied the anxiety in his eyes. She lifted her fingers to her mouth, and that little gesture, covering her lips as if with an alarmed modesty, made all the world right. It was something Sita did—a reflex so delicate and personal to her that for him it seemed an intimate signature. Seeing it this evening, spying it here, almost hurt him with gladness. It certainly aroused him.

Her parents relinquished her with looks of mingled relief and concern. "We must greet our guests," she said, approaching him and touching his arm lightly.

He nodded and the silver helmet nearly tumbled into his hands. "When can I take this damn thing off?" he whispered more fiercely than he'd intended. "It weighs a ton. And I feel like the schoolroom dunce." He smiled to make the plea into a joke.

Lips pressed tight, she shook her head. "Stop, please, Gerald. Haven't we been through this? Come, come—there's no taking it off. Family tradition is family tradition. The bloody thing must be endured."

"Only for you," he murmured.

She cocked her head to the side, acknowledging his tenderness with a little smile. It stabbed him with the pain of his own love for her. And it also forced him to dodge once again the awareness that though she loved him—he dared not doubt it—it was not with an intensity that could match his own.

Touching his arm once more, Sita steered him toward one cluster of guests and then another. Although conversation was almost entirely in English, its sounds had been shaped locally, like the graft of a foreign plant onto sturdy new roots, and Gerald's ear hadn't yet been trained to make sense of them—he missed much of what was said, even when directly to him. On the other hand, no one seemed put off by his awkwardness. They smiled and nodded. They thought it charming that he'd learned to press his palms together and salute them with an earnest *Namaste*—charming as a child may be both charming and silly. Like a tolerant, even doting nurse, Sita beamed and steered him proudly about.

Gerald stifled as best he could a swelling resentment. Charming, yes—he'd certainly intended to generate seas of good will on behalf of this woman and her family. But not by being a source of amusement, first for Ravi and now these others. In general, he prided himself on his equanimity, his good will. It had been hard won. Margot's death after five years of battling breast cancer, its remission, its return and blasted triumph, had all but swamped him with despair. To that moment he could trace a chasm spreading between himself and his children, one that had never entirely healed. But his spirits did slowly revive, broadening into an unexpected contentedness in middle age, along with a considerable financial success. Discovering Sita and then persuading her to marry him—these only increased his sense of rare fortune. He was perfectly willing to offer patience and generosity to the world about him. But, but: playing the fool for these wealthy Indians, whatever good will it might earn, was wearing his patience thin.

With a sough like a gathering wind, the crowd's attention swerved away from the bridal couple. Gerald too turned and spotted a silver Ambassador, still the car of official India, with darkened windows and little flags flickering on its fenders, draw to the painted gates of the wedding pavilion. Like an electric spark, word leapt across the sea of craning faces: Gangaswami had arrived! A celebrity among celebrities, the holy man and political guru alone was permitted to be driven this far. Ravi bestowed this honor on him because of the honor that Gangaswami brought in turn to the family by appearing and even participating in the ceremony.

A young boy, fourteen perhaps, with a shaggy head of hair and dressed in a gray jacket and tight pants, scrambled from a front seat and hurried to open the car's rear door. Heavy curtains blocked any glimpse inside. A massive hand thrust out into the night air wielding a heavy black stick, which it planted in the dust. Another hand grasped at the boy's neck and shoulders, part caress and part throttle, threatening to drag him back into the dark maw of the automobile. But the boy braced himself, one hand against the doorframe, legs leveraged into the dirt. Slowly, by stages, an arm, a leg, the gradual shifting of the great bulk of his torso, Gangaswami emerged. Immense in girth, jovial and commanding, he raised a hand in the air and thus allowed the multitude of servants and guests to breathe again. Until that moment they'd been unaware of having ceased in anticipation.

Gerald had first met the god man (as he'd seem him called in the Indian papers, partly in tribute, partly ridicule), shortly after arriving in Delhi. Hurrying to the door of his house, Ravi Singh had grasped the visitor's arm and helped him cross the threshold. As a favor to the rising young political star and scion of one of India's lordliest families, Gangaswami had offered to consult personally on the wedding now being planned. Ravi ushered him through to a salon specially prepared for the audience.

It wasn't until their guest had been settled monumentally onto a vast sofa that the orientation of the room, its deep chairs and other furnishings, came clear to Gerald. He himself had been steered to a solitary, hard settee. Sita was perched across the way, impossibly distant. A family crescent seemed to stretch along Gangaswami's arm span—father and mother, several aunts and uncles and who-knew-else—gathered neatly on either side. Ravi remained standing behind the sofa, sometimes leaning casually to whisper in his guest's ear.

For the sake of politeness, Gangaswami picked at the delicacies and sweets set beside him on a platter, sipped at a glass of water. At last he turned his gaze fully on Gerald Knapper. Behind heavy black spectacles his eyes were small and set too closely together for the amount of flesh about them. Yet they were sharp and full of good humor. He beamed more broadly at the American, and suddenly Gerald was washed by an astonishing flood of warmth. The power of the guru's personality, his sheer presence, was oddly comforting at the same time it was overwhelming. Almost a physical pummeling, it unsettled Gerald in his seat. He felt vulnerable, almost naked before him. Yet he also had to resist an urge to rise and hurry toward the man. This was new—Gerald had dealt with the rich and powerful, but never anyone with such a force. Now he glimpsed how Gangaswami had gathered so much influence, so many proteges among the political elite, from prime ministers to high tech moguls.

"I do not see that it makes any difference," Gangaswami was saying with a toss of his hand, tilting his head first to one side of the family audience and then to other without yet taking his eyes off of Gerald. His voice was itself a surprise:

nasal and reedy, almost childishly high-pitched. "If we want to make a proper wedding, there is no reason not to do so. What do the gods of his parents matter so long as he does not reject ours?"

"Sorry?" said Gerald, looking first at the guru and then to Sita. She was staring into her lap. Her parents, the elder Singh and his wife, looked as startled as Gerald. They didn't seem able to respond.

Ravi understood at once. He glanced at his father and then spoke to Gerald. "We of course originally agreed with the notion of a civil wedding, because a traditional one— a Hindu wedding—seemed out of the question. But now that our eminent friend has opened our eyes to what is possible, the family will be happy to welcome you as one of its sons in the traditional way. No one will dare challenge Shri Gangaswami's ruling."

"Sita?" Gerald said. Still she wouldn't face him but blushed deeply and gave the hint of a shrug. "Sorry," he said again. "But this is a little too quick, a little too, well, crazy. You're not giving me a chance to catch up."

"My friend," said Gangaswami with patience and generous good will, "this is a great and unusual honor my friends, Ravi Singh's family, are offering you. We do not say you must give up your gods that you were raised with. Simply that you say welcome to ours, and they will welcome you as well."

Gerald shook his head, but no one seemed to notice. Was this possible? Could he do such a thing? He hadn't been to shul since Margot's death, and never very vigorously before. To what degree did he feel himself bound to have no gods before one who, after all, had been perfectly pleased to keep his own distance? Gerald realized he wasn't much concerned with betraying that God of his youth. Still—he worried whether he might be betraying something of himself in the bargain.

Like moths to a swollen candle, the wedding guests found themselves fluttering toward and about Gangaswami. He was leaning heavily on his cane as he waded through the enveloping crowd. Beaming, his head wagging from side to side, he moved forward, taking notice—making contact, however brief—with apparently everyone. His presence glowed through the throng. The servants, carrying platters of food, circling with beverages, could hardly draw their gaze from the god man.

Gerald's eyes sought out Ravi Singh. Left hand stylishly jabbed in his jacket pocket—who is he, the goddam Prince of Wales? Gerald wondered—Ravi appeared delighted by the delight and distraction of his guests. He was smiling slightly as he observed the melee. Another move in his complicated choreography was playing out as designed. This time he made no move to welcome his eminent guest personally. He was content—more than content—to stand at a distance and savor ripples of excitement radiating through the crowd of politicians, industrialists, artists in dinner jackets, Italian suits, blue silk *kurtas*, the many beautiful women in golden saris and silver *shalwar-kameez*. Such electricity could only brighten Ravi's own star for having arranged it. No doubt the evening was already a grand success for the young man's ambitions. Gerald wondered whether what was to come—a wedding—could be anything more than an afterthought.

For the moment, however, any ceremony seemed far from imminent. And beckoning to Gerald was an entire tent filled with heavily-laden tables. He hadn't eaten since mid-day. As he discovered his hunger it became overpowering. He spied steaming bowls of shrimp in a pungent green mint and chili sauce; roasted chickens sliced on platters; eggplants and mushrooms and spinach. They perfumed the night with ginger and cumin and spices Gerald couldn't identify. He didn't care. Ravenous beyond reason, all he wanted was to stuff his belly. And too, he spied certain gentleman guests who knew how to conjure a magic phrase, sipping tall glasses of whiskey and soda rather than the lemonade and other juices in public circulation. Whiskey, too: he could use a quick dash.

Sita snagged his sleeve as he hesitated. "Come," she said, "come," tugging him away. He resisted, leaning half a step toward the food. But she jerked his arm more sharply. At her touch, the invisibility that had cloaked him since Gangaswami's arrival, and which he'd been enjoying, dissolved like so much mist.

Still the crowd of guests was swelling, hundreds it seemed, surging through tents and across lawns, more and more arriving as the evening grew late. Gerald felt their eyes upon him and Sita as they made their way up toward two high-backed wooden chairs on the terrace of the ancient monument. The grayish hewn stones and few surviving fragments of the emperor's delicate inlay had been incorporated into a high platform overlooking Ravi's party, flowing with explosions of winter flowers—roses, orange and red and peach, purple orchids, strings of marigolds beyond count. Stepping awkwardly, worried about tripping on the uneven stones, feeling that they, he and Sita, were somehow trespassing, Gerald allowed her to lead him along a narrow path that wound toward the throne-like chairs.

"Now what?" he whispered. "Is it time for the ceremony?"

"What a fuss you keep making. One must be patient," she hissed as she turned to sit.

Sita's eyes remained focused on the tips of her toes in their crimson sandals. Faithfully, obstinately, she gripped fast to her role as young bride: joyful, innocent, a tiny bit frightened, she might only have met the man who was to be her husband once or twice during the match-making interviews, and was certainly still a virgin. Gerald didn't know whether to laugh or cry aloud with rage. He was too old for such pretense. *She* was too old.

"What about dinner? I'm starving." Immediately he hated his own voice—whining and petulant.

Sita chose not to answer, but her stiffness and displeasure at his performance thus far were plain enough.

Bravely, as bravely as he could muster, he righted the headdress and prepared himself for what was to come.

What came was slow to the point of madness. While guests plundered food and drink, greeted each other with kisses, slipped off together for urgent consultations or covert assignations—the view from the monument stripped away the feints of ordinary pretense—the wedding couple received tribute. Among the first to rush up toward them, unseemly in their haste and eager enthusiasm, were women who had been Sita's colleagues in the English department at Lady Shri Ram College before she went to America to finish her Ph.D. Gerald was delighted to meet them at last, Kasturi, and Meenakshi and Gopa, so much had he heard about them, though he couldn't begin to match name to face.

Kasturi—it *was* Kasturi?—abruptly grabbed his hand, shook it powerfully in both her own, and looked him straight in the eye in a way that no one, certainly no woman, had done in better than a month. "You are certainly a lucky man, Mr.

Knapper. I hope you will be a good one as well. In that case we shall be friends."

Ravi had materialized somehow onto the platform. Sita's friends sensed his presence behind them, and when he leaned ever-so-slightly in their direction, smiling, they startled into flight with little cries and waves and promises to call on her.

Now the central ceremony of the evening elaborated itself. An old man, perhaps five feet tall, with a heavily pocked face and bulbous nose, slowly climbed the stone steps. He wore an elegantly tailored black Indian jacket. At his hip floated a willowy young woman, perhaps twenty-five and a foot taller than her escort, in a peacock-blue sari. The old man bowed toward Gerald but said nothing, and kissed Sita on both cheeks. He flicked a wrist into the cool night air, and into it a trailing servant placed a thick silken packet. The old man tugged the knot and drew out a single crisp ten-thousand rupee note, one of a thick company. He leaned forward and tucked the bill like a bright kerchief into Gerald's breast pocket. The packet he laid in Sita's lap with another short bow and then turned away. Gerald wondered whether he would go so far as to brush Ravi's shoes with his fingers as he passed.

"Don't touch that," snapped Sita under her breath.

Gerald's own fingers froze. "I can't leave this thing sticking out of my pocket—it's humiliating. I'm not some boy desperate for a buck."

"It isn't about you. They don't know anything about you. Such things are a matter of form."

"It's all a matter of making a fuss over Ravi's sister, is what it is. And of shaming me, or putting me in my place, though I haven't figured out why or what he's after."

"Oh, Gerald." She sighed. She glanced at him despite herself. "He's my brother. He's not after anything except my happiness."

Before he could respond the next pair of guests was already upon them. Two by two they continued to appear, all greeting the couple and bearing gifts. It was hard to tell—and there was no opportunity to ask—but Gerald guessed that most were strangers to Sita as well. Some touched their gifts only at the last instant, receiving the wrapped boxes or stuffed envelopes from a servant and handing them in turn to Sita. Nearly all dropped a few golden coins in their laps or stuck notes of large denomination in pockets and creases and even in the silver headdress. Gerald battled grimly not to blush or shout or stalk off the stage entirely. Sita passed the gifts to a family servant who was constructing a small castle of unopened treasures behind the wooden thrones. And two by two the guests made their way to greet Ravi and be acknowledged for their loyalty and largesse.

Gerald couldn't help but snatch glimpses of Sita's brother as the queue jerked spasmodically along. A prince indeed, it seemed, so at ease was Ravi, so coolly warm in his greetings and deflections. Here was no politician of an American stripe. He received the tributes of these people as his due, for which he was pleased but not indebted.

Well past midnight the last of the visitors paid homage, turning like all the others from wedding couple to host, and then quickly descending into the floodlit darkness below. Gerald rose stiffly. Peering from the lip of the monument, he saw that the tents and tables and buffets of food had grown largely deserted. A general detritus of fallen flowers, of napkins and scattered glasses lay strewn about. Members of the family were gathered in tight fists of conversations. Sita's parents slumped wearily on fabric chairs that had been ferried from the main house, with nieces and nephews, cousins and brothers gathered about for support.

With a daring pat on Sita's knee—and no glance to gauge her response—Gerald rose and strode quickly toward Ravi. He was standing by himself, watching something at the other end of the monument or not watching anything at all. Gerald lifted the silver helmet from his head and thrust it forward.

"Your turn now, don't you think?"

Ravi laughed lightly. "I wondered how long you'd put up with that bloody thing." He made no move to accept this particular gift. "Besides, you haven't finished with it yet. There are still the priests to satisfy."

"Surely your friend Mr. Gangaswami won't fuss if I'm not wearing the family armor." He tossed the headdress toward Ravi, who had little choice but to catch it. His eyes glittered, but the pleasant little smile never wavered.

Out beyond the last of the tents, safely beyond the precincts of the stone tombs of vanished Muslim rulers, flaring tapers kept the night at bay. A larger blaze snapped and smoked in a shallow pit. As Sita and Gerald finally approached the fire, with her family gathered at the threshold of shadows just beyond, Gangaswami lurched up from several large pillows with the help of his young assistant. Plates were scattered on the ground near his cushions. It was unclear how long he'd sought refuge out here in wilderness and exile. Perhaps he'd fled the unceasing homage and pleas for advice or blessing amidst the crowd.

"My friends," he cried in a voice that, nasal and reedy, startled Gerald each time he heard it, "this will be a great moment for you and for your family. And for your friends too, yes, and I am only too happy, so happy, to count myself among the latter."

He grabbed Sita's hand and placed it in Gerald's, drawing them toward the holy fire and the path that twined about it. Gangaswami signaled for two Brahmin priests in attendance to approach. And without another word, the god man turned and strolled heavily away into the night. The practicalities of the affair he would leave to others.

As he trudged the prescribed path around the fire for the third—or was it fourth?—time, Gerald's head was swimming with fatigue and hunger and a faint dizziness, as if a renewed bout of jet lag had swept him up and beyond himself. This woman at his side—who was she?

This disturbing intuition from earlier in the evening, of Sita become someone else, a stranger, had never entirely disappeared. It wasn't merely the kohl around her eyes or the diamond in her nose, nor that he was glimpsing an undiscovered aspect of her character, one he'd never had the chance to encounter in her American exile. No—he'd prepared himself for that possibility before ever boarding the plane for India. No—what unnerved him now in the late blue-black night of these Delhi gardens was the way she carried herself, the different lilt to her voice, an unrecognizable inflection in her eyes. He feared some more profound transformation of her character that he would no longer understand. Yet none of this—not for a moment—lessened his desire for her. And he reminded himself that these doubts and worries might well be simply a measure of his weariness.

Weariness apparently had yet to graze Sita. A gauzy gold-and-crimson *dupatta* was draped over her head and across the lower half of her face. Through most of the months they had all but lived together she'd worn jeans or longish dresses, yet tonight she seemed released by the very constrictions of the tightly wound sari. She floated, she *danced* the prescribed steps around the fire as if she'd trained for this moment all her life, in all her dreams.

Which she had, which she probably had, Gerald silently conceded.

Stranger or lover, both she might be, but her simple presence at his side on the path called to him, bound him, delighted him, stoked him, crushed muscle in his chest and groin with yearning. A thought of what lay ahead in the night once they were finally, finally set free (for this the smoke and strange chants and confusion of dance and dust could all be endured), turned him hard, brilliantly and unreservedly hard, as if he were an adolescent boy again and not a man into his fifties. He was simultaneously proud and a trifle embarrassed. (Surely no one could spy the truth.)

He hadn't slept with Sita in something more than four weeks. Why this was so he hadn't quite fathomed. Ravi had assigned them separate rooms of course, for the sake of appearances. Beyond this formality her brother paid no attention. And whatever their roots in rural Bihar, the elder Singhs were Delhi-wallahs of many decades—more sophisticated, more worldly than Sita had led him to expect. They were under no illusions about the life their daughter had been living, nor were they particularly troubled by it. Yet each night for four long weeks she'd slipped free of his increasingly urgent goodnight kisses—reluctantly, yearningly, but with absolute conviction. He did not understand but was willing to go along with her wishes, her instincts—her playacting, if that's what it was.

In America he'd also been occasionally embarrassed by his passion for this woman. Never in his life (though he wouldn't admit it to his children, or even Larry Tomsich and other pals at the club) had he been so truly intoxicated with love. A glimpse of her, an accidental brush of her elbow or knee, smote him to foolishness. And all he could do was grin and shrug and accept the truth of his foolishness and his delight.

Janice Stein, wife of one of his partners and an academic, had drunkenly accused him one evening of being attracted to Sita because she was exotic—an oriental, full of mystery and potent sexuality. "It's all illusion. It's all in the sick minds of western men," she'd mocked over dinner.

Not intending to make an enemy, Gerald had done the unpardonable: he laughed. A strong deep laugh of astonishment and pleasure in just how silly Janice's notion was. Because that was just it: with Sita he felt a marrow-deep harmony more intense than with any person he'd ever known, even Margot. There was no mystery, nothing exotic, beyond the simple, blissful necessity of there being this woman with whom he could find the best part of himself.

Happily, he'd given up all for her—or, really, given up nothing. His partnership provided money beyond his needs, even with generous tokens of affection (and guilt) to three grown and rather demanding offspring. The work itself no longer provided any satisfaction in itself, rarely much beyond a means to fill his days, which had been so important after Margot died. Better now to let Sita fill his days!

To India then he came.

And came to himself in mid stumble, waking on a narrow serpentine path that wound about the Brahmin flames. His forehead was smeared with orange and yellow paste. Wreaths of marigolds were draped around his neck. Was it Sita who had changed or he himself? The uncertainty rocked him.

He glanced up and in the shadows he made out Ravi watching languorously, hardly paying attention. A sudden searing resentment flared. He grasped with fresh clarity just how Ravi had been twisting and spinning him like a baited animal since his arrival. All while making a pretense of treating him as a new brother, a man to be honored for his own sake, not simply because he was marrying Sita, sister and daughter of the household.

Sacrificing home and family—that had only been an initial gesture, though this too he hadn't properly realized until this moment. They'd forgone a secular wedding in Columbus; he'd agreed to come to India to accomplish the marriage as part of an extended stay (no particular length had ever been mentioned and hadn't concerned him); his children, all the family that remained for him, felt no need to attend a wedding they neither understood nor approved.

As he considered this brief history, humiliations large and small seemed to gather themselves into the ludicrous struggle over the silver headdress. Humiliations large and small—most he hadn't even consciously sensed at the moment, though now they returned with a thousand tiny stings. What had been Ravi's point? What purpose? Merely a rich young man's whim, toying with an American too besotted with his sister to realize the easy sport he made?

No, weighing the past month, Gerald didn't feel that he'd merely been pricked and prodded for sport. He might have been able to laugh that off or arrange a playful revenge. Instead, he'd been stripped and scoured by a thousand goads as by grains of a coarse abrasive. Astonished at himself, that it had taken this long to penetrate his smitten attention, he saw now that Ravi on behalf of his family had undertaken a deliberate process: it was a kind of cleansing, and through it Gerald had been transformed into someone else altogether, at least as far as the world of Sita and her family were concerned. Like some young bride leaving hearth and kin behind, he was being prepared to become part of a new family on its own terms. His wealth—and he grimaced as this occurred to him—was dowry enough for the Singhs to overlook so much else that might compromise the choice of a middle-aged American.

Just as he was reaching the limit of endurance, summoning outrage enough to hurl marigolds from his throat, to cry out some mammoth defiance, to stalk away into a night he didn't begin to understand, the wedding ceremony ended. Sita and he were handed earthenware mugs of holy water. They dribbled some into the fire, which sputtered and sparked. One of the priests followed at their heels and casually dumped out a bucket of less precious liquid. The flame hissed, disappearing into a curl of smoke reeking and fetid.

*

Guests and revelers had long since departed. A few servants were rolling up carpets, offering token gestures with brooms and wicker baskets, but even Gerald could see that they were only waiting of the Singhs to make their way home. Anything of value had already been whisked away. Just beyond the fringe of shadows he spied, here and there, pairs of eager eyes, young and old, waiting. Once the site was abandoned, the local poor would descend and neatly, precisely scavenge anything abandoned. This was their due.

Strings of electric lights suddenly disappeared into blackness. Only a few torches guttered on wobbly stands.

Sita's mother and father were walking slowly toward a car that would carry them back to the main house. Bent and weary, they seemed oblivious to the world about them. All energy was husbanded for the remainder of this journey. Gerald trailed along after them because he did not know what else to do. Sita had once again disappeared. Nor was there any sign of her brother. Tired, wretched, near tears with frustration, Gerald again imagined himself as a bride learning a first lesson even while being brought roughly into the family: stripped of his past, expected to make a place for himself and be useful. He recognized the absurd self-pity of such an image, but the recognition in no way freed or soothed him.

A sudden clutch at his elbow. He jerked sharply as if bitten. Panting in surprise, he discovered that Sita had magically materialized at his side once more. She slipped her hand through his arm, drawing close. The gauzy *dupatta* had fallen from her head and she smiled up at him as she hadn't been able to smile for weeks.

"Thank you, thank you," she murmured into his ear. "You were wonderful. I'm so grateful."

For a moment it was as if he couldn't quite understand her—what was she chattering about? All the tensions, all the resentments that had been building in him through the evening—for better than four weeks in truth—blistered at this instant, hot to the touch and threatening to burst. His transformation hadn't taken after all. He was fifty-six years old and too old for such a change. Disoriented and miserable, he was swelling with an anger that wasn't like him at all.

He panted, he panted, he wouldn't, couldn't quite look at her yet, but walked along with her at his side. Finally, calming a bit, he had to speak. "What was all this, really? Some kind of test? Or am I initiated good and properly now, a member of your family?" The bitterness naked here was as much an outburst as he'd allow himself.

But Sita wouldn't let him spoil her own sense of relief and release and satisfaction. "My dearest. I told you before—it wasn't about you. Believe it or not. It was for my family. And yes, it was for me too. It was selfish and I'm sorry—oh, but it was fun and wonderful. Believe me, I promise to find lots of ways to make it up to you." She brought her hand to her mouth, but it didn't hide the wicked little smile she beamed at him.

"It won't be easy," he said. He wondered whether she herself had known what Ravi was up to. Was she in on the conspiracy? But already his misery and dourness had been lanced, not by Sita directly but by the joy sweeping up and over him that this woman should love him, that he should know such a love for her. If scouring his allegiances, even his character clean away had been a necessary price to make a new life with her possible, then he was grateful for it.

"We'll have some fun figuring out just how you'll manage it," he murmured.

David Lynn is the author of two earlier collections of stories, *Year of Fire*, published by Harcourt, and *Fortune Telling*, from Carnegie Mellon University Press. A 2016 recipient of an O. Henry Prize for the story "Divergence," he is also the author of *Wrestling with Gabriel*, a novel, and *The Hero's Tale: Narrators in the Early Modern Novel*, a critical study. His stories and essays have appeared in magazines and journals in the U.S., the U.K., India, and Australia. Since 1994 he has been the editor of *The Kenyon Review*, an international journal of literature, culture and the arts. A Professor of English at Kenyon College, David Lynn lives in Gambier, Ohio with his wife, Wendy Singer, a distinguished historian of India.

CPSIA information can be obtained
at www.ICGtesting.com
Printed in the USA
FFHW021926080419
51617471-57038FF